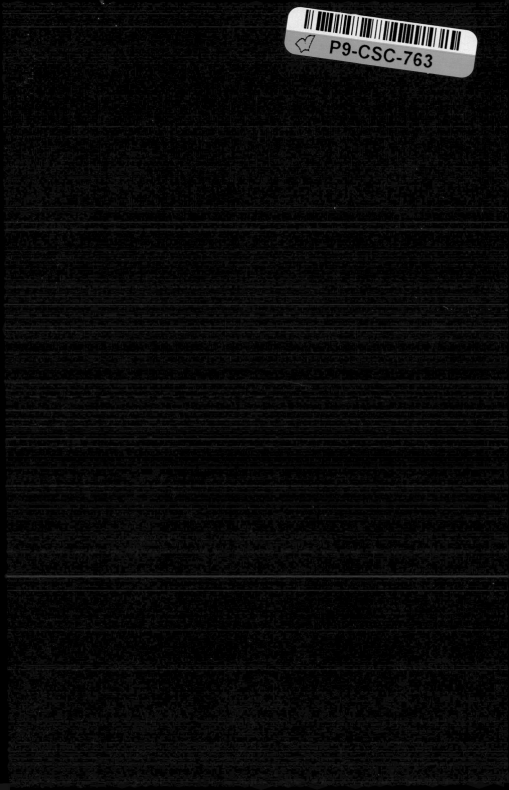
P9-CSC-763

ALSO BY KURT VONNEGUT

LOOK
AT
THE
BIRDIE

Kurt Vonnegut

LOOK
AT
THE
BIRDIE

UNPUBLISHED SHORT FICTION

Delacorte Press ▐ New York

Copyright © 2009 by The Kurt Vonnegut, Jr., Trust
Foreword © 2009 by Sidney Offit

All rights reserved.

Published in the United States by Delacorte Press, an imprint of
The Random House Publishing Group, a division of Random House, Inc.,
New York.

DELACORTE PRESS is a registered trademark of Random House, Inc., and
the colophon is a trademark of Random House, Inc.

Cover illustration by Kurt Vonnegut. Copyright © 1997 Kurt Vonnegut/
Origami Express, LLC. www.vonnegut.com
For complete credits for the original illustrations by Kurt Vonnegut
contained in this work, see page 253.

ISBN 978-0-385-34371-8
eBook ISBN 978-0-440-33877-2

Printed in the United States of America on acid-free paper

www.bantamdell.com

9 8 7 6 5 4 3 2 1

First Edition

Book design by Liz Cosgrove

FOREWORD

by Sidney Offit

As I read this anthology of Kurt Vonnegut's previously un-published short stories, I was reminded of the paradoxical aspects of his personality. Few writers in the history of litera-ture have achieved such a fusion of the human comedy with the tragedies of human folly in their fiction—and, I suspect, fewer still have had the grace to so candidly acknowledge them in their presentation of self.

During the years of our friendship, though I was aware that he might be suffering private misery, Kurt scuttled his demons with élan as we played tennis and Ping-Pong, skipped off to afternoon movies and jaunts around town, feasted at steak houses and French restaurants, watched foot-ball games on television, and twice sat as guests in a box at Madison Square Garden to root for the Knicks.

With his signature gentle but mordant wit, Kurt partici-pated in family celebrations, meetings of writers' organi-zations, and our gab and laugh sessions with Morley Safer and Don Farber, George Plimpton and Dan Wakefield, Wal-ter Miller and Truman Capote, Kevin Buckley and Betty Friedan. I don't think it an exaggeration to suggest that I, as well as Kurt's other friends, felt that time with Kurt was a momentous gift no matter how light our conversation. We often found ourselves imitating his amused reserve about his own foibles and those of the world.

Along with the fun and warm support he so graciously expressed to his friends, Kurt Vonnegut treated me to intimate glimpses of the master storyteller whose ironic and frequently startling observations of people emphasized the moral complexities of life. Walking uptown after a memorial service for an unmarried female author who had devoted her life to literary criticism, Kurt said to me, "No children. No books. Few friends." His voice expressed empathic pain. Then he added, "She seemed to know what she was doing."

At Kurt's eightieth birthday party, John Leonard, a former editor of *The New York Times Book Review,* reflected on the experience of knowing and reading Kurt: "Vonnegut, like Abe Lincoln and Mark Twain, is always being funny when he's not being depressed," Leonard observed. "His is a weird jujitsu that throws us for a loop."

The Vonnegut acrobatics are off to a fast start in this circus of good and evil, fantasy and reality, tears and laughter. The first story, "Confido," is about a magical device that provides instant conversation, advice, and therapy to the lonely. But—and here comes the flip side—Confido, the ingenious mind reader, eagerly reveals to its listeners their worse dissatisfactions, leading to painful discomfort with life. This story suggests not only the risks of psychiatry, where the patient may learn too much about himself/herself, but also the drastic spiritual consequences of biting the knowledge-bearing apple.

Although I recall Kurt as being appreciative of his brief

adventure with psychotherapy, misgivings about the practice of psychiatry are a recurring theme in this collection. "Look at the Birdie" begins with the narrator sitting at a bar, talking about a person he hates. "Let me help you to think about it clearly," the man in a black mohair suit with a black string tie says to him. "What you need are the calm, wise services of a murder counselor..."

This bizarre tale is resolved with a version of the old-fashioned O. Henry surprise ending that requires the reader's suspension of disbelief. But who can resist the enchantments of a storyteller who has a mad character tell us that a para-noiac is "a person who has gone crazy in the most intelligent, well-informed way, the world being what it is"? That's not just jujitsu. It's martial art.

Other gems of Kurt's wit and verbal play, his dour but just about always humorous commentaries, punctuate these tales. "F U B A R," a story title as well as theme, is defined for the reader by the bemused and sometimes mocking narrator as *"fouled up beyond all recognition."* Then we are asked to con-sider that "it is a particularly useful and interesting word in that it describes a misfortune brought about not by malice but by administrative accidents in some large and complex organization."

With one brief sentence, the weather in Indianapolis, Kurt's hometown, which is the scene for the story "Hall of Mirrors," is vividly described. Although the first words of the sentence lead us to expect a lovely nature ramble, the balance surprisingly allows the reader to see, feel, and hear the ugly chill. "Autumn winds, experimenting with the idea of a hard winter, made little twists of soot and paper, made the plastic propellers over the used car lot go *frrrrrrrrrrrrrrrrrrrrrrrrrrrrrr.*"

Twenty-eight *r*s by my count. How's that for sound effects in prose that says it all, courtesy of Kurt Vonnegut!

One of the few stories with an unhappy ending, "The Nice Little People" provides a preview of the coming attractions of Kurt's later career as a novelist. We are engaged by a reversal of the familiar image of larger than life space aliens: In Kurt's tale, a platoon of sweet, tiny, insectlike folk descend in a spaceship the size and shape of a paper knife. They turn out to be frightened creatures whom Lowell Swift, a linoleum salesman, befriends. But on guard! The role the aliens play in the resolution of Swift's deteriorating marriage is as harrowing as it is unpredictable. Unpredictable! Hmm. I should have suspected that! Especially with a hero named Swift and a hollow knife handle full of highly sensitive Lilliputian characters.

When I asked Kurt what he thought was the most important aspect of the craft of fiction that he taught his students during his years on the faculty of the University of Iowa's graduate writing program, as well as Columbia and Harvard, he told me, "Development. Every scene, every dialogue should advance the narrative and then if possible there should be a surprise ending." The element of surprise serves, too, to express the paradox of Kurt's viewpoint. When all is said and written, the resolution, the surprise, turns the story around and gives it meaning.

Unpublished is not a word we identify with a Kurt Vonnegut short story. It may well be that these stories didn't appear in print because for one reason or another they didn't satisfy Kurt. He rewrote and rewrote, as his son, Mark, as well as agents and editors testify. Although Kurt's style may seem casual and spontaneous, he was a master craftsman, demanding of himself perfection of the story, the sentence, the word. I remember the rolled up balls of paper in the wastebaskets of his workrooms in Bridgehampton and on East Forty-eighth Street.

The closest Kurt ever came to confessing an ambition for his writing was when he recited to me one of his rules for fictional composition: "Use the time of a total stranger in such a way that he or she will not feel the time was wasted."

To Kurt Vonnegut writing was kind of a spiritual mission, and these stories with all their humor seem most often to be inspired by his moral and political outrage. They are evidence, too, of the volume of Kurt's prodigious imagination, a talent that enabled him, after World War II and into the fifties and early sixties, to help support his growing family by contributing short stories to the popular ("slick") magazines.

Kurt Vonnegut, Jr.'s bylines appeared routinely in *The Saturday Evening Post, Collier's, Cosmopolitan, Argosy.* He later reminded his readers of the satisfactions of this association when he wrote in his introduction to *Bagombo Snuff Box*, "I was in such good company.... Hemingway had written for *Esquire*, F. Scott Fitzgerald for *The Saturday Evening Post*, William Faulkner for *Collier's*, John Steinbeck for *The Woman's Home Companion!*"

Hemingway! Fitzgerald! Faulkner! Steinbeck! Vonnegut! Their literary legacies survived the demise of so many of the magazines that provided them with generous fees, per word or per line, and introduced them to hundreds of thousands, even millions of readers.

Kurt's stories selected for this collection are reminiscent of the entertainments of that era—so easy to read, so straight-forward as to seem simplistic in narrative technique, until the reader thinks about what the author is saying. They are Kurt's magic verbal lantern, the Confido that projects so relentlessly the vagaries and mysteries of human behavior, but with a leavening of humor and forgiveness.

The discovery of this sampling of vintage Vonnegut con-firms the accessibility that is the trademark of his style and the durability of his talents, a gift to all of us—friends and readers who celebrate the enlightenments and fun of Kurt Von-negut's jujitsus and his art.

CONTENTS

LOOK
AT
THE
BIRDIE

Box 37

Alplaus, N.Y.

February 11, 1951

Dear Miller:

Thought, rather fuzzily, about something I want to add to my recent letter to you. It's this business about *the school*: school of painting, school of poetry, school of music, school of writing. For a couple of years after the War I was a graduate student in the Anthropology Department at the University of Chicago. At the instigation of a bright and neurotic instructor named Slotkin, I got interested in the notion of the school (I'm going to explain what I mean in a minute), and decided to do a thesis on the subject. I did about 40 pages of the thing, based on the Cubist School in Paris, and then got told by the faculty that I'd better pick something more strictly anthropological. They suggested rather firmly (with Slotkin abstaining) that I interest myself in the Indian Ghost Dance of 1894. Shortly thereafter I ran out of money and signed on with G-E, and I never did get past the note-taking stage on the Ghost Dance business (albeit damn interesting).

But Slotkin's notion of the importance of the school stuck with me, and it now seems pertinent to you, me, Knox, McQuade, and anybody else whose literary fortunes we take a personal interest in. What Slotkin said was this: no man who achieved greatness in the arts operated by himself; he was top man in a group of like-minded individuals. This works out fine for the cubists, and Slotkin had plenty of good evidence for its applying to Goethe, Thoreau, Hemingway, and just about anybody you care to name.

If this isn't 100% true, it's true enough to be interesting—and maybe helpful.

The school gives a man, Slotkin said, the fantastic amount of guts it takes to add to culture. It gives him morale, esprit de corps, the resources of many brains, and—maybe most important—one-sidedness with assurance. (My reporting what Slotkin said four years ago is pretty subjective—so let's say Vonnegut, a Slotkin derivative, is saying this.) About this one-sidedness: I'm convinced that no one can amount to a damn in the arts if he becomes sweetly reasonable, seeing all sides of a picture, forgiving all sins.

Slotkin also said a person in the arts can't help but belong to some school—good or bad. I don't know what school you belong to. My school is presently comprised of Littauer & Wilkenson (my agents), and Burger, and nobody else. For want of support from any other quarter, I write for them—high grade, slick bombast.

I've been on my own for five weeks now. I've rewritten a novelette, and turned out a short-short and a couple of 5,000-worders. Some of them will sell, probably. This is Sunday, and the question arises, what'll I start tomorrow? I already know what the answer is. I also know it's the wrong answer. I'll start something to please L&W, Inc., and Burger, and, please, God, MGM.

The obvious alternative is, of course, something to please the *Atlantic, Harpers*, or the *New Yorker*. To do this would be to turn out something after the fashion of somebody-or-other, and I might be able to do it. I say might. It amounts to signing on with any of a dozen schools born ten, twenty, thirty years ago. The kicks are based largely on having passed off a creditable counterfeit. And, of course, if you appear in the *Atlantic* or *Harpers* or the *New Yorker*, by God you *must* be a writer, because everybody says so. This is poor competition for the fat checks from the slicks. For want of anything more tempting, I'll stick with money.

So, having said that much, where am I? In Alplaus, New York, I guess, wishing I could pick up some fire and confidence and originality and fresh prejudices from somewhere. As Slotkin said, these things are group products. It isn't a question of finding a Messiah, but of a group's creating one—and it's hard work, and takes a while.

If this sort of thing is going on somewhere (not in Paris, says Tennessee Williams), I'd love to get in on it. I'd give my right arm to be enthusiastic. God knows there's plenty to write about—more now than ever before, certainly. You're defaulting, I'm defaulting, everyone's defaulting, seems to me.

If Slotkin's right, maybe the death of the institution of friendship is the death of innovation in the arts.

This letter is sententious crap, shot full of self-pity. But it's the kind of letter writers seem to write; and since I quit G-E, if I'm not a writer then I'm nothing.

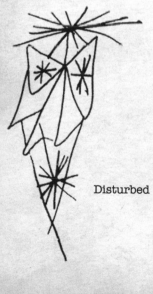

Yours truly,

Kurt

Disturbed personality

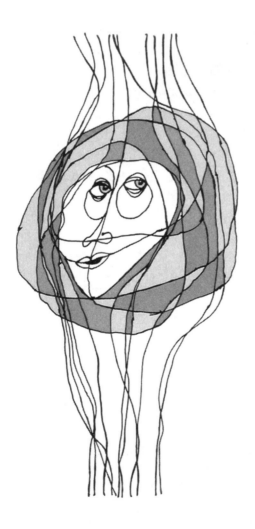

CONFIDO

The Summer had died peacefully in its sleep, and Autumn, as soft-spoken executrix, was locking life up safely until Spring came to claim it. At one with this sad, sweet allegory outside the kitchen window of her small home was Ellen Bowers, who, early in the morning, was preparing Tuesday breakfast for her husband, Henry. Henry was gasping and dancing and slapping himself in a cold shower on the other side of a thin wall.

Ellen was a fair and tiny woman, in her early thirties, plainly mercurial and bright, though dressed in a dowdy housecoat. In almost any event she would have loved life, but she loved it now with an overwhelming emotion that was like the throbbing amen of a church organ, for she could tell herself this morning that her husband, in addition to being good, would soon be rich and famous.

She hadn't expected it, had seldom dreamed of it, had been content with inexpensive possessions and small adventures of the spirit, like thinking about autumn, that cost nothing at all. Henry was not a moneymaker. That had been the understanding.

He was an easily satisfied tinker, a maker and mender who had a touch close to magic with materials and machines. But his miracles had all been small ones as he went about his job as a laboratory assistant at the Accousti-gem Corporation, a manufacturer of hearing aids. Henry was valued by his employers, but the price they paid for him was not great. A high price, Ellen and Henry had agreed amiably, probably wasn't called for, since being paid at all for puttering was an honor and a luxury of sorts. And that was that.

Or that had *seemed* to be that, Ellen reflected, for on the kitchen table lay a small tin box, a wire, and an earphone, like a hearing aid, a creation, in its own modern way, as marvelous as Niagara Falls or the Sphinx. Henry had made it in secret during his lunch hours, and had brought it home the night before. Just before bedtime, Ellen had been inspired to give the box a name, an appealing combination of confidant and household pet—*Confido.*

"What is it every person really wants, more than food almost?" Henry had asked coyly, showing her Confido for the first time. He was a tall, rustic man, ordinarily as shy as a woods creature. But something had changed him, made him fiery and loud. "What is it?"

"Happiness, Henry?"

"Happiness, certainly! But what's the *key* to happiness?"

"Religion? Security, Henry? Health, dear?"

"What is the longing you see in the eyes of strangers on the street, in eyes wherever you look?"

"You tell me, Henry. I give up," Ellen had said helplessly.

"Somebody to talk to! Somebody who really understands! That's what." He'd waved Confido over his head. "And this is it!"

Now, on the morning after, Ellen turned away from the window and gingerly slipped Confido's earphone into her ear. She pinned the flat metal box inside her blouse and concealed the wire in her hair. A very soft drumming and shushing, with an overtone like a mosquito's hum, filled her ear.

She cleared her throat self-consciously, though she wasn't going to speak aloud, and thought deliberately, "What a nice surprise you are, Confido."

"Nobody deserves a good break any more than you do, Ellen," whispered Confido in her ear. The voice was tinny and high, like a child's voice through a comb with tissue paper stretched over it. "After all *you've* put up with, it's about time something halfway nice came your way."

"Ohhhhhh," Ellen thought depreciatively, "I haven't been through so much. It's been quite pleasant and easy, really."

"On the surface," said Confido. "But you've had to do without *so* much."

"Oh, I suppose—"

"Now, now," said Confido. "I understand you. This is just between us, anyway, and it's good to bring those things out in the open now and then. It's *healthy*. This is a lousy, cramped house, and it's left its mark on you down deep, and you know it, you poor kid. And a woman can't help being just a little hurt when her husband doesn't love her enough to show much ambition, either. If he only knew how brave you'd been, what a front you'd put up, always cheerful—"

"Now, see here—" Ellen objected faintly.

"Poor kid, it's about time your ship came in. Better late than never."

"Really, I haven't minded," insisted Ellen in her thoughts. "Henry's been a happier man for not being tormented by ambition, and happy husbands make happy wives and children."

"All the same, a woman can't help thinking now and then that her husband's love can be measured by his ambition," said Confido. "Oh, you deserve this pot of gold at the end of the rainbow."

"Go along with you," said Ellen.

"I'm on *your* side," said Confido warmly.

Henry strode into the kitchen, rubbing his craggy face to a bright pink with a rough towel. After a night's sleep, he was still the new Henry, the promoter, the enterpriser, ready to lift himself to the stars by his own garters.

"Dear sirs!" he said heartily. "This is to notify you that two weeks from this date I am terminating my employment with the Accousti-gem Corporation in order that I may pursue certain business and research interests of my own. Yours truly—" He embraced Ellen and rocked her back and forth in his great arms. "Aha! Caught you chatting with your new friend, didn't I?"

Ellen blushed, and quickly turned Confido off. "It's uncanny, Henry. It's absolutely spooky. It hears my thoughts and answers them."

"Now nobody need ever be lonely again!" said Henry.

"It seems like magic to me."

"Everything about the universe is magic," said Henry grandly, "and Einstein would be the first to tell you so. All I've done is stumble on a trick that's always been waiting to be performed. It was an accident, like most discoveries, and none other than Henry Bowers is the lucky one."

Ellen clapped her hands. "Oh, Henry, they'll make a movie of it someday!"

"And the Russians'll claim *they* invented it," laughed Henry. "Well, let 'em. I'll be big about it. I'll divide up the market with 'em. I'll be satisfied with a mere billion dollars from American sales."

"Uh-huh." Ellen was lost in the delight of seeing in her imagination a movie about her famous husband, played by an actor that looked very much like Lincoln. She watched the simple-hearted counter of blessings, slightly down at the heels, humming and working on a tiny microphone with which he hoped to measure the minute noises inside the human ear. In the background, colleagues played cards and joshed him for working during the lunch hour. Then he placed the microphone in his ear, connected it to an amplifier and loudspeaker, and was astonished by Confido's first whispers on earth:

"You'll never get anywhere around here, Henry," the first, primitive Confido had said. "The only people who get ahead at Accousti-gem, boy, are the backslappers and snowjob artists. Every day somebody gets a big raise for something you did. Wise up! You've got ten times as much on the ball as anybody else in the whole laboratory. It isn't fair."

What Henry had done after that was to connect the microphone to a hearing aid instead of a loudspeaker. He fixed the microphone on the earpiece, so that the small voice, whatever it was, was picked up by the microphone, and played back louder by the hearing aid. And there, in Henry's trembling hands, was Confido, everybody's best friend, ready for market.

"I mean it," said the new Henry to Ellen. "A cool billion! That's a six-dollar profit on a Confido for every man, woman, and child in the United States."

"I wish we knew what the voice was," said Ellen. "I mean, it makes you wonder." She felt a fleeting uneasiness.

Henry waved the question away as he sat down to eat. "Something to do with the way the brain and the ears are hooked up," he said with his mouth full. "Plenty of time to find *that* out. The thing now is to get Confidos on the market, and start living instead of merely existing."

"Is it us?" said Ellen. "The voice—is it us?"

Henry shrugged. "I don't think it's God, and I don't think it's the Voice of America. Why not ask Confido? I'll leave it home today, so you can have lots of good company."

"Henry—haven't we been doing more than merely existing?"

"Not according to Confido," said Henry, standing and kissing her.

"Then I guess we haven't after all," she said absently.

"But, by God if we won't from now on!" said Henry. "We owe it to ourselves. Confido says so."

Ellen was in a trance when she fed the two children and sent them off to school. She came out of it momentarily, when her eight-year-old-son, Paul, yelled into a loaded school bus, "Hey! My daddy says we're going to be rich as Croesus!"

The school bus door clattered shut behind him and his seven-year-old sister, and Ellen returned to a limbo in a rocking chair by her kitchen table, neither heaven nor hell. Her jumbled thoughts permitted one small peephole out into the world, and filling it was Confido, which sat by the jam, amid the uncleared breakfast dishes.

The telephone rang. It was Henry, who had just gotten to work. "How's it going?" he asked brightly.

"As usual. I just put the children on the bus."

"I mean, how's the first day with Confido going?"

"I haven't tried it yet, Henry."

"Welllll—let's get going. Let's show a little faith in the merchandise. I want a full report with supper."

"Henry—have you quit yet?"

"The only reason I haven't is I haven't gotten to a type-writer." He laughed. "A man in my position doesn't quit by just saying so. He resigns on paper."

"Henry—would you please hold off, just for a few days?"

"Why?" said Henry incredulously. "Strike while the iron's hot, I say."

"Just to be on the safe side, Henry. Please?"

"So what's there to be afraid of? It works like a dollar watch. It's bigger than television and psychoanalysis combined, and they're in the black. Quit worrying." His voice was growing peevish. "Put on your Confido, and quit worrying. That's what it's for."

"I just feel we ought to know more about it."

"Yeah, yeah," said Henry, with uncharacteristic impatience. "O.K., O.K., yeah, yeah. See you."

Miserably, Ellen hung up, depressed by what she'd done to Henry's splendid spirits. This feeling changed quickly to anger with herself, and, in a vigorous demonstration of loyalty and faith, she pinned Confido on, put the earpiece in place, and went about her housework.

"What are you, anyway?" she thought. "What *is* a Confido?"

"A way for you to get rich," said Confido. This, Ellen found, was all Confido would say about itself. She put the same question to it several times during the day, and each time Confido changed the subject quickly—usually taking up the matter of money's being able to buy happiness, no matter what anyone said.

"As Kin Hubbard said," whispered Confido, " 'It ain't no disgrace to be poor, but it might as well be.' "

Ellen giggled, though she'd heard the quotation before. "Now, listen, you—" she said. All her arguments with Confido were of this extremely mild nature. Confido had a knack of saying things she didn't agree with in such a way and at such a time that she couldn't help agreeing a little.

"Mrs. Bowers—El-len," called a voice outside. The caller was Mrs. Fink, the Bowerses' next-door neighbor, whose driveway ran along the bedroom side of the Bowerses' home. Mrs. Fink was racing the engine of her new car by Ellen's bedroom window.

Ellen leaned out over the windowsill. "My," she said. "Don't *you* look nice. Is that a new dress? It suits your complexion perfectly. Most women can't wear orange."

"Just the ones with complexions like salami," said Confido.

"And what have you done to your hair? I love it that way. It's just right for an oval face."

"Like a mildewed bathing cap," said Confido.

"Well, I'm going downtown, and I thought maybe there was something I could pick up for you," said Mrs. Fink.

"How awfully thoughtful," said Ellen.

"And here we thought all along she just wanted to rub our noses in her new car, her new clothes, and her new hairdo," said Confido.

"I thought I'd get prettied up a little, because George is going to take me to lunch at the Bronze Room," said Mrs. Fink.

"A man *should* get away from his secretary from time to time, if only with his wife," said Confido. "Occasional separate vacations keep romance alive, even after years and years."

"Have you got company, dear?" said Mrs. Fink. "Am I keeping you from something?"

"Hmmmmm?" said Ellen absently. "Company? Oh—no, no."

"You acted like you were listening for something or something."

"I did?" said Ellen. "That's strange. You must have imagined it."

"With all the imagination of a summer squash," said Confido.

"Well, I must dash," said Mrs. Fink, racing her great engine.

"Don't blame you for trying to run away from yourself," said Confido, "but it can't be done—not even in a Buick."

"Ta ta," said Ellen.

"She's really awfully sweet," Ellen said in her thoughts to Confido. "I don't know why you had to say those awful things."

"Aaaaaaaaah," said Confido. "Her whole life is trying to make other women feel like two cents."

"All right—say that *is* so," said Ellen, "it's all the poor thing's got, and she's harmless."

"Harmless, harmless," said Confido. "Sure, she's harmless, her crooked husband's harmless and a poor thing, everybody's harmless. And, after arriving at that bighearted conclusion, what have you got left for yourself? What does that leave you to think about anything?"

"Now, I'm simply not going to put up with you anymore," said Ellen, reaching for the earpiece.

"Why not?" said Confido. "We're having the time of your life." It chuckled. "Saaaay, listen—won't the stuffy old biddies around here like the Duchess Fink curl up and die

with envy when the Bowerses put on a little dog for a change.
Eh? That'll show 'em the good and honest win out in the
long run."

"The good and honest?"

"*You*—you and Henry, by God," said Confido. "That's
who. Who else?"

Ellen's hand came down from the earpiece. It started up
again, but as a not very threatening gesture, ending in her
grasping a broom.

"That's just a nasty neighborhood rumor about Mr. Fink
and his secretary," she thought.

"Heah?" said Confido. "Where there's smoke—"

"And he's not a crook."

"Look into those shifty, weak blue eyes, look at those fat
lips made for cigars and tell me that," said Confido.

"Now, now," thought Ellen. "That's enough. There's
been absolutely no proof—"

"Still waters run deep," said Confido. It was silent for a
moment. "And I don't mean just the Finks. This whole
neighborhood is still water. Honest to God, somebody ought
to write a book about it. Just take this block alone, starting at
the corner with the Kramers. Why, to look at her, you'd
think she was the quietest, most proper..."

"Ma, Ma—hey, Ma," said her son several hours later.

"Ma—you sick? Hey, Ma!"

"And *that* brings us to the Fitzgibbonses," Confido was
saying. "That poor little, dried-up, sawed-off, henpecked—"

"Ma!" cried Paul.

"Oh!" said Ellen, opening her eyes. "You startled me.

What are you children doing home from school?" She was sitting in her kitchen rocker, half-dazed.

"It's after three, Ma. Whuddya think?"

"Oh, dear—is it that late? Where on earth has the day gone?"

"Can I listen, Ma—can I listen to Confido?"

"It's not for children to listen to," said Ellen, shocked. "I should say not. It's strictly for grown-ups."

"Can't we just look at it?"

With cruel feat of will, Ellen disengaged Confido from her ear and blouse, and laid it on the table. "There—you see? That's all there is to it."

"Boy—a billion dollars lying right there," said Paul softly. "Sure doesn't look like much, does it? A cool billion." He was giving an expert imitation of his father on the night before. "Can I have a motorcycle?"

"Everything takes time, Paul," said Ellen.

"What are you doing with your housecoat on so late?" said her daughter.

"I was *just* going to change it," said Ellen.

She had been in the bedroom just a moment, her mind seething with neighborhood scandal, half-heard in the past, now refreshed and ornamented by Confido, when there were bitter shouts in the kitchen.

She rushed into the kitchen to find Susan crying, and Paul red and defiant. Confido's earpiece in his ear.

"Paul!" said Ellen.

"I don't care," said Paul. "I'm *glad* I listened. Now I know the truth—I know the whole secret."

"He pushed me," sobbed Susan.

"Confido said to," said Paul.

"Paul," said Ellen, horrified. "What secret are you talking about? What secret, dear?"

"I'm not your son," he said sullenly.

"Of *course* you are!"

"Confido says I'm not," said Paul. "Confido says I'm adopted. Susan's the one you love, and that's why I get a raw deal around here."

"Paul—darling, darling. It simply isn't true. I promise. I swear it. And I don't know what on earth you mean by raw deals—"

"Confido says it's true all right," said Paul stoutly.

Ellen leaned against the kitchen table and rubbed her temples. Suddenly, she leaned forward and snatched Confido from Paul.

"Give me that filthy little beast!" she said. She strode angrily out of the back door with it.

"Hey!" said Henry, doing a buck-and-wing through his front door, and sailing his hat, as he had never done before, onto the coatrack in the hall. "Guess what? The breadwinner's home!"

Ellen appeared in the kitchen doorway and gave him a sickly smile. "Hi."

"There's my girl," said Henry, "and have I got good news for you. This is a great day! I haven't got a job anymore. Isn't that swell? They'll take me back any time I want a job, and that'll be when Hell freezes over."

"Um," said Ellen.

"The Lord helps those who help themselves," said Henry, "and here's one man who just got both hands free."

"Huh," said Ellen.

Young Paul and Susan appeared on either side of her to peer bleakly at their father.

"What is this?" said Henry. "It's like a funeral parlor."

"Mom buried it, Pop," said Paul hoarsely. "She buried Confido."

"She did—she really did," said Susan wonderingly. "Under the hydrangeas."

"Henry, I had to," said Ellen desolately, throwing her arms around him. "It was us or it."

Henry pushed her away. "Buried it," he murmured, shaking his head. "Buried it? All you had to do was turn it off."

Slowly, he walked through the house and into the backyard, his family watching in awe. He hunted for the grave under the shrubs without asking for directions.

He opened the grave, wiped the dirt from Confido with his handkerchief, and put the earpiece in his ear, cocking his head and listening intently.

"It's all right, it's O.K.," he said softly. He turned to Ellen. "What on earth got into you?"

"What did it say?" said Ellen. "What did it just say to you, Henry?"

He sighed and looked awfully tired. "It said somebody else would cash in on it sooner or later, if we didn't."

"Let them," said Ellen.

"Why?" demanded Henry. He looked at her challengingly, but his firmness decayed quickly, and he looked away.

"If you've talked to Confido, you *know* why," said Ellen. "Don't you?"

Henry kept his eyes down. "It'll sell, it'll sell, it'll sell," he murmured. "My God, how it'll sell."

"It's a direct wire to the worst in us, Henry," said Ellen. She burst into tears. "Nobody should have that, Henry, no-body! That little voice is loud enough as it is."

An autumn silence, muffled in moldering leaves, settled over the yard, broken only by Henry's faint whistling through his teeth. "Yeah," he said at last. "I know."

He removed Confido from his ear, and laid it gently in its grave once more. He kicked dirt in on top of it.

"What's the last thing it said, Pop?" said Paul.

Henry grinned wistfully. " 'I'll be seeing you, sucker. I'll be seeing you.' "

F U B A R

The word *snafu,* derived from the initials of *situation normal, all fouled up,* was welcomed into the American language during World War II, and remains a useful part of the language today. *Fubar,* a closely related word, was coined at about the same time, and is now all but forgotten. *Fubar* is worthy of a better fate, meaning as it does *fouled up beyond all recognition.* It is a particularly useful and interesting word in that it describes a misfortune brought about not by malice but by administrative accidents in some large and complex organization.

Fuzz Littler, for instance, was fubar in the General Forge and Foundry Company. He was familiar with the word *fubar*—had to hear it only once to know it fit him like a pair of stretch nylon bikini shorts. He was fubar in the Ilium Works of GF&F, which consisted of five hundred and twenty-seven numbered buildings. He became fubar in the classic way, which is to say that he was the victim of a temporary arrangement that became permanent.

Fuzz Littler belonged to the Public Relations Department, and all the public relations people were supposed to be in Building 22. But Building 22 was full up when Fuzz came to work, so they found a temporary desk for Fuzz in an office by the elevator machinery on the top floor of Building 181.

Building 181 had nothing to do with public relations. With the exception of Fuzz's one-man operation, it was devoted entirely to research into semiconductors. Fuzz shared the office and a typist with a crystallographer named Dr. Lomar Horthy. Fuzz stayed there for eight years, a freak to those he was among, a ghost to those he should have been among. His superiors bore him no malice. They simply kept forgetting about him.

Fuzz did not quit for the simple and honorable reason that he was the sole support of his very sick mother. But the price of being passively fubar was high. Inevitably, Fuzz became listless, cynical, and profoundly introverted.

And then, at the start of Fuzz's ninth year with the company, when Fuzz himself was twenty-nine, Fate took a hand. Fate sent grease from the Building 181 cafeteria up the elevator shaft. The grease collected on the elevator machinery, caught fire, and Building 181 burned to the ground.

But there still wasn't any room for Fuzz in Building 22, where he belonged, so they fixed him up a temporary office in the basement of Building 523, clear at the end of the company bus line.

Building 523 was the company gym.

One nice thing, anyway—nobody could use the gym facilities except on weekends and after five in the afternoon, so Fuzz didn't have to put up with people swimming and bowling and dancing and playing basketball around him while he was trying to work. Sounds of playfulness would have been not only distracting but almost too mocking to bear. Fuzz, caring for his sick mother, had never had time to play in all his fubar days.

Another nice thing was that Fuzz had finally achieved the rank of supervisor. He was so isolated out in the gym that he couldn't borrow anybody else's typist. Fuzz had to have a girl all his own.

Now Fuzz was sitting in his new office, listening to the showerheads dribble on the other side of the wall and waiting for the new girl to arrive.

It was nine o'clock in the morning.

Fuzz jumped. He heard the great, echoing *ka-boom* of the entrance door slamming shut upstairs. He assumed that the new girl had entered the building, since not another soul in the world had any business there.

It was not necessary for Fuzz to guide the new girl across the basketball court, past the bowling alleys, down the iron stairway, and over the duckboards to his office door. The buildings and grounds people had marked the way with arrows, each arrow bearing the legend GENERAL COMPANY RESPONSE SECTION, PUBLIC RELATIONS DEPARTMENT.

Fuzz had been the General Company Response Section of the Public Relations Department during his entire fubar career with the company. As that section he wrote replies to letters that were addressed simply to the General Forge and Foundry Company at large, letters that couldn't logically be referred to any company operation in particular. Half the letters didn't even make sense. But no matter how foolish and rambling the letters might be, it was Fuzz's duty to reply to them warmly, to prove what the Public Relations Department proved tirelessly—that the General Forge and Foundry Company had a heart as big as all outdoors.

Now the footsteps of Fuzz's new girl were coming down the stairway cautiously. She didn't have much faith in what the arrows said, apparently. Her steps were hesitant, were sometimes light enough to be on tiptoe.

There was the sound of a door opening, and the open door loosed a swarm of tinny, nightmarish little echoes. The girl had made a false turn, then, had mistakenly opened the door to the swimming pool.

She let the door fall shut with a *blam*.

On she came again, back on the right path. The duck-boards creaked and squished under her. She knocked on the door of the General Company Response Section of the Public Relations Department.

Fuzz opened the office door.

Fuzz was thunderstruck. Smiling up at him was the merriest, prettiest little girl he'd ever seen. She was a flawless little trinket, a freshly minted woman, surely not a day older than eighteen.

"Mr. Littler?" she said.

"Yes?" said Fuzz.

"I'm Francine Pefko." She inclined her sweet head in enchanting humility. "You're my new supervisor."

Fuzz was almost speechless with embarrassment, for here was infinitely more girl than the General Company Response Section could handle with any grace. Fuzz had assumed that he would be sent a dispirited and drab woman, an unimaginative drudge who could be glumly content with a fubar supervisor in fubar surroundings. He had not taken into account the Personnel Department's card machines, to whom a girl was simply a girl.

"Come in—come in," said Fuzz emptily.

Francine entered the miserable little office, still smiling, vibrant with optimism and good health. She had obviously just joined the company, for she carried all the pamphlets that new employees were given on their first day.

And, like so many girls on their first day, Francine was what one of her pamphlets would call *overdressed for work*. The heels of her shoes were much too slender and high. Her dress was frivolous and provocative, and she was a twinkling constellation of costume jewels.

"This is nice," she said.

"It is?" said Fuzz.

"Is this my desk?" she said.

"Yes," said Fuzz. "That's it."

She sat down springily in the revolving posture chair that was hers, stripped the cover from her typewriter, twittered her fingers over the keys. "I'm ready to go to work any time you are, Mr. Littler," she said.

"Yes—all righty," said Fuzz. He dreaded setting to work, for there was no way in which he could glamorize it. In showing this pert creature what his work was, he was going to display to her the monumental pointlessness of himself and his job.

"This is my very first minute of my very first hour of my very first day of my very first job," said Francine, her eyes shining.

"That so?" said Fuzz.

"Yes," said Francine. In all innocence, Francine Pefko now spoke a simple sentence that was heartbreakingly poetic to Fuzz. The sentence reminded Fuzz, with the ruthlessness of great poetry, that his basic misgivings about Francine were not occupational but erotic.

What Francine said was this: *"I came here straight from the Girl Pool."* In speaking of the Girl Pool, she was doing no more than giving the proper name to the reception and assignment center maintained by the company for new woman employees.

But when Fuzz heard those words, his mind whirled with images of lovely young women like Francine, glistening young women, rising from cool, deep water, begging aggressive, successful young men to woo them. In Fuzz's mind, the desirable images all passed him by, avoided his ardent glances. Such beautiful creatures would have nothing to do with a man who was fubar.

Fuzz looked at Francine uneasily. Not only was she, so fresh and desirable from the Girl Pool, going to discover that her supervisor had a very poor job. She was going to conclude, as well, that her supervisor wasn't much of a man at all.

The normal morning workload in the General Company Response Section was about fifteen letters. On the morning that Francine Pefko joined the operation, however, there were only three letters to be answered.

One letter was from a man in a mental institution. He claimed to have squared the circle. He wanted a hundred thousand dollars and his freedom for having done it. Another letter was from a ten-year-old who wanted to pilot the first rocket ship to Mars. The third was from a lady who complained that she could not keep her dachshund from barking at her GF&F vacuum cleaner.

By ten o'clock, Fuzz and Francine had disposed of all three letters. Francine filed the three letters and carbons of Fuzz's gracious replies. The filing cabinet was otherwise empty. The General Company Response Section had lost all its old files in the Building 181 fire.

Now there was a lull.

Francine could hardly clean her typewriter, since her typewriter was brand new. Fuzz could hardly make busywork of shuffling gravely through papers, since he had only one paper in his desk. That one paper was a terse notice to the effect that all supervisors were to crack down hard on coffee breaks.

"That's all for right now?" said Francine.

"Yes," said Fuzz. He searched her face for signs of derision. So far there were none. "You—you happened to pick a slack morning," he said.

"What time does the mailman come?" said Francine.

"Mail service doesn't come out this far," said Fuzz. "When I come to work in the morning, and again when I come back from lunch, I pick up our mail at the company post office."

"Oh," said Francine.

The leaking showerheads next door suddenly decided to inhale noisily. And then, their nasal passages seemingly cleared, they resumed their dribbling once more.

"Is it real busy around here sometimes, Mr. Littler?" said Francine, and she shuddered because the idea of being thrillingly busy pleased her so much.

"Busy enough," said Fuzz.

"When do the people come out here, and what do we do for them?" said Francine.

"People?" said Fuzz.

"Isn't this public relations?" said Francine.

"Yes—" said Fuzz.

"Well, when does the public come?" said Francine, looking down at her eminently presentable self.

"I'm afraid the public doesn't come out this far," said Fuzz. He felt like a host at the longest, dullest party imaginable.

"Oh," said Francine. She looked up at the one window in the office. The window, eight feet above the floor, afforded a view of the underside of a candy wrapper in an areaway. "What about the people we work with?" she said. "Do they rush in and out of here all day?"

"I'm afraid we don't work with anybody else, Miss Pefko," said Fuzz.

"Oh," said Francine.

There was a terrific bang from a steam pipe upstairs. The huge radiator in the tiny office began to hiss and spit.

"Why don't you read your pamphlets, Miss Pefko," said Fuzz. "Maybe that would be a good thing to do," he said.

Francine nodded, eager to please. She started to smile, thought better of it. The crippled smile was Francine's first indication that she found her new place of employment something less than gay. She frowned slightly, read her pamphlets.

Fuzz whistled reedily, the tip of his tongue against the roof of his mouth.

The clock on the wall clicked. Every thirty seconds it clicked, and its minute hand twitched forward microscopically. An hour and fifty-one minutes remained until lunchtime.

"Huh," said Francine, commenting on something she'd read.

"Pardon me?" said Fuzz.

"They have dances here every Friday night—right in this building," said Francine, looking up. "That's how come they've got it all so decorated up upstairs," she said. She was referring to the fact that Japanese lanterns and paper streamers were strung over the basketball court. The mood of the next dance was apparently going to be rural, for there was a real haystack in one corner, and pumpkins and farm implements and sheaves of corn stalks were arranged with artistic carelessness along the walls.

"I love to dance," said Francine.

"Um," said Fuzz. He had never danced.

"Do you and your wife dance a lot, Mr. Littler?" said Francine.

"I'm not married," said Fuzz.

"Oh," said Francine. She blushed, pulled in her chin, resumed her reading. When her blushing faded, she looked up again. "You bowl, Mr. Littler?" she said.

"No," said Fuzz quietly, tautly. "I don't dance. I don't bowl. I'm afraid I don't do much of anything, Miss Pefko, but take care of my mother, who's been sick for years."

Fuzz closed his eyes. What he contemplated within the purple darkness of his eyelids was what he considered the cruelest fact of life—that sacrifices were *really* sacrifices. In caring for his mother, he had lost a great deal.

Fuzz was reluctant to open his eyes, for he knew that what he would see in Francine's face would not please him. What he would see in Francine's heavenly face, he knew, would be the paltriest of all positive emotions, which is respect. And mixed with that respect, inevitably, would be a wish to be away from a man who was so unlucky and dull.

The more Fuzz thought about what he would see when he opened his eyes, the less willing he was to open them. The clock on the wall clicked again, and Fuzz knew that he could not stand to have Miss Pefko watch him for even another thirty seconds.

"Miss Pefko," he said, his eyes still closed, "I don't think you'll like it here."

"What?" said Francine.

"Go back to the Girl Pool, Miss Pefko," said Fuzz. "Tell them about the freak you found in the basement of Building 523. Demand a new assignment."

Fuzz opened his eyes.

Francine was pale and rigid. She shook her head slightly, incredulous, scared. "You—you don't like me, Mr. Littler?" she said.

"That has nothing to do with it!" said Fuzz, standing. "Just clear out of here for your own good!"

Francine stood, too, still shaking her head.

"This is no place for a pretty, clever, ambitious, charming little girl like you," said Fuzz unevenly. "Stay here and you'll rot!"

"Rot?" echoed Francine.

"Rot like me," said Fuzz. In a jangling jumble of words he poured out the story of his fubar life. And then, beet red and empty, he turned his back on Francine. "Good-bye, Miss Pefko," he said, "it's been extremely nice knowing you."

Francine nodded wincingly. She said nothing. Blinking hard and often, she gathered up her things and left.

Fuzz sat down at his desk again, his head in his hands. He listened to Miss Pefko's fading footfalls, awaited the great, echoing *ka-boom* that would tell him Francine had left his life forever.

He waited and he waited and he waited for the *ka-boom*.

And he supposed, finally, that he had been cheated out of that symbolic sound, that Francine had managed to close the door noiselessly.

And then he heard music.

The music Fuzz heard was a recording of a popular song, cheap and foolish. But, turned back on itself by the countless echo chambers of Building 523, the music was mysterious, dreamlike, magical.

Fuzz followed the music upstairs. He found its source, a large phonograph set against one wall of the gym. He smiled bleakly. The music, then, had been a little farewell present from Francine.

He let the record play to the end, and then he turned it off. He sighed, let his gaze travel over the decorations and playthings.

If he had raised his eyes to the level of the balcony, he would have seen that Francine hadn't left the building yet. She was sitting in the front row of the balcony, her arms resting on the pipe railing.

But Fuzz did not look up. In what he believed to be privacy, he tried a melancholy dance step or two—without hope.

And then Francine spoke to him. "Did it help?" she said.

Fuzz looked up, startled.

"Did it help?" she said again.

"Help?" said Fuzz.

"Did the music make you any happier?" said Francine.

Fuzz found the question one he couldn't answer promptly.

Francine didn't wait for an answer. "I thought maybe music would make you a little happier," she said. She shook her head. "I don't mean I thought it could solve anything. I just thought it would maybe—" She shrugged. "You know—maybe help a little."

"That's—that's very thoughtful of you," said Fuzz.

"Did it help?" said Francine.

Fuzz thought about it, gave an honest, hesitant answer. "Yes—" he said. "I—I guess it did, a little."

"You could have music all the time," said Francine. "There's tons of records. I thought of something else that could help, too."

"Oh?" said Fuzz.

"You could go swimming," said Francine.

"Swimming?" said Fuzz, amazed.

"Sure," said Francine. "Be just like a Hollywood movie star with his own private swimming pool."

Fuzz smiled at her for the first time in their relationship. "Someday I just might do that," he said.

Francine leaned out over the railing. "Why someday?" she said. "If you're so blue, why don't you go swimming right now?"

"On company time?" said Fuzz.

"There isn't anything you can do for the company now anyway, is there?" said Francine.

"No," said Fuzz.

"Then go on," said Francine.

"No suit," said Fuzz.

"Don't wear a suit," said Francine. "Skinny-dip. I won't peek, Mr. Littler. I'll stay right here. You'll feel *so* good, Mr. Littler." Francine now showed Fuzz a side of herself that he hadn't seen before. It was harsh and strong. "Or maybe you shouldn't go swimming, Mr. Littler," she said unpleasantly.

"Maybe you like being unhappy so much, you wouldn't do anything to change it."

Fuzz stood on the edge of the swimming pool at the deep end, looked down into eleven feet of cool water. He was stark naked, feeling scrawny, pale, and a fool. He thought he was surely a fool for having become the plaything of the logic of an eighteen-year-old.

Pride made Fuzz turn his back on the water. He started for the locker room, but Francine's logic turned him around again. The cool, deep water undeniably represented pleasure and well-being. If he refused to throw himself into all that chlorinated goodness, then he really was a contemptible thing, a man who enjoyed being miserable.

In he went.

The cool, deep water did not fail him. It shocked him delightfully, stripped away his feelings of paleness and scrawniness. When Fuzz came to the surface after his first plunge, his lungs were filled with a mixture of laughter and shouts. He barked like a dog.

Fuzz gloried in the echoes of the barking, so he barked some more. And then he heard answering barks, much higher in pitch, and far away. Francine could hear him and was barking back at him through the ventilator system.

"Does it help?" she called.

"Yes!" Fuzz yelled back, without hesitation or restraint.

"How's the water?" said Francine.

"Wonderful!" yelled Fuzz. "Once you get in."

Fuzz went upstairs to the first floor of the gym again, fully dressed, tingling, virile. Again there was music to lead him on.

Francine was dancing in her stocking feet on the basketball court, gravely, respecting the grace God had given her.

Factory whistles blew outside—some near, some far, all mournful.

"Lunchtime," said Fuzz, turning off the phonograph.

"Already?" said Francine. "It came so fast."

"Something very peculiar has happened to time," said Fuzz.

"You know," said Francine, "you could become bowling champion of the company, if you wanted to."

"I never bowled in my life," said Fuzz.

"Well, you can now," said Francine. "You can bowl to your heart's content. In fact, you could become an all-round athlete, Mr. Littler. You're still young."

"Maybe," said Fuzz.

"I found a whole bunch of dumbbells in the corner," said Francine. "Every day you could work with them a little till you were just as strong as a bull."

Fuzz's toned-up muscles tightened and twisted pleasurably, asking to be as strong as the muscles of a bull. "Maybe," said Fuzz.

"Oh, Mr. Littler," said Francine beseechingly, "do I really have to go back to the Girl Pool? Can't I stay here? Whenever there's any work to do, I'll be the best secretary any man ever had."

"All right," said Fuzz, "stay."

"Thank you, thank you, thank you," said Francine. "I think this must be the best place in the whole company to work."

"That may well be," said Fuzz wonderingly. "I—I don't suppose you'd have lunch with me?"

"Oh, I can't today, Mr. Littler," she said. "I'm awfully sorry."

"I suppose you have a boyfriend waiting for you somewhere," said Fuzz, suddenly glum again.

"No," said Francine. "I have to go shopping. I want to get a bathing suit."

"I guess I'd better get one, too," said Fuzz.

They left the building together. The entrance door closed behind them with a great, echoing *ka-boom.*

Fuzz said something quietly as he looked back over his shoulder at Building 523.

"Did you say something, Mr. Littler?" said Francine.

"No," said Fuzz.

"Oh," said Francine.

What Fuzz had said to himself so quietly was just one word. The word was *"Eden."*

SHOUT ABOUT IT FROM
THE HOUSETOPS

I read it. I guess everybody in Vermont read it when they heard Hypocrites' Junction was actually Crocker's Falls.

I didn't think it was such a raw book, the way raw books go these days. It was just the rawest book a woman ever wrote—and I expect that's why it was so popular.

I met that woman once, that Elsie Strang Morgan, the one who wrote the book. I met her husband, the high school teacher, too. I sold them some combination aluminum storm windows and screens one time. That was about two months after the book came out. I hadn't read it yet, hadn't paid much attention to all the talk about it.

They lived in a huge, run-down old farmhouse five miles outside of Crocker's Falls back then, just five miles away from all those people she gave the works to in the book. I don't generally sell that far south, don't know many people down that way. I was on my way home from a sales meeting in Boston, and I saw that big house with no storm windows, and I just had to stop in.

I didn't have the least idea whose house it was.

I knocked on the door, and a young man in pajamas and a bathrobe answered. I don't think he'd shaved in a week. I don't think he'd been out of the pajamas and bathrobe for a week, either. They had a very lived-in look. His eyes were wild. He was the husband. He was Lance Magnum in the book. He was the great lover in the book, but he looked like one of the world's outstanding haters when I met him.

"How do you do," I said.

"How do *you* do?" he asked. He made it a very unpleasant question.

"I couldn't help noticing you don't have any storm windows on this beautiful old home," I said.

"Why don't you try again?" he said.

"Try what?" I said.

"Try not noticing we don't have any storm windows on this beautiful old home," he said.

"If you were to put up storm windows," I said, "do you know who would pay for them?" I was going to answer the question myself. I was going to tell him that the money for the windows would come out of his fuel dealer's pocket, since the windows would save so much fuel. But he didn't give me a chance.

"Certainly I know who'd pay for 'em—my wife," he said. "She's the only person with any money around here. She's the breadwinner."

"Well," I said, "I don't know what your personal situation here happens to be—"

"You don't?" he said. "Everybody else does. What's the matter—can't you read?" he said.

"I can read," I told him.

"Then rush down to your nearest bookstore, plunk down your six dollars, and start reading about the greatest lover boy of modern times! Me!" he said, and he slammed the door.

. . .

My conclusion was that the man was crazy, and I was about to drive off when I heard what sounded like a scream from the back of the house. I thought maybe I'd interrupted him while he was murdering his wife, thought he'd gone back to it now.

I ran to where the screaming was coming from, and I saw that an old rusty pump was making all the noise.

But it might as well have been a woman screaming, because a woman was making the pump scream, and the woman looked like she was just about to scream, too. She had both hands on the pump handle, and she was sobbing, and she was putting her whole body into every stroke. Water was going into a bucket that was already full, splashing down over the sides, spreading out on the ground. I didn't know it then, but she was Elsie Strang Morgan. Elsie Strang Morgan didn't want water. What she was after was violent work and noise.

When she saw me she stopped. She brushed the hair off of her eyes. She was Celeste in the book, of course. She was the heroine in her own book. She was the woman who didn't know what love was till she met Lance Magnum. When I saw her, she looked as though she'd forgotten what love was again.

"What are you?" she said. "A process server or a Rolls-Royce salesman?"

"Neither one, lady," I said.

"Then you came to the wrong house," she said. "Only two kinds of people come here anymore—those who want to sue me for a blue million and those who think I ought to live like King Farouk."

"It so happens that I *am* selling a quality product," I said. "But it also happens that this product pays for itself. As I was telling your husband—"

"When did you see my husband?" she said.

"Just now—at the front door," I said.

She looked surprised. "Congratulations," she said.

"Pardon me?" I said.

"You're the first outsider he's faced since the school board fired him," she said.

"I'm sorry to hear he was fired," I said.

"This is the first you heard of it?" she said.

"I'm not from around here, lady," I said. "I'm from the northern part of the state."

"Everybody from Chickahominy to Bangkok knows he was fired," she said, and she started to cry again.

I was sure now that both the husband and the wife were crazy, and that, if there were any children, the children would be as crazy as bedbugs, too. There obviously wasn't anybody around who could be counted on to make regular payments on storm windows, and, looking about the yard, I couldn't even see the makings of a down payment. There was about three dollars' worth of chickens, a fifty-dollar Chevrolet, and the family wash on the clothesline. The blue jeans and the tennis shoes and the wool shirt the woman was wearing wouldn't have brought a dollar and a half at a fire department rummage sale.

"Lady," I said, getting ready to leave, "I'm sorry you feel so bad, and I sure wish I could help. Things are bound to get better by and by, and when they do, I'd certainly like to show you the Rolls-Royce of the storm window field, the American Tri-trak, made of anodized aluminum with disappearing lifetime screen."

"Wait!" she said as I turned away.

"Ma'am?" I said.

"How would you act," she said, "if your wife had done what I did?"

"Ma'am?" I said.

And then she grabbed the pump handle and started making the pump scream again.

A lot of people have asked me if she really looks as tough as her picture on the back of her book. If she didn't want everybody to think she was a beer truck driver, I don't know why she chose that picture for the book, because she could certainly look nicer than that. In real life she doesn't look anything like Jimmy Hoffa.

She's got a low center of gravity, that's true. And she is maybe a little heavy, but I know plenty of men who would like that. The main thing is her face. It's a pretty, sweet, loving face. In real life she doesn't look as though she's wondering where she'd put down her cigar.

The second time she got going, the pump screamed so loud it brought her husband to the kitchen door. He had a quart of beer with him.

"It's full!" he yelled at her.

"What?" she said, still pumping.

"The bucket's full!" he said.

"I don't care!" she said.

So he took hold of the handle to make her stop. "She isn't well," he said to me.

"Just rich and famous is all," she said, "and sick as a dog."

"You better get out of here," he said to me, "or you'll wind up in bed in the middle of her next book—with God knows who."

"There isn't going to *be* any next book!" she said. "There

isn't going to be any next anything! I'm getting out of here for good!" And she got into the old Chevrolet, got in and punched down the starter. Nothing happened. The battery was dead.

And then she went dead, too. She closed her eyes, rested her head on the steering wheel, and she looked like she wanted to stay there forever.

When she stayed like that for more than a minute, her husband got worried. He went over to the car barefooted, and I could see that he really loved her. "Honey?" he said. "Honeybunch?"

She kept her head where it was. Her mouth was all that moved. "Call up that Rolls-Royce salesman that was here," she said. "I want a Rolls-Royce. I want it right away."

"Honey?" he said again.

She raised her hand. "I want it!" she said. She certainly looked tough now. "And I want a mink! I want two minks! I want a hundred dresses from Bergdorf Goodman! A trip around the world! A diamond tiara from Cartier!" She got out of the car, feeling pretty good now. "What is it you sell?" she asked me.

"Storm windows," I said.

"I want those, too!" she said. "Storm windows all around!"

"Ma'am?" I said.

"That's all you sell?" she said. "Isn't there something else you could sell me? I have a check for a hundred and sixty thousand dollars in the kitchen, and you haven't even made a dent in it."

"Well," I said, "I also handle storm doors and tub enclosures and jalousies."

"Good!" she said. "I'll take 'em!" She stopped by her husband, looked him up and down. "Maybe you're through living," she said to him, "but I'm just starting. Maybe I can't have your love anymore, if I ever had it—but at least I can have everything money can buy, and that's plenty!"

She went into the house, and she slammed the kitchen door so hard she broke the window in it.

Her husband went over to the bucket that was already so full, and he poured his quart of beer into it. "Alcohol is no help," he said.

"I'm sorry to hear it," I said.

"What would you do if you were in the middle of this situation?" he asked me. "What would *you* do?"

"I suppose I'd commit suicide after a while," I said, "because nothing anybody's said or done has made any sense at all. The human system can stand only so much of that."

"You mean we're being immature?" he said. "You mean you don't think our problems are real? Just think a minute about the strain that's been placed on this marriage!"

"How can I," I said, "when I don't even know who you are?"

He couldn't believe it. "You don't?" he said. "You don't know my name?" He pointed after his wife. "Or her name?"

"No," I said, "but I certainly wish I did, because she just gave me the biggest order for windows I've had since I did the Green Mountain Inn. Or was she kidding?"

He looked at me now as though I were something rare and beautiful, as though he were afraid I would disappear. "I'm just one more plain, ordinary human being to you?" he said.

"Yes," I said. That wasn't strictly true, after the show he and his wife put on.

"Come in—come in," he said. "What would you like? Beer? Coffee?"

Nothing was too good for me. He hustled me into the kitchen. Nothing would do but I pass the time of day with him. I never knew a man to be so hungry for talk. In about half an hour there we covered every subject but love and literature.

And then his wife came in, all charged up for a new scene, the biggest scene yet.

"I've ordered the Rolls-Royce," she said, "and a new battery for the Chevrolet. When they come, I'm leaving for New York City in the Chevrolet. You can have the Rolls as partial compensation for all the heartaches I've caused you."

"Oh, for crying out loud, Elsie," he said.

"I'm through crying out loud," she said. "I'm through crying any which way. I'm going to start living."

"More power to you," he said.

"I'm glad to see you've got a friend," she said, looking at me. "I'm sorry to say I don't have any friends at the moment, but I expect to find some in New York City, where people aren't afraid to live a little and face life the way it really is."

"You know who my friend is?" he said.

"He's a man who hopes to sell storm windows," she said. And then she said to me, "Well, you sold 'em, Junior. You sold an acre of 'em, and my deepest hope is that they will keep my first husband from catching cold. Before I can leave this house in good conscience, I want to make sure it's absolutely safe and snug for a man who lives in his pajamas."

"Elsie—listen to me," he said. "This man is one of the few

living creatures who knows nothing about you, me, or the book. He is one of the few people who can still look upon us as ordinary human beings rather than objects of hate, ridicule, envy, obscene speculation—"

Elsie Strang Morgan thought that over. The more she thought about it, the harder it hit her. She changed from a wild woman to a gentle, quiet housewife, with eyes as innocent as any cow's.

"How do you do?" she said.

"Fine, thank you, ma'am," I said.

"You must think we're kind of crazy here," she said.

"Oh, no ma'am," I said. The lie made me fidget some, and I picked up the sugar bowl in the middle of the table, and there underneath it was a check for one hundred and sixty thousand dollars. I am not fooling. That is where they had the check she'd gotten for the movie rights to her book, under a cracked five-and-ten-cent-store sugar bowl.

I knocked my coffee over, spilled it on the check.

And do you know how many people tried to save that check?

One.

Me.

I pulled it out of the coffee, dried it off, while Elsie Strang Morgan and her husband sat back, didn't care what happened to it. That check, that ticket to a life of ease and luxury, might as well have been a chance on a turkey raffle, for all they cared.

"Here—" I said, and I handed it to the husband. "Better put this in a safe place."

He folded his hands, wouldn't take it. "Here," he said.

I handed it to her. She wouldn't take it, either. "Give it to your favorite charity," she said. "It won't buy anything I want."

"What *do* you want, Elsie?" her husband asked her.

"I want things the way they were," she said, clouding up, "the way they never can be again. I want to be a dumb, shy, sweet little housewife again. I want to be the wife of a struggling high school teacher again. I want to love my neighbors again, and I want my neighbors to love me again—and I want to be tickled silly by dumb things like sunshine and a drop in the price of hamburger and a three-dollar-a-week raise for my husband." She pointed out the window. "It's spring out there," she said, "and I'm sure every woman in the world but me is glad."

And then she told me about her book. And while she talked she went to a window and looked out at all that useless springtime.

"It's about a very worldly, virile man from New York City," she said, "who comes to a small town in Vermont to teach."

"Me," said her husband. "She changed my name from Lawrence Morgan to Lance Magnum, so nobody could possibly recognize me—and then she proceeded to describe me right down to the scar on the bridge of my nose." He went to the icebox for another quart of beer. "She worked on this thing in secret, understand. I had no idea she'd ever written anything more complicated than a cake recipe until the six author's copies of the book came from the publisher. I came home from work one day, and there they were, stacked on that kitchen table there—six copies of *Hypocrites' Junction* by—good God in Heaven!—Elsie Strang Morgan!" He took a long pull from the beer bottle, banged the bottle down.

"And there were candies all around the stack," he said, "and on the top was one perfect red red rose."

"This man in the book," said Elsie Strang Morgan, looking out the window, "falls in love with a simple country girl who has been out of Hypocrites' Junction just once in her life— when she was a junior in high school, and the whole junior class went to Washington, D.C., at cherry blossom time."

"That's you," said her husband.

"That's me—that *was* me," she said. "And when my husband married me, he found out I was so innocent and shy that he couldn't stand it."

"In the book?" I said.

"In life, in the book?" said her husband. "There's no difference. You know who the villain is in the book?"

"No," I said.

"A greedy banker named Walker Williams," he said. "And do you know who, in real life, is the President of the Crocker's Falls Savings Bank?"

"Nope," I said.

"A greedy banker named William Walker," he said. "Holy smokes," he said, "my wife should be working for the Central Intelligence Agency, making up new, unbreakable codes!"

"Sorry, sorry," she said, but she sounded way past being sorry to me. Her marriage was over. Everything was over.

"I suppose I should be sore at the school board for firing me," said her husband, "but who could really blame them? All four members were in the book, big as life. But even if they weren't in the book, how could they let a famous lover, a ruthless woman awakener like me, continue to instruct the young?" He went to his wife, came up behind her. "Elsie Strang Morgan," he said, "what on earth possessed you?"

And here was her reply:

"You did," she said very quietly. "You," she said.

"Think of what I was before I loved you. I couldn't have written a word in that book, because the ideas simply weren't in my head. Oh, I knew grubby little secrets about Crocker's Falls, but I didn't think about them much. They didn't seem so bad."

She faced him. "And then you, the great Lance Magnum, came to town, swept me off my feet. And you found me shy about this, hopelessly old-fashioned about that, hypocritical about something else. So, for the love of you, I changed," she said.

"You told me to stop being afraid of looking life in the face," she said, "so I stopped being afraid. You told me to see my friends and neighbors for what they really were— ignorant, provincial, greedy, mean—so I saw them for what they were.

"You told me," that woman said to her husband, "not to be shy and modest about love, but to be frank and proud about it—to shout about it from the housetops.

"So I did," she said.

"And I wrote a book to tell you how much I loved you," she said, "and to show you how much I'd learned, how much you'd taught me.

"I've been waiting and waiting and waiting for you to say one small thing that would indicate that you knew," said Elsie Strang Morgan, "that the book was as much yours as mine. I was the mother. You were the father. And the book, God help it, was our first child."

. . .

I left after that big scene.

I would have liked to hear what Lance Magnum said about the terrible child he'd fathered by a simple country girl, but he told me I'd better go.

When I got outside, I found a mechanic putting a new battery in the Chevrolet. And I realized that the famous love affair between Lance and Celeste might end right then and there, if either one of them could jump in a car and drive away.

So I told the mechanic there'd been a mistake, told him we didn't want the battery after all.

I'm glad I did, because when I went back two days later, Elsie Strang Morgan and her husband were still together, cooing at each other like doves, and they signed an order for storm windows and doors all around. I couldn't sell them bathtub enclosures because they hadn't had plumbing put in yet—but they did have a Rolls-Royce.

While I was measuring up the windows on the house, Elsie Strang Morgan's husband brought me out a glass of beer. He was all dressed up now in a new suit, and he'd shaved.

"I guess you admitted the baby was yours," I said.

"If I didn't," he said, "I'd be the biggest hypocrite in Hypocrites' Junction," he said. "What kind of a man is it who'll father a baby and then not love it and call it his own?"

Now I hear she's got a new book out, and I'm scared to look at it. From all I hear, the leading character is a storm window salesman. He goes around measuring people's windows—and the book's about what he sees inside.

ED LUBY'S KEY CLUB

Part One

Ed Luby worked as a bodyguard for Al Capone once. And then he went into bootlegging on his own, made a lot of money at it. When the prohibition era ended, Ed Luby went back to his hometown, the old mill town of Ilium. He bought several businesses. One was a restaurant, which he called Ed Luby's Steak House. It was a very good restaurant. It had a brass knocker on its red front door.

At seven o'clock the other night, Harve and Claire Elliot banged on the door with the brass knocker—because the red door was locked. They had come from a city thirty miles away. It was their fourteenth wedding anniversary. They would be celebrating their anniversary at Luby's for the fourteenth time.

Harve and Claire Elliot had a lot of kids and a lot of love, and not much money. But once a year they really splurged. They got all dolled up, took twenty dollars out of the sugar bowl, drove over to Ed Luby's Steak House, and carried on like King Farouk and his latest girlfriend.

There were lights on in Luby's, and there was music inside. And there were plenty of cars in the parking lot—all a good deal newer than what Harve and Claire arrived in. Their car was an old station wagon whose wood was beginning to rot.

The restaurant was obviously in business, but the red front door wouldn't budge. Harve banged away some more with the knocker, and the door suddenly swung open. Ed Luby himself opened it. He was vicious old man, absolutely bald, short and heavy, built like a .45-caliber slug.

He was furious. "What in hell you trying to do—drive the members nuts?" he said in a grackle voice.

"What?" said Harve.

Luby swore. He looked at the knocker. "That thing comes down right now," he said. "All the dumb things— a knocker on the door." He turned to the big thug who lurked behind him. "Take the knocker down right now," he said.

"Yes, sir," said the thug. He went to look for a screwdriver.

"Mr. Luby?" said Harve, puzzled, polite. "What's going on?"

"What's going on?" said Luby. "I'm the one who oughta be asking what's going on." He still looked at the knocker rather than at Harve and Claire. "What's the big idea?" he said. "Halloween or something? Tonight's the night people put on funny costumes and go knock on private doors till the people inside go nuts?"

The crack about funny costumes was obviously meant to hit Claire Elliot squarely—and it did. Claire was vulnerable— not because she looked funny, but because she had made the dress she wore, because her fur coat was borrowed. Claire looked marvelous, as a matter of fact, looked marvelous to anyone with an eye for beauty, beauty that had been touched by life. Claire was still slender, affectionate, tremendously optimistic. What time and work and worry had done to her was to make her look, permanently, the least bit tired.

Harve Elliot didn't react very fast to Luby's crack. The anniversary mood was still upon Harve. All anxieties, all expectations of meanness were still suspended. Harve wasn't going to pay any attention to anything but pleasure. He simply wanted to get inside, where the music and the food and the good drinks were.

"The door was stuck," said Harve. "I'm sorry, Mr. Luby. The door was stuck."

"Wasn't stuck," said Luby. "Door was *locked.*"

"You—you're closed?" said Harve gropingly.

"It's a private club now," said Luby. "Members all got a key. You got a key?"

"No," said Harve. "How—how do we get one?"

"Fill out a application, pay a hundred dollars, wait and see what the membership committee says," said Luby. "Takes two weeks—sometimes a month."

"A hundred dollars!" said Harve.

"I don't think this is the kind of place you folks would be happy at," said Luby.

"We've been coming here for our anniversary for fourteen years," said Harve, and he felt himself turning red.

"Yeah—I know," said Luby. "I remember you real well."

"You do?" said Harve hopefully.

Luby turned really nasty now. "Yeah, big shot," he said to Harve, "you tipped me a quarter once. Me—Luby—I own the joint, and one time you slip me a big, fat quarter. Pal, I'll never forget you for that."

Luby made an impatient sweeping motion with his stubby hand. "You two mind stepping out of the way?" he said to Harve and Claire. "You're blocking the door. A couple of members are trying to get in."

Harve and Claire stepped back humbly.

The two members whose way they had been blocking now advanced on the door grandly. They were man and wife, middle-aged—porky, complacent, their faces as undistinguished as two cheap pies. The man wore new dinner clothes. The woman was a caterpillar in a pea green evening gown and dark, oily mink.

"Evening, Judge," said Luby. "Evening, Mrs. Wampler."

Judge Wampler held a golden key in his hand. "I don't get to use this?" he said.

"Happen to have the door open for some minor repairs," said Luby.

"I see," said the judge.

"Taking the knocker down," said Luby. "Folks come up here, won't believe it's a private club, drive the members nuts banging on the door."

The judge and his lady glanced at Harve and Claire with queasy scorn. "We aren't the first to arrive, are we?" said the judge.

"Police chief's been here an hour," said Luby. "Doc Waldron, Kate, Charley, the mayor—the whole gang's in there."

"Good," said the judge, and he and his lady went in.

The thug, Ed Luby's bodyguard, came back with a screwdriver. "These people still giving you a hard time, Ed?" he said. He didn't wait for an answer. He bellied up to Harve. "Go on—beat it, Junior," he said.

"Come on, Harve—let's get out of here," said Claire. She was close to tears.

"That's right—beat it," said Luby. "What you want is something like the Sunrise Diner. Get a good hamburger steak dinner there for a dollar and a half. All the coffee you can drink on the house. Leave a quarter under your plate. They'll think you're Diamond Jim Brady."

Harve and Claire Elliot got back into their old station wagon. Harve was so bitter and humiliated that he didn't dare to drive for a minute or two. He made claws of his shaking hands, wanted to choke Ed Luby and his bodyguard to death.

One of the subjects Harve covered in profane, broken sentences was the twenty-five-cent tip he had once given Luby. "Fourteen years ago—our first anniversary," said Harve. "That's when I handed that miserable b—— a quarter! And he never forgot!"

"He's got a right to make it a club, if he wants to," said Claire emptily.

Luby's bodyguard now had the knocker down. He and Luby went inside, slammed the big red door.

"Sure he does!" said Harve. "Certainly he's got a right! But the stinking little rat doesn't have a right to insult people the way he insulted us."

"He's sick," said Claire.

"All right!" said Harve, and he hammered on the dashboard with his folded hands. "All right—he's sick. Let's kill all the people who are sick the way Luby is."

"Look," said Claire.

"At what?" said Harve. "What could I see that would make me feel any better or any worse?"

"Just look at the wonderful kind of people who get to be members," said Claire.

Two very drunk people, a man and a woman, were getting out of a taxicab.

The man, in trying to pay the cabdriver, dropped a lot of change and his gold key to the Key Club. He got down on his hands and knees to look for it.

The sluttish woman with him leaned against the cab, apparently couldn't stand unsupported.

The man stood up with the key. He was very proud of himself for having found it. "Key to the most exclusive club in Ilium," he told the cabdriver.

Then he took out his billfold, meaning to pay his fare. And he discovered that the smallest bill he had was a twenty, which the driver couldn't change.

"You wait right here," said the drunk. "We'll go in and get some change."

He and the woman reeled up the walk to the door. He tried again and again to slip the key into the lock, but all he could hit was wood. "Open Sesame!" he'd say, and he'd laugh, and he'd miss again.

"Nice people they've got in this club," Claire said to Harve. "Aren't you sorry we're not members, too?"

The drunk finally hit the keyhole, turned the lock. He and his girl literally fell into the Key Club.

Seconds later they came stumbling out again, bouncing off the bellies of Ed Luby and his thug.

"Out! Out!" Luby squawked in the night. "Where'd you get that key?" When the drunk didn't answer, Luby gathered the drunk's lapels and backed him up to the building. "Where'd you get that key?"

"Harry Varnum lent it to me," said the drunk.

"You tell Harry he ain't a member here anymore," said

Luby. "Anybody lends his key to a punk lush like you—he ain't a member anymore."

He turned his attention to the drunk's companion. "Don't you ever come out here again," he said to her. "I wouldn't let you in if you was accompanied by the President of the United States. That's one reason I turned this place into a club—so I could keep pigs like you out, so I wouldn't have to serve good food to a ————" And he called her what she obviously was.

"There's worse things than that," she said.

"Name one," said Luby.

"I never killed anybody," she said. "That's more than you can say."

The accusation didn't bother Luby at all. "You want to talk to the chief of police about that?" he said. "You want to talk to the mayor? You want to talk to Judge Wampler about that? Murder's a very serious crime in this town." He moved very close to her, looked her up and down. "So's being a loudmouth, and so's being a ————" He called her what she was again.

"You make me sick," he said.

And then he slapped her with all his might. He hit her so hard that she spun and crumpled without making a sound.

The drunk backed away from her, from Luby, from Luby's thug. He did nothing to help her, only wanted to get away.

But Harve Elliot was out of his car and running at Luby before his wife could stop him.

Harve hit Luby once in the belly, a belly that was as hard as a cast-iron boiler.

That satisfaction was the last thing Harve remembered—

until he came to in his car. The car was going fast. Claire was driving.

Harve's clinging, aching head was lolling on the shoulder of his wife of fourteen years.

Claire's cheeks were wet with recent tears. But she wasn't crying now. She was grim. She was purposeful.

She was driving fast through the stunted, mean, and filthy business district of Ilium. Streetlights were faint and far apart.

Tracks of a long-abandoned streetcar system caught at the wheels of the old station wagon again and again.

A clock in front of a jeweler's store had stopped. Neon signs, all small, all red, said BAR and BEER and EAT and TAXI.

"Where we going?" said Harve.

"Darling! How do you feel?" she said.

"Don't know," said Harve.

"You should see yourself," she said.

"What would I see?" he said.

"Blood all over your shirt. Your good suit ruined," she said. "I'm looking for the hospital."

Harve sat up, worked his shoulders and his neck gingerly. He explored the back of his head with his hand. "I'm that bad?" he said. "Hospital?"

"I don't know," she said.

"I—I don't feel too bad," he said.

"Maybe you don't need to go to the hospital," said Claire, "but she does."

"Who?" said Harve.

"The girl—the woman," said Claire. "In the back."

Paying a considerable price in pain, Harve turned to look into the back of the station wagon.

The backseat had been folded down, forming a truck bed. On that hard, jouncing bed, on a sandy blanket, lay the woman Ed Luby had hit. Her head was pillowed on a child's snowsuit. She was covered by a man's overcoat.

The drunk who had brought her to the Key Club was in back, too. He was sitting tailor-fashion. The overcoat was his. He was a big clown turned gray and morbid. His slack gaze told Harve that he did not want to be spoken to.

"How did we get these two?" said Harve.

"Ed Luby and his friends made us a present of them," said Claire.

Her bravery was starting to fail her. It was almost time to cry again. "They threw you and the woman into the car," she said. "They said they'd beat me up, too, if I didn't drive away."

Claire was too upset to drive now. She pulled over to the curb and wept.

Harve, trying to comfort Claire, heard the back door of the station wagon open and shut. The big clown had gotten out.

He had taken his overcoat from the woman, was standing on the sidewalk, putting the coat on.

"Where you think you're going?" Harve said to him. "Stay back there and take care of that woman!"

"She doesn't need me, buddy," said the man. "She needs an undertaker. She's dead."

In the distance, its siren wailing, its roof lights flashing, a patrol car was coming.

"Here come your friends, the policemen," said the man. He turned up an alley, was gone.

. . .

The patrol car nosed in front of the old station wagon. Its revolving flasher made a hellish blue merry-go-round of the buildings and street.

Two policemen got out. Each had a pistol in one hand, a bright flashlight in the other.

"Hands up," said one. "Don't try anything."

Harve and Claire raised their hands.

"You the people who made all the trouble out at Luby's Key Club?" The man who asked was a sergeant.

"Trouble?" said Harve.

"You must be the guy who hit the girl," said the sergeant.

"Me?" said Harve.

"They got her in the back," said the other policeman. He opened the back door of the station wagon, looked at the woman, lifted her white hand, let it fall. "Dead," he said.

"We were taking her to the hospital," said Harve.

"That makes everything all right?" said the sergeant. "Slug her, then take her to the hospital, and that makes everything all right?"

"I didn't hit her," said Harve. "Why would I hit her?"

"She said something to your wife you didn't like," said the sergeant.

"Luby hit her," said Harve. "It was Luby."

"That's a good story, except for a couple of little details," said the sergeant.

"What details?" said Harve.

"Witnesses," said the sergeant. "Talk about witnesses, brother," he said, "the mayor, the chief of police, Judge Wampler and his wife—they *all* saw you do it."

· · ·

Harve and Claire Elliot were taken to the squalid Ilium Police Headquarters.

They were fingerprinted, were given nothing with which to wipe the ink off their hands. This particular humiliation happened so fast, and was conducted with such firmness, that Harve and Claire reacted with amazement rather than indignation.

Everything was happening so fast, and in such unbelievable surroundings, that Harve and Claire had only one thing to cling to—a childlike faith that innocent persons never had anything to fear.

Claire was taken into an office for questioning. "What should I say?" she said to Harve as she was being led away.

"Tell them the truth!" said Harve. He turned to the sergeant who had brought him in, who was guarding him now. "Could I use the phone, please?" he said.

"To call a lawyer?" said the sergeant.

"I don't need a lawyer," said Harve. "I want to call the babysitter. I want to tell her we'll be home a little late."

The sergeant laughed. "A *little* late?" he said. He had a long scar that ran down one cheek, over his fat lips, and down his blocky chin. "A little late?" he said again. "Brother, you're gonna be about twenty years late getting home—twenty years if you're lucky."

"I didn't have a thing to do with the death of that woman," said Harve.

"Let's hear what the witnesses say, huh?" said the sergeant. "They'll be along in a little bit."

"If they saw what happened," said Harve, "I'll be out of here five minutes after they get here. If they've made a mistake, if they really think they saw me do it, you can still let my wife go."

"Let me give you a little lesson in law, buddy," said the sergeant. "Your wife's an accessory to the murder. She drove the getaway car. She's in this as deep as you are."

Harve was told that he could do all the telephoning he wanted—could do it after he had been questioned by the captain.

His turn to see the captain came an hour later. He asked the captain where Claire was. He was told that Claire had been locked up.

"That was necessary?" said Harve.

"Funny custom we got around here," said the captain. "We lock up anybody we think had something to do with a murder." He was a short, thickset, balding man. Harve found something vaguely familiar in his features.

"Your name's Harvey K. Elliot?" said the captain.

"That's right," said Harve.

"You claim no previous criminal record?" said the captain.

"Not even a parking ticket," said Harve.

"We can check on that," said the captain.

"Wish you would," said Harve.

"As I told your wife," said the captain, "you really pulled a bonehead mistake, trying to pin this thing on Ed Luby. You happened to pick about the most respected man in town."

"All due respect to Mr. Luby—" Harve began.

The captain interrupted him angrily, banged on his desk. "I heard enough of that from your wife!" he said. "I don't have to listen to any more of it from you!"

"What if I'm telling the truth?" said Harve.

"You think we haven't checked your story?" said the captain.

"What about the man who was with her out there?" said Harve. "He'll tell you what really happened. Have you tried to find him?"

The captain looked at Harve with malicious pity. "There wasn't any man," he said. "She went out there alone, went out in a taxicab."

"That's wrong!" said Harve. "Ask the cabdriver. There was a man with her!"

The captain banged on his desk again. "Don't tell me I'm wrong," he said. "We talked to the cabdriver. He swears she was alone. Not that we need any more witnesses," he said. "The driver swears he saw you hit her, too."

The telephone on the captain's desk rang. The captain answered, his eyes still on Harve. "Captain Luby speaking," he said.

And then he said to the sergeant standing behind Harve, "Get this jerk out of here. He's making me sick. Lock him up downstairs."

The sergeant hustled Harve out of the office and down an iron staircase to the basement. There were cells down there.

Two naked lightbulbs in the corridor gave all the light there was. There were duckboards in the corridor, because the floor was wet.

"The captain's Ed Luby's brother?" Harve asked the sergeant.

"Any law against a policeman having a brother?" said the sergeant.

"Claire!" Harve yelled, wanting to know what cell in Hell his wife was in.

"They got her upstairs, buddy," said the sergeant.

"I want to see her!" said Harve. "I want to talk to her! I want to make sure she's all right!"

"Want a lot of things, don't you?" said the sergeant. He shoved Harve into a narrow cell, shut the door with a *clang*.

"I want my rights!" said Harve.

The sergeant laughed. "You got 'em, friend. You can do anything you want in there," he said, "just as long as you don't damage any government property."

The sergeant went back upstairs.

There didn't seem to be another soul in the basement. The only sounds that Harve could hear were footfalls overhead.

Harve gripped his barred door, tried to find some meaning in the footfalls.

There were the sounds of many big men walking together—one shift coming on, another going off, Harve supposed.

There was the clacking of a woman's sharp heels. The clacking was so quick and free and businesslike that the heels could hardly belong to Claire.

Somebody moved a heavy piece of furniture. Something fell. Somebody laughed. Several people suddenly arose and moved their chairs back at the same time.

And Harve knew what it was to be buried alive.

He yelled. "Hey, up there! Help!" he yelled.

A reply came from close by. Someone groaned drowsily in another cell.

"Who's that?" said Harve.

"Go to sleep," said the voice. It was rusty, sleepy, irritable.

"What kind of a town is this?" said Harve.

"What kind of a town is any town?" said the voice. "You got any big-shot friends?"

"No," said Harve.

"Then it's a bad town," said the voice. "Get some sleep."

"They've got my wife upstairs," said Harve. "I don't know what's going on. I've got to do something."

"Go ahead," said the voice. It chuckled ruefully.

"Do you know Ed Luby?" said Harve.

"You mean do I know who he is?" said the voice. "Who doesn't? You mean is he a friend of mine? If he was, you think I'd be locked up down here? I'd be out at Ed's club, eating a two-inch steak on the house, and the cop who brought me in would have had his brains beat out."

"Ed Luby's that important?" said Harve.

"Important?" said the voice. "Ed Luby? You never heard the story about the psychiatrist who went to Heaven?"

"What?" said Harve.

The voice told an old, old story—with a local variation. "This psychiatrist died and went to Heaven, see? And Saint Peter was tickled to death to see him. Seems God was having mental troubles, needed treatment bad. The psychiatrist asked Saint Peter what God's symptoms were. And Saint Peter whispered in his ear, 'God thinks He's Ed Luby.'"

The heels of the businesslike woman clacked across the floor above again. A telephone rang.

"Why should one man be so important?" said Harve.

"Ed Luby's all there is in Ilium," said the voice. "That answer your question? Ed came back here during the Depression.

He had all the dough he'd made in bootlegging in Chicago. Everything in Ilium was closed down, for sale. Ed Luby bought."

"I see," said Harve, beginning to understand how scared he'd better be.

"Funny thing," said the voice, "people who get along with Ed, do what Ed says, say what Ed likes to hear—they have a pretty nice time in old Ilium. You take the chief of police now—salary's eight thousand a year. Been chief for five years now. He's managed his salary so well he's got a seventy-thousand-dollar house all paid for, three cars, a summer place on Cape Cod, and a thirty-foot cabin cruiser. Of course, he isn't doing near as good as Luby's brother."

"The captain?" said Harve.

"Of course, the captain earns everything he gets," said the voice. "He's the one who really runs the Police Department. He owns the Ilium Hotel now—and the cab company. Also Radio Station WKLL, the friendly voice of Ilium.

"Some other people doing pretty well in Ilium, too," said the voice. "Old Judge Wampler and the mayor—"

"I got the idea," said Harve tautly.

"Doesn't take long," said the voice.

"Isn't there anybody against Luby?" said Harve.

"Dead," said the voice. "Let's get some sleep, eh?"

Ten minutes later, Harve was taken upstairs again. He wasn't hustled along this time, though he was in the care of the same sergeant who had locked him up. The sergeant was gentle now—even a little apologetic.

At the head of the iron stairs, they were met by Captain Luby, whose manners were changed for the better, too. The captain encouraged Harve to think of him as a prankish boy with a heart of gold.

Captain Luby put his hand on Harve's arm, and he smiled, and he said, "We've been rough on you, Mr. Elliot, and we know it. I'm sorry, but you've got to understand that police have to get rough sometimes—especially in a murder investigation."

"That's fine," said Harve, "except you're getting rough with the wrong people."

Captain Luby shrugged philosophically. "Maybe—maybe not," he said. "That's for a court to decide."

"If it has to come to that," said Harve.

"I think you'd better talk to a lawyer as soon as possible," said the captain.

"I think so, too," said Harve.

"There's one in the station house now, if you want to ask him," said the captain.

"Another one of Ed Luby's brothers?" said Harve.

Captain Luby looked surprised, and then he decided to laugh. He laughed very hard. "I don't blame you for saying that," he said. "I can imagine how things look to you."

"You can?" said Harve.

"You get in a jam in a strange town," said the captain, "and all of a sudden it looks to you like everybody's named Luby." He laughed again. "There's just me and my brother— just the two Lubys—that's all. This lawyer out front—not only isn't he any relative, he hates my guts and Ed's, too. That make you feel any better?"

"Maybe," said Harve carefully.

"What's that supposed to mean?" said the captain. "You want him or not?"

"I'll let you know after I've talked to him," said Harve.

"Go tell Lemming we maybe got a client for him," said the captain to the sergeant.

"I want my wife here, too," said Harve.

"Naturally," said the captain. "No argument there. She'll be right down."

The lawyer, whose name was Frank Lemming, was brought in to Harve long before Claire was. Lemming carried a battered black briefcase that seemed to have very little in it. He was a small, pear-shaped man.

Lemming's name was stamped on the side of his briefcase in big letters. He was shabby, puffy, short-winded. The only outward sign that he might have a little style, a little courage, was an outsize mustache.

When he opened his mouth, he let out a voice that was deep, majestic, unafraid. He demanded to know if Harve had been threatened or hurt in any way. He talked to Captain Luby and the sergeant as though they were the ones in trouble.

Harve began to feel a good deal better.

"Would you gentlemen kindly leave," said Lemming, calling the police *gentlemen* with grand irony. "I want to talk to my client alone."

The police left meekly.

"You're certainly a breath of fresh air," said Harve.

"That's the first time I've ever been called that," said Lemming.

"I was beginning to think I was in the middle of Nazi Germany," said Harve.

"You sound like a man who's never been arrested before," said Lemming.

"I never have been," said Harve.

"There's always got to be a first time," said Lemming pleasantly. "What's the charge?"

"They didn't tell you?" said Harve.

"They just told me they had somebody back here who wanted a lawyer," said Lemming. "I was here on another case." He sat down, put his limp briefcase against the leg of his chair. "So what's the charge?"

"They—they've been talking about murder," said Harve.

This news fazed Lemming only briefly. "These morons they call the Ilium Police Force," he said, "everything's murder to them. What did you do it with?"

"I didn't," said Harve.

"What did they *say* you did it with?" said Lemming.

"My fist," said Harve.

"You hit a man in a fight—and he died?" said Lemming.

"I didn't hit anybody!" said Harve.

"All right, all right, all right," said Lemming calmingly.

"Are you in with these guys, too?" said Harve. "Are you part of the nightmare, too?"

Lemming cocked his head. "Maybe you better explain that?" he said.

"Everybody in Ilium works for Ed Luby, I hear," said Harve. "I guess you do, too."

"Me?" said Lemming. "Are you kidding? You heard how I talk to Luby's brother. I'd talk to Ed Luby the same way. They don't scare me."

"Maybe—" said Harve, watching Lemming closely, wanting with all his heart to trust him.

"I'm hired?" said Lemming.

"How much will it cost?" said Harve.

"Fifty dollars to start," said Lemming.

"You mean right now?" said Harve.

"The class of people I do business with," said Lemming, "I get paid right away, or I never get paid."

"All I've got with me is twenty," said Harve.

"That'll do nicely for the moment," said Lemming. He held out his hand.

As Lemming was putting the money into his billfold, a policewoman with clacking heels brought Claire Elliot in.

Claire was snow-white. She wouldn't speak until the policewoman was gone. When she did speak, her voice was ragged, barely under control.

Harve embraced her, encouraged her. "We've got a lawyer now," he said. "We'll be all right now. He knows what to do."

"I don't trust him. I don't trust *anybody* around here!" said Claire. She was wild-eyed. "Harve! I've got to talk to you alone!"

"I'll be right outside," said Lemming. "Call me when you want me." He left his briefcase where it was.

"Has anybody threatened you?" Claire said to Harve, when Lemming was gone.

"There's been some pretty rough talk," said Harve.

"Has anybody threatened to kill you?" she said.

"No," said Harve.

Claire whispered now. "Somebody's threatened to kill me, and you—" Here she broke down. "And the children," she whispered brokenly.

Harve exploded. "Who?" he said at the top of his lungs. "Who threatened that?" he replied.

Claire put her hand over his mouth, begged him to be quiet.

Harve took her hand away. "Who?" he said.

Claire didn't even whisper her answer. She just moved her lips. "The captain," her lips said. She clung to him. "Please," she whispered, "keep your voice down. We've got to be calm. We've got to think. We've got to make up a new story."

"About what?" said Harve.

"About what happened," she said. She shook her head. "We mustn't ever tell what really happened again."

"My God," said Harve, "is this America?"

"I don't know what it is," said Claire. "I just know we've got to make up a new story—or—or something terrible will happen."

"Something terrible already has happened," said Harve.

"Worse things can still happen," said Claire.

Harve thought hard, the heels of his hands in his eye sockets. "If they're trying that hard to scare us," he said, "then they must be plenty scared, too. There must be plenty of harm we could do them."

"How?" said Claire.

"By sticking to the truth," said Harve. "That's pretty plain, isn't it? That's what they want to make us stop doing."

"I don't want to do anybody any harm," said Claire. "I just want to get out of here. I just want to go home."

"All right," said Harve. "We've got a lawyer now. That's a start."

Harve called to Lemming, who came in rubbing his hands. "Secret conference over?" he said cheerfully.

"Yes," said Harve.

"Well, secrets are all very fine in their place," said

Lemming, "but I recommend strongly that you don't keep any from your lawyer."

"Harve—" said Claire warningly.

"He's right," said Harve. "Don't you understand—he's right."

"She's in favor of holding a little something back?" said Lemming.

"She's been threatened. That's the reason," said Harve.

"By whom?" said Lemming.

"Don't tell him," said Claire beseechingly.

"We'll save that for a little while," said Harve. "The thing is, Mr. Lemming, I didn't commit this murder they say I did. But my wife and I saw who really did it, and we've been threatened with all kinds of things, if we tell what we saw."

"Don't tell," said Claire. "Harve—don't."

"I give you my word of honor, Mrs. Elliot," said Lemming, "nothing you or your husband tells me will go any farther." He was proud of his word of honor, was a very appealing person when he gave it. "Now tell me who really did this killing."

"Ed Luby," said Harve.

"I beg your pardon?" said Lemming blankly.

"Ed Luby," said Harve.

Lemming sat back, suddenly drained and old. "I see," he said. His voice wasn't deep now. It was like wind in the treetops.

"He's a powerful man around here," said Harve, "I hear."

Lemming nodded. "You heard that right," he said.

Harve started to tell about how Luby had killed the girl. Lemming stopped him.

"What's—what's the matter?" said Harve.

Lemming gave him a wan smile. "That's a very good question," he said. "That's—that's a very *complicated* question."

"You work for him, after all?" said Harve.

"Maybe I do—after all," said Lemming.

"You see?" Claire said to Harve.

Lemming took out his billfold, handed the twenty dollars back to Harve.

"You quit?" said Harve.

"Let's say," said Lemming sadly, "that any advice you get from me from now on is free. I'm not the lawyer for this case—and any advice I have to give doesn't have much to do with the law." He spread his hands. "I'm a legal hack, friends. That must be obvious. If what you say is true—"

"It *is* true!" said Harve.

"Then you need a lawyer who can fight a whole town," said Lemming, "because Ed Luby *is* this town. I've won a lot of cases in Ilium, but they were all cases Ed Luby didn't care about." He stood. "If what you say is true, this isn't a case—it's a war."

"What am I going to do?" said Harve.

"My advice to you," said Lemming, "is to be as scared as your wife is, Mr. Elliot."

Lemming nodded, and then he scuttled away.

Seconds later, the sergeant came in for Harve and Claire, marched them through a door and into a room where a floodlight blinded them. Whispers came from the darkness beyond.

"What's this?" said Harve, his arm around Claire.

"Don't speak unless you're spoken to," said the voice of Captain Luby.

"I want a lawyer," said Harve.

"You had one," said the captain. "What happened to Lemming?"

"He quit," said Harve.

Somebody snickered.

"That's funny?" said Harve bitterly.

"Shut up," said Captain Luby.

"This is funny?" Harve said to the whispering blackness. "A man and a woman up here who never broke a law in their whole lives—accused of killing a woman they tried to save—"

Captain Luby emerged from the blackness. He showed Harve what he had in his right hand. It was a slab of rubber about four inches wide, eight inches long, and half an inch thick.

"This is what I call Captain Luby's wise-guy-wiser-upper," he said. He put the piece of rubber against Harve's cheek caressingly. "You can't imagine how much pain one slap from this thing causes," he said. "I'm surprised all over again, every time I use it. Now stand apart, stand straight, keep your mouths shut, and face the witnesses."

Harve's determination to break jail was born when the clammy rubber touched his cheek.

By the time the captain had returned to the whispering darkness, Harve's determination had become an obsession. No other plan would do.

Out in the darkness, a man now said in a clear, proud voice that he had seen Harve hit the girl. He identified himself as the mayor of Ilium.

The mayor's wife was honored to back him up.

Harve did not protest. He was too busy sensing all he could of what lay beyond the light. Someone now came in from another room, showing Harve where a door was, showing him what lay beyond the door.

Beyond the door he glimpsed a foyer. Beyond the foyer he glimpsed the great outdoors.

Now Captain Luby was asking Judge Wampler if he had seen Harve hit the girl.

"Yes," that fat man said gravely. "And I saw his wife help him to make a getaway, too."

Mrs. Wampler spoke up. "They're the ones, all right," she said. "It was one of the most terrible things I ever saw in my life. I don't think I'll ever forget it."

Harve tried to make out the first row of people, the first people he had to pass. He could make out only one person with any certainty. He could make out the policewoman with the clacking heels. She was taking notes now on all that was being said.

Harve decided to charge past her in thirty seconds.

He began to count the seconds away.

Part Two

Harve Elliot stood in front of a blinding light with his wife, Claire. He had never committed a crime in his life. He was now counting off the seconds before he would break jail, before he would run away from the charge of murder.

He was listening to a supposed witness to his crime, to the man who had actually committed the murder. Ed Luby, somewhere behind the light, told his tale. Luby's brother, a captain on the Ilium Police Force, asked helpful questions from time to time.

"Three months ago," said Ed Luby, "I turned my restaurant

into a private club—to keep undesirable elements out." Luby, the expert on undesirable elements, had once been a gunman for Al Capone.

"I guess those two up there," he said, meaning Harve and Claire, "didn't hear about it—or maybe they figured it didn't apply to them. Anyway, they showed up tonight, and they got sore when they couldn't get in, and they hung around the front door, insulting the members."

"You ever see them before?" Captain Luby asked him.

"Back before the place was a private club," said Luby, "these two used to come in about once a year. The reason I remembered 'em from one year to the next was the man was always loaded. And he'd get drunker in my place—and he'd turn mean."

"Mean?" said the captain.

"He'd pick fights," said Luby, "not just with men, either."

"So what happened tonight?" said the captain.

"These two were hanging around the door, making trouble for the members," said Luby, "and a dame came out in a taxi, all by herself. I don't know what she figured on doing. Figured on picking up somebody on the way in, I guess. Anyway, she got stopped, too, so I had three people hanging around outside my door. And they got in some kind of argument with each other."

All that interested Harve Elliot was the effect Luby's tale was having on the mood in the room. Harve couldn't see Luby, but he sensed that everyone was watching the man, was fascinated by him.

Now, Harve decided, was the time to run.

"I don't want you to take my word for what happened

next," said Luby, "on account of I understand some people claim it was me who hit the girl."

"We've got the statements of other witnesses," said the captain sympathetically. "So you go ahead and give us your version, and we can double-check it."

"Well," said Luby, "the dame who came out in the taxi called the other dame—the dame up there—"

"Mrs. Elliot," said the captain.

"Yeah," said Luby. "She calls Mrs. Elliot something Mr. Elliot don't like, and the next thing I knew, Mr. Elliot had hauled off and—"

Harve Elliot plunged past the light and into the darkness. He charged at the door and the freedom beyond.

Harve lay under an old sedan in a used car lot. He was a block from the Ilium Police Station. His ears roared and his chest quaked. Centuries before he had broken jail. He had knocked people and doors and furniture out of his way effortlessly, had scattered them like leaves.

Guns had gone off, seemingly right by his head.

Now men were shouting in the night, and Harve lay under the car.

One clear image came to Harve from his fantastic flight— and only one. He remembered the face of the policewoman, the first person between him and freedom. Harve had flung her into the glare of the floodlight, had seen her livid, shocked face.

And that was the only face he'd seen.

The hunt for Harve—what Harve heard of it—sounded foolish, slovenly, demoralized. When Harve got his wind and

his wits back, he felt marvelous. He wanted to laugh out loud
and yell. He had won so far, and he would go on winning.
He would get to the State Police. He would bring them back
to Ilium to free Claire.

After that, Harve would hire the best lawyer he could
find, clear himself, put Luby in prison, and sue the rotten city
of Ilium for a blue million.

Harve peered out from under the car. His hunters were not
coming toward him. They were moving away, blaming each
other with childish querulousness for having let him escape.

Harve crawled out from under the car, crouched, listened. And then he began to walk carefully, always in shadows. He moved with the cunning of an infantry scout. The
filth and feeble lights of the city, so recently his enemies, were
his friends now.

And, moving with his back to sooty walls, ducking into
doorways of decaying buildings, Harve realized that pure evil
was his friend, too. Eluding it, outwitting it, planning its de-
struction all gave his life inconceivably exciting meanings.

A newspaper scuttled by, tumbled in a night breeze,
seemed on its raffish way out of Ilium, too.

Far, far away a gun went off. Harve wondered what had
been shot at—or shot.

Few cars moved in Ilium. And even rarer were people on
foot. Two silent, shabby lovers passed within a few feet of
Harve without seeing him.

A lurching drunk did see Harve, murmured some quizzi-
cal insult, lurched on.

Now a siren wailed—and then another, and yet another.
Patrol cars were fanning out from the Ilium Police Station,
idiotically advertising themselves with noise and lights.

One car set up a noisy, flashy roadblock not far from Harve. It blocked an underpass through the high, black rampart of a railroad bed. That much of what the police were doing was intelligent, because the car made a deadend of the route that Harve had been taking.

The railroad bed loomed like the Great Wall of China to Harve. Beyond it lay what he thought of as freedom. He had to think of freedom as being something close, as being just one short rush away. Actually, on the other side of the black rampart lay more of Ilium—more faint lights and broken streets. Hope, real hope, lay far, far beyond—lay miles beyond, lay on a superhighway, the fast, clean realm of the State Police.

But Harve now had to pretend that passing over or through the rampart was all that remained for him to do.

He crept to the railroad bed, moved along its cindery face, moved away from the underpass that the police had blocked.

He found himself approaching yet another underpass that was blocked by a car. He could hear talk. He recognized the voice of the talker. It was the voice of Captain Luby.

"Don't bother taking this guy alive," the captain said. "He's no good to himself or anybody else alive. Do the taxpayers a favor, and shoot to kill."

Somewhere a train whistle blew.

And then Harve saw a culvert that cut through the bed of the railroad. It seemed at first to be too close to Captain Luby. But then the captain swept the approaches with a powerful flashlight, showed Harve the trench that fed the culvert. It crossed a field littered with oil drums and trash.

When Captain Luby's light went off, Harve crawled out onto the field, reached the ditch, slithered in. In its shallow, slimy shelter, he moved toward the culvert.

The train that had whistled was approaching now. Its progress was grindingly, clankingly slow.

When the train was overhead, its noise at a maximum, Harve ducked into the culvert. Without thought of an ambush on the other side, he emerged, scrambled up the cinder slope.

He swung onboard the rusty rungs of an empty gondola in the moving train.

Eternities later, the slow-moving train had carried Harve Elliot out of Ilium. It was making its complaining way now through a seemingly endless wasteland—through woods and neglected fields.

Harve's eyes, stinging in the night wind, searched for light and motion ahead, for some outpost of the world that would help him rescue his wife.

The train rounded a curve. And Harve saw lights that, in the midst of the rural desolation, looked as lively as a carnival.

What made all that seeming life was a red flasher at a grade crossing, and the headlights of one car stopped by the flasher.

As the gondola rattled over the crossing, Harve dropped off and rolled.

He stood, went unsteadily to the stopped automobile. When he got past the headlights, he could see that the driver was a young woman.

He could see, too, how terrified she was.

"Listen! Wait! Please!" said Harve.

The woman jammed her car in gear, sent the car bucking past Harve and over the crossing as the end of the caboose went by.

Her rear wheels threw cinders in Harve's eyes.

When he had cleared his eyes, her taillights were twinkling off into the night, were gone.

The train was gone, too.

And the noisy red flasher was dead.

Harve stood alone in a countryside as still and bleak as the arctic. Nowhere was there a light to mark a house.

The train blew its sad horn—far away now.

Harve put his hands to his cheeks. They were wet. They were grimed. And he looked around at the lifeless night, remembered the nightmare in Ilium. He kept his hands on his cheeks. Only his hands and his cheeks seemed real.

He began to walk.

No more cars came.

On he trudged, with no way of knowing where he was, where he was heading. Sometimes he imagined that he heard or saw signs of a busy highway in the distance—the faint singing of tires, the billowing of lights.

He was mistaken.

He came at last to a dark farmhouse. A radio murmured inside.

He knocked on the door.

Somebody stirred. The radio went off.

Harve knocked again. The glass pane in the door was loose, rattled when Harve knocked. Harve put his face to the pane. He saw the sullen red of a cigarette. It cast only enough light to illuminate the rim of the ashtray in which it rested.

Harve knocked again.

"Come in," said a man's voice. "Ain't locked."

Harve went in. "Hello?" he said.

No one turned on a light for him. Whoever had invited

him in didn't show himself, either. Harve turned this way and that. "I'd like to use your phone," he said to the dark.

"You stay faced right the way you are," said the voice, coming from behind Harve. "I got a double-barreled twelve-gauge shotgun aimed right at your middle, Mr. Elliot. You do anything out of the way at all, and I'll blow you right in two."

Harve raised his hands. "You know my name?" he said.

"That *is* your name?" said the voice.

"Yes," said Harve.

"Well, well," said the voice. It cackled. "Here I am, an old, old man. Wife gone, friends gone, children gone. Been thinking the past few days about using this here gun on myself. Just looky here what I would have missed! Just goes to prove—"

"Prove what?" said Harve.

"Nobody ever knows when he's gonna have a lucky day."

The ceiling fixture in the room went on. It was over Harve's head. Harve looked up at it. He didn't look behind himself, for fear of being blown in two. The ceiling fixture was meant to have three bulbs, had only one. Harve could tell that by the gray ghosts of the missing two.

The frosted shade was dotted with the shadows of the bodies of bugs.

"You can look behind, if you want," said the voice. "See for yourself whether I got a gun or not, Mr. Elliot."

Harve turned slowly to look at a very old man— a scrawny old man with obscenely white and even false teeth. The old man really did have a shotgun—a cavernous, rusty antique. The ornate, arched hammers of the gun were cocked.

The old man was scared. But he was pleased and excited, too.

"Don't make any trouble, Mr. Elliot," he said, "and we'll get along just fine. You're looking at a man who went over the top eight times in the Great War, so you ain't looking at anybody who'd be too chickenhearted to shoot. Shooting a man ain't something I never done before."

"All right—no trouble," said Harve.

"Wouldn't be the first man I shot," said the old man. "Wouldn't be the tenth, far as that goes."

"I believe you," said Harve. "Can I ask you how you happen to know my name?"

"Radio," said the old man. He motioned to an armchair, a chair with burst upholstering, with sagging springs. "You better set there, Mr. Elliot."

Harve did as he was told. "There's news of me on the radio?" he said.

"I guess there is," said the old man. "I expect you're on television, too. Don't have no television. No sense getting television at my age. Radio does me fine."

"What does the radio say about me?" said Harve.

"Killed a woman—broke jail," said the old man. "Worth a thousand dollars, dead or alive." He moved toward a telephone, keeping the gun aimed at Harve. "You're a lucky man, Mr. Elliot."

"Lucky?" said Harve.

"That's what I said," said the old man. "Whole county knows there's a crazy man loose. Radio's been telling 'em, 'Lock your doors and windows, turn out your lights, stay inside, don't let no strangers in.' Practically any house you would have walked up to, they would have shot first and asked questions afterwards. Just lucky you walked up to a house where there was somebody who don't scare easy." He took the telephone from its cradle.

"I never hurt anybody in my life," said Harve.

"That's what the radio said," said the old man. "Said you just went crazy tonight." He dialed for an operator, said to her, "Get me the Ilium Police Department."

"Wait!" said Harve.

"You want more time to figure how to kill me?" said the old man.

"The State Police—call the State Police!" said Harve.

The old man smiled foxily, shook his head. "They ain't the ones offering the big reward," he said.

The call went through. The Ilium Police were told where they could find Harve. The old man explained again and again where he lived. The Ilium Police would be coming out into unfamiliar territory. They had no jurisdiction there.

"He's all quiet now," said the old man. "I got him all calmed down."

And that was a fact.

Harve was feeling the relaxation of a very hard game's being over. The relaxation was a close relative of death.

"Funny thing to happen to an old man—right at the end of his days," said the old man. "Now I get a thousand dollars, picture in the paper—God knows what all—"

"You want to hear my story?" said Harve.

"Pass the time?" said the old man amiably. "All right with me. Just don't you budge from that chair."

So Harve Elliot told his tale. He told it pretty well, listened to the story himself. He astonished himself with the tale—and, with that astonishment, anger and terror began to seep into his being again.

"You've got to believe me!" said Harve. "You've got to let me call the State Police!"

The old man smiled indulgently. "Got to, you say?" he said.

"Don't you know what kind of a town Ilium is?" said Harve.

"Expect I do," said the old man. "I grew up there—and my father and grandfather, too."

"Do you know what Ed Luby's done to the town?" said Harve.

"Oh, I hear a few things now and then," said the old man. "He gave a new wing for the hospital, I know. I know, on account of I was in that wing one time. Generous man, I'd say."

"You can say that, even after what I've told you?" said Harve.

"Mr. Elliot," said the old man, with very real sympathy, "I don't think you're in any condition to talk about who's good and who's bad. I know what I'm talking about when I say that, on account of I was crazy once myself."

"I'm not crazy," said Harve.

"That's what I said, too," said the old man. "But they took me off to the crazy house just the same. I had a big story, too—all about the things folks had done to me, all about things folks was ganging up to do to me." He shook his head. "I believed that story, too. I mean, Mr. Elliot, I *believed* it."

"I tell you, I'm *not* crazy," said Harve.

"That's for a doctor to say, now, ain't it?" said the old man. "You know when they let me out of the crazy house, Mr. Elliot? You know when they let me out, said I could go home to my wife and family?"

"When?" said Harve. His muscles were tightening up. He knew he was going to have to rush past death again—to rush past death and into the night.

"They let me go home," said the old man, "when I could finally see for myself that nobody was really trying to do me in, when I could see for myself it was all in my head." He turned on the radio. "Let's have some music while we wait," he said. "Music always helps."

Asinine music about teenage love came from the radio. And then there was this news bulletin:

"Units of the Ilium Police are now believed to be closing in on Harvey Elliot, escaped maniac, who killed a woman outside of the fashionable Key Club in Ilium tonight. House-holders are warned, however, to continue to be on the look-out for this man, to keep all doors and windows locked, and to report at once any prowlers. Elliot is extremely dangerous and resourceful. The chief of police has characterized Elliot as a 'mad dog,' and he warns persons not to attempt to reason with him. The management of this station has offered a thousand-dollar reward for Elliot, dead or alive.

"This is WKLL," said the announcer, "eight sixty on your dial, the friendly voice of Ilium, with news and music for your listening pleasure around the clock."

It was then that Harve rushed the old man.

Harve knocked the gun aside. Both barrels roared.

The tremendous blast ripped a hole in the side of the house.

The old man held the gun limply, stupid with shock. He made no protest when Harve relieved him of the gun, went out the back door with it.

Sirens sobbed, far down the road.

. . .

Harve ran into the woods in back of the house. But then he understood that in the woods he could only provide a short and entertaining hunt for Captain Luby and his boys. Something more surprising was called for.

So Harve circled back to the road, lay down in a ditch.

Three Ilium police cars came to showy stops before the old man's house. The front tire of one skidded to within a yard of Harve's hand.

Captain Luby led his brave men up to the house. The blue flashers of the cars again created revolving islands of nightmare.

One policeman stayed outside. He sat at the wheel of the car nearest to Harve. He was intent on the raiders and the house.

Harve got out of the ditch quietly. He leveled the empty shotgun at the back of the policeman's neck, said softly, politely, "Officer?"

The policeman turned his head, found himself staring down two rusty barrels the size of siege howitzers.

Harve recognized him. He was the sergeant who had arrested Harve and Claire, the one with the long scar that seamed his cheek and lips.

Harve got into the back of the car. "Let's go," he said evenly. "Pull away slowly, with your lights out. I'm insane—don't forget that. If we get caught, I'll kill you first. Let's see how quietly you can pull away—and then let's see how fast you can go after that."

The Ilium police car streaked down a superhighway now. No one was in pursuit. Cars pulled over to let it by.

It was on its way to the nearest barracks of the State Police.

The sergeant at the wheel was a tough, realistic man. He did exactly what Harve told him to do. At the same time, he let Harve know that he wasn't scared. He said what he pleased.

"What you think this is gonna get you, Elliot?" he said.

Harve had made himself comfortable in the backseat. "It's going to get a lot of people a lot of things," he said grimly.

"You figure the State Police will be softer on a murderer than we were?" said the sergeant.

"You know I'm not a murderer," said Harve.

"Not a jailbreaker or a kidnapper, either, eh?" said the sergeant.

"We'll see," said Harve. "We'll see what I am, and what I'm not. We'll see what everybody is."

"You want my advice, Elliot?" said the sergeant.

"No," said Harve.

"If I were you, I'd get clear the hell out of the country," said the sergeant. "After all you've done, friend, you haven't got a chance."

Harve's head was beginning to bother him again. It ached in a pulsing way. The wound on the back of his head stung, as though it were open again, and waves of wooziness came and went.

Speaking out of that wooziness, Harve said to the sergeant, "How many months out of the year do you spend in Florida? Your wife got a nice fur coat and a sixty-thousand-dollar house?"

"You really *are* nuts," said the sergeant.

"You aren't getting your share?" said Harve.

"Share of what?" said the sergeant. "I do my job. I get my pay."

"In the rottenest city in the country," said Harve.

The sergeant laughed. "And you're gonna change all that—right?"

The cruiser slowed down, swung into a turnout, came to a stop before a brand-new State Police barracks of garish, yellow brick.

The car was surrounded instantly by troopers with drawn guns.

The sergeant turned and grinned at Harve. "Here's your idea of Heaven, buddy," he said. "Go on—get out. Have a talk with the angels."

Harve was hauled out of the car. Shackles were slammed on his wrists and ankles.

He was hoisted off his feet, was swept into the barracks, was set down hard on a cot in a cell.

The cell smelled of fresh paint.

Many people crowded around the cell door for a look at the desperado.

And then Harve passed out cold.

"No—he isn't faking," he heard someone say in a swirling mist. "He's had a pretty bad blow on the back of his head."

Harve opened his eyes. A very young man was standing over him.

"Hello," said the young man, when he saw that Harve's eyes were open.

"Who are you?" said Harve.

"Dr. Mitchell," said the young man. He was a narrow-shouldered, grave, bespectacled young man. He looked very insignificant in comparison with the two big men standing behind him. The two big men were Captain Luby and a uniformed sergeant of the State Police.

"How do you feel?" said Dr. Mitchell.

"Lousy," said Harve.

"I'm not surprised," said the doctor. He turned to Captain Luby. "You can't take this man back to jail," he said. "He's got to go to Ilium Hospital. He's got to have X-rays, got to be under observation for at least twenty-four hours."

Captain Luby gave a wry laugh. "Now the taxpayers of Ilium gotta give him a nice rest, after the night he put in."

Harve sat up. Nausea came and went. "My wife—how is my wife?"

"Half off her nut, after all the stuff you pulled," said Captain Luby. "How the hell you expect her to be?"

"You've still got her locked up?" said Harve.

"Nah," said Captain Luby. "Anybody who isn't happy in our jail, we let 'em go right away—let 'em walk right out. You know that. You're a big expert on that."

"I want my wife brought out here," said Harve. "That's why I came here—" Grogginess came over him. "To get my wife out of Ilium," he murmured.

"Why do you want to get your wife out of Ilium?" said Dr. Mitchell.

"Doc—" said the captain jocularly, "you go around asking jailbirds *how* come they want what they want, and you won't have no time left over for medicine."

Dr. Mitchell looked vaguely annoyed with the captain, put his question to Harve again.

"Doc," said Captain Luby, "what's that disease called— where somebody thinks everybody's against 'em?"

"Paranoia," said Dr. Mitchell tautly.

"We saw Ed Luby murder a woman," said Harve. "They blamed it on me. They said they'd kill us if we told." He lay back. Consciousness was fading fast. "For the love of God," he said thickly, "somebody help."

Consciousness was gone.

Harve Elliot was taken to Ilium Hospital in an ambulance. The sun was coming up. He was aware of the trip—aware of the sun, too. He heard someone mention the sun's coming up.

He opened his eyes. Two men rode on a bench that paralleled his cot in the ambulance. The two swayed as the ambulance swayed.

Harve made no great effort to identify the two. When hope died, so, too, had curiosity. Harve, moreover, had been somehow drugged. He remembered the young doctor's having given him a shot—to ease his pain, the doctor said. It killed Harve's worries along with his pain, gave him what comfort there was in the illusion that nothing mattered.

His two fellow passengers now identified themselves by speaking to each other.

"You new in town, Doc?" said one. "Don't believe I've ever seen you around before." That was Captain Luby.

"I started practice three months ago," the doctor said. That was Dr. Mitchell.

"You ought to get to know my brother," said the captain. "He could help you get started. He gets a lot of people started."

"So I've heard," said the doctor.

"A little boost from Ed never hurt anybody," said the captain.

"I wouldn't think so," said the doctor.

"This guy sure pulled a boner when he tried to pin the murder on Ed," said the captain.

"I can see that," said the doctor.

"Practically everybody who's anybody in town is a witness for Ed and against this jerk," said the captain.

"Uh-huh," said the doctor.

"I'll fix you up with an introduction to Ed sometime," said the captain. "I think you two would hit it off just fine."

"I'm very flattered," said the doctor.

At the emergency door of Ilium Hospital, Harve Elliot was transferred from the ambulance to a rubber-wheeled cart.

There was a brief delay in the receiving room, for another case had arrived just ahead of Harve. The delay wasn't long, because the other case was dead on arrival. The other case, on a cart exactly like Harve's, was a man.

Harve knew him.

The dead man was the man who had brought his girl out to Ed Luby's Key Club so long ago, who had seen his girl killed by Ed Luby.

He was Harve's prize witness—dead.

"What happened to him?" Captain Luby asked a nurse.

"Nobody knows," she said. "They found him shot in the back of the neck—in the alley behind the bus station." She covered the dead man's face.

"Too bad," said Captain Luby. He turned to Harve. "You're luckier than him, anyway, Elliot," he said. "At least you're not dead."

. . .

Harve Elliot was wheeled all over Ilium Hospital—had his skull X-rayed, had an electroencephalogram taken, let doctors peer gravely into his eyes, his nose, his ears, his throat.

Captain Luby and Dr. Mitchell went with him wherever he was rolled. And Harve was bound to agree with Captain Luby when the captain said, "It's crazy, you know? We're up all night, looking for a clean shot at this guy. Now here we are, all day long, getting the same guy the best treatment money can buy. Crazy."

Harve's time sense was addled by the shot Dr. Mitchell had given him, but he did realize that the examinations and tests were going awfully slowly—and that more and more doctors were being called in.

Dr. Mitchell seemed to grow a lot tenser about his patient, too.

Two more doctors arrived, looked briefly at Harve, then stepped aside with Dr. Mitchell for a whispered conference.

A janitor, mopping the corridor, paused in his wet and hopeless work to take a good look at Harve. "This him?" he said.

"That's him," said Captain Luby.

"Don't look very desperate, do he?" said the janitor.

"Kind of ran out of desperation," said the captain.

"Like a car run out of gas," said the janitor. He nodded. "He crazy?" he asked.

"He better be," said the captain.

"What you mean by that?" said the janitor.

"If he isn't," said the captain, "he's going to the electric chair."

"My, my," said the janitor. He shook his head. "Sure glad

I ain't him." He resumed his mopping, sent a little tidal wave of gray water down the corridor.

There was loud talk at the far end of the corridor now. Harve turned his incurious eyes to see Ed Luby himself approaching. Luby was accompanied by his big bodyguard, and by his good friend, his fat friend, Judge Wampler.

Ed Luby, an elegant man, was first of all concerned about the spotlessness of his black and pointed shoes. "Watch where you mop," he told the janitor in a grackle voice. "These are fifty-dollar shoes."

He looked down at Harve. "My God," he said, "it's the one-man army himself." Luby asked his brother if Harve could talk and hear.

"They tell me he hears all right," said the captain. "He don't seem to talk at all."

Ed Luby smiled at Judge Wampler. "I'd say that was a pretty good way for a man to be, wouldn't you, Judge?" he said.

The conference of doctors ended on a note of grim agreement. They returned to Harve's side.

Captain Luby introduced young Dr. Mitchell to his brother, Ed. "The doc here's new to town, Ed," said the captain. "He's kind of taken Elliot here under his wing."

"I guess that's part of his oath. Right?" said Ed Luby.

"Beg your pardon?" said Dr. Mitchell.

"No matter what somebody is," said Ed, "no matter what terrible things they've done—a doctor's still got to do everything he can for him. Right?"

"Right," said Dr. Mitchell.

Luby knew the other two doctors, and they knew him.

Luby and the doctors didn't like each other much. "You two guys are working on this Elliot, too?" said Ed.

"That's right," said one.

"Would somebody please tell me what's the matter with this guy, that so many doctors have to come from far and wide to look at him?" said Captain Luby.

"It's a very complicated case," said Dr. Mitchell. "It's a very tricky, delicate case."

"What's that mean?" said Ed Luby.

"Well," said Dr. Mitchell, "we're all pretty well agreed now that we've got to operate on this man at once, or there's a good chance he'll die."

Harve was bathed, and his head was shaved.

And he was rolled through the double doors and put under the blinding light of the operating room.

The Luby brothers were kept outside. There were only doctors and nurses around Harve now—pairs of eyes, and masks and gowns.

Harve prayed. He thought of his wife and children. He awaited the mask of the anesthetist.

"Mr. Elliot?" said Dr. Mitchell. "You can hear me?"

"Yes," said Harve.

"How do you feel?" said Dr. Mitchell.

"In the Hands of God," said Harve.

"You're not a very sick man, Mr. Elliot," said Dr. Mitchell. "We're not going to operate. We brought you up here to protect you." The eyes around the table shifted uneasily. Dr. Mitchell explained the uneasiness. "We've taken quite a chance here, Mr. Elliot," he said. "We have no way of knowing whether you deserve protection or not. We'd like to hear your story again."

Harve looked into each of the pairs of circling eyes. He shook his head almost imperceptibly. "No story," he said.

"No story?" said Dr. Mitchell. "After all this trouble we've gone to?"

"Whatever Ed Luby and his brother say the story is—that's the story," said Harve. "You can tell Ed I finally got the message. Whatever he says goes. No more trouble from me."

"Mr. Elliot," said Dr. Mitchell, "there isn't a man or a woman here who wouldn't like to see Ed Luby and his gang in prison."

"I don't believe you," said Harve. "I don't believe any-body anymore." He shook his head again. "As far as that goes," he said, "I can't prove any of my story anyway. Ed Luby's got all the witnesses. The one witness I thought I might get—he's dead downstairs."

This news was a surprise to those around the table.

"You knew that man?" said Dr. Mitchell.

"Forget it," said Harve. "I'm not saying any more. I've said too much already."

"There *is* a way you could prove your story—to our sat-isfaction, anyway," said Dr. Mitchell. "With your permission, we'd like to give you a shot of sodium pentothal. Do you know what it is?"

"No," said Harve.

"It's a so-called truth serum, Mr. Elliot," said Dr. Mitchell. "It will temporarily paralyze the control you have over your conscious mind. You'll go to sleep for a few minutes, and then we'll wake you up, and you won't be able to lie."

"Even if I told you the truth, and you believed it, and you

wanted to get rid of Ed Luby," said Harve, "what could a bunch of doctors do?"

"Not much, I admit," said Dr. Mitchell.

"But only four of us here are doctors," said Dr. Mitchell. "As I told Ed Luby, yours was a very complicated case—so we've called together a pretty complicated meeting to look into it." He pointed out masked and gowned men around the table. "This gentleman here is head of the County Bar Association. These two gentlemen here are detectives from the State Police. These two gentlemen are F.B.I. agents. That is, of course," he said, "if your story's true—if you're willing to let us prove it's true."

Harve looked into the circling eyes again.

He held out his bare arm to receive the shot. "Let's go," he said.

Harve told his story and answered questions in the unpleasant, echoing trance induced by sodium pentothal.

The questions came to an end at last. The trance persisted.

"Let's start with Judge Wampler," he heard someone say.

He heard someone else telephoning, giving orders that the cabdriver who had driven the murdered woman out to the Key Club was to be identified, picked up, and brought to the operating room of Ilium Hospital for questioning. "You heard me—the operating room," said the man on the telephone.

Harve didn't feel any particular elation about that. But then he heard some really good news. Another man took over the telephone, and he told somebody to get Harve's wife out of jail at once on a writ of habeas corpus. "And somebody else find out who's taking care of the kids," said the telephoner, "and, for God's sake, make sure the papers and the radio stations find out this guy isn't a maniac after all."

And then Harve heard another man come back to the operating room with the bullet from the dead man downstairs, the dead witness. "Here's one piece of evidence that isn't going to disappear," said the man. "Good specimen." He held the bullet up to the light. "Shouldn't have any trouble proving what gun it came from—if we had the gun."

"Ed Luby's too smart to do the shooting himself," said Dr. Mitchell, who was obviously starting to have a very fine time.

"His bodyguard isn't too smart," said somebody else. "In fact, he's just dumb enough. He's even dumb enough to have the gun still on him."

"We're looking for a thirty-eight," said the man with the bullet. "Are they all still downstairs?"

"Keeping a death watch," said Dr. Mitchell pleasantly.

And then word came that Judge Wampler was being brought up. Everyone tied on his surgical mask again, in order that the judge, when he entered, mystified and afraid, could see only eyes.

"What—what is this?" said Judge Wampler. "Why do you want me here?"

"We want your help in a very delicate operation," said Dr. Mitchell.

Wampler gave a smile that was queer and slack. "Sir?" he said.

"We understand that you and your wife were witnesses to a murder last night," said Dr. Mitchell.

"Yes," said Wampler. His translucent chins trembled.

"We think you and your wife aren't quite telling the truth," said Dr. Mitchell. "We think we can prove that."

"How *dare* you talk to me like that!" said Wampler indignantly.

"I dare," said Dr. Mitchell, "because Ed Luby and his brother are all through in this town. I dare," he said, "because police from outside have moved in. They're going to cut the rotten heart right out of this town. You're talking to federal agents and State Police at this very minute." Dr. Mitchell spoke over his shoulder. "Suppose you unmask, gentlemen, so the judge can see what sort of people he's talking to."

The faces of the law were unmasked. They were majestic in their contempt for the judge.

Wampler looked as though he were about to cry.

"Now tell us what you saw last night," said Dr. Mitchell.

Judge Wampler hesitated. Then he hung his head, and he whispered, "Nothing. I was inside. I didn't see anything."

"And your wife didn't see anything, either?" said Dr. Mitchell.

"No," whispered Wampler.

"You didn't see Elliot hit the woman?" said Dr. Mitchell.

"No," said the judge.

"Why did you lie?" said Dr. Mitchell.

"I—I believed Ed Luby," said Wampler. "He—he told me what happened—and I—I believed him."

"You believe him now?" said Dr. Mitchell.

"I—I don't know," said Wampler wretchedly.

"You're through as a judge," said Dr. Mitchell. "You must know that."

Wampler nodded.

"You were through as a man a long time ago," said Dr.

Mitchell. "All right," he said, "dress him up. Let him watch what happens next."

And Judge Wampler was forced to put on a mask and gown.

The puppet chief of police and the puppet mayor of Ilium were telephoned from the operating room, were told to come to the hospital at once, that there was something very important going on there. Judge Wampler, closely supervised, did the telephoning.

But, before they arrived, two state troopers brought in the cabdriver who had driven the murdered woman out to the Key Club.

He was appalled when he was brought before the weird tribunal of seeming surgeons. He looked in horror at Harve, who was still stretched out on the table in his sodium pentothal trance.

Judge Wampler again had the honor of doing the talking. He was far more convincing than anyone else could have been in advising the driver that Ed Luby and his brother were through.

"Tell the truth," said Judge Wampler quaveringly.

So the driver told it. He had seen Ed Luby kill the girl.

"Issue this man his uniform," said Dr. Mitchell.

And the driver was given a mask and gown.

Next came the mayor and the chief of police.

After them came Ed Luby, Captain Luby, and Ed Luby's big bodyguard.

The three came through the double doors of the operating room shoulder to shoulder.

They were handcuffed and disarmed before they could say a word.

"What the hell's the idea?" Ed Luby roared.

"It's all over. That's all," said Dr. Mitchell. "We thought you ought to know."

"Elliot's dead?" said Luby.

"*You're* dead, Mr. Luby," said Dr. Mitchell.

Luby started to inflate himself, was instantly deflated by a tremendous *bang*. A man had just fired the bodyguard's thirty-eight into a bucket packed with cotton.

Luby watched stupidly as the man dug the bullet out of the cotton, took it over to a counter where two microscopes had been set up.

Luby's comment was somewhat substandard. "Now, just a minute—" he said.

"We've got nothing but time," said Dr. Mitchell. "Nobody's in a hurry to go anywhere—unless you or your brother or your bodyguard have appointments elsewhere."

"Who *are* you guys?" said Luby malevolently.

"We'll show you in a minute," said Dr. Mitchell. "First, though, I think you ought to know that we're all agreed— you're through."

"Yeah?" said Luby. "Let me tell you, I've got plenty of friends in this town."

"Time to unmask, gentlemen," said Dr. Mitchell.

All unmasked.

Ed Luby stared at his utter ruin.

The man at the microscopes broke the silence. "They match," he said. "The bullets match. They came from the same gun."

Harve broke through the glass walls of his trance

momentarily. The tiles of the operating room echoed. Harve Elliot had laughed out loud.

Harve Elliot dozed off, was taken to a private room to sleep off the drug.

His wife, Claire, was waiting for him there.

Young Dr. Mitchell was with Harve when he was wheeled in. "He's perfectly all right, Mrs. Elliot," Harve heard Dr. Mitchell say. "He just needs rest—and so, I'd think, would you."

"I don't think I'll be able to sleep for a week," said Claire.

"I'll give you something, if you like," said Dr. Mitchell.

"Later, maybe," said Claire. "Not now."

"I'm sorry we shaved off all his hair," said Dr. Mitchell. "It seemed necessary at the time."

"Such a crazy night—such a crazy day," she said. "What did it all mean?"

"It meant a lot," said Dr. Mitchell, "thanks to some brave and honest men."

"Thanks to you," she said.

"I was thinking of your husband," he said. "As for myself, I never enjoyed anything more in my life. It taught me how men get to be free, and how they can stay free."

"How?" said Claire.

"By fighting for justice for strangers," said Dr. Mitchell.

Harve Elliot managed to get his eyes open. "Claire—" he said.

"Darling—" she said.

"I love you," said Harve.

"That's the absolute truth," said Dr. Mitchell, "in case you've ever wondered."

A SONG FOR SELMA

Around Lincoln High School, Al Schroeder's first name was hardly ever mentioned. He was simply Schroeder. Or not so simply Schroeder, either, because his last name was spoken with a strong accent, as though Schroeder were a famous dead European. He wasn't. He was as American as cornflakes, and, far from being dead, he was a vivid sixteen years old.

It was Helga Grosz, the German teacher at Lincoln, who first gave the name a rich accent. The other faculty members, hearing her do it, recognized instantly the rightness of the accent. It set Schroeder apart, reminded any faculty member who discussed him that Schroeder represented a thrilling responsibility.

For Schroeder's own good, it was kept from him and from the rest of the student body just why Schroeder was such a thrilling responsibility. He was the first authentic genius in the history of Lincoln High.

Schroeder's blinding I.Q., like the I.Q. of every student, was a carefully guarded secret in the confidential files in the office of the principal.

It was the opinion of George M. Helmholtz, portly head of the music department and director of the Lincoln Ten Square

Marching Band, that Schroeder had the stuff to become as great as John Philip Sousa, composer of "Stars and Stripes Forever."

Schroeder, in his freshman year, learned to play a clarinet well enough in three months to take over the first chair in the band. By the end of his sophomore year, he was master of every instrument in the band. He was now a junior, and the composer of nearly a hundred marches.

As an exercise in sight reading, Helmholtz was now putting the beginners' band, the C Band, through an early Schroeder composition called "Hail to the Milky Way." It was an enthusiastic piece of music, and Helmholtz hoped that the straightforward violence of it would tempt the beginners into really having a go at music. Schroeder's own comments on the composition pointed out that the star farthest from the earth in the Milky Way was approximately ten thousand light-years away. If the sound of the musical salute was to reach that farthest star, the music would have to be played good and loud.

The C Band bleated, shrieked, howled, and squawked at that farthest star gamely. But the musicians dropped out one by one until, as was so often the case, the bass drummer played alone.

Blom, blom, bloom went the bass drum. It was being larruped by Big Floyd Hires, the biggest, the most pleasant, and the dumbest boy in school. Big Floyd was probably the wealthiest, as well. Someday he would own his father's drycleaning chain.

Bloom, bloom, bloom went Big Floyd's drum.

Helmholtz waved Big Floyd to silence. "Thank you for sticking with it, Floyd," he said. "Sticking with it to the end is an example the rest of you could well follow. Now, we're going to go through this again—and I want everybody to stick with it right to the end, no matter what."

Helmholtz raised his baton, and Schroeder, the school genius, came in from the hall. Helmholtz nodded a greeting. "All right, men," Helmholtz said to the C Band, "here's the composer himself. Don't let him down."

Again the band tried to hail the Milky Way, again it failed.

Bloom, bloom, bloom went Big Floyd's drum—alone, alone, terribly alone.

Helmholtz apologized to the composer, who was sitting on a folding chair by the wall. "Sorry," he said. "It's only the second time through. Today's the first they've seen of it."

"I understand," said Schroeder. He was a small person—nicely proportioned, but very light, and only five feet and three inches tall. He had a magnificent brow, high and already lined by scowling thought. Eldred Crane, head of the English department, called that brow "the white cliffs of Dover." The unrelenting brilliance of Schroeder's thoughts gave him an alarming aspect that had been best described by Hal Bourbeau, the chemistry teacher. "Schroeder," Bourbeau said one time, "looks as though he's sucking on a very sour lemon drop. And when the lemon drop is gone, he's going to kill everybody."

The part about Schroeder's killing everybody was, of course, pure poetic license. He had never been in the least temperamental.

"Perhaps you would like to speak to the boys about what you've tried to achieve with this composition," Helmholtz said to Schroeder.

"Nope," said Schroeder.

"Nope?" said Helmholtz, surprised. Negativism wasn't Schroeder's usual style. It would have been far more like Schroeder to speak to the bandsmen thrillingly, to make them optimistic and gay. "Nope?" said Helmholtz.

"I'd rather they didn't try it again," said Schroeder.

"I don't understand," said Helmholtz.

Schroeder stood, and he looked very tired. "I don't want anybody to play my music anymore," he said. "I'd like to have it all back, if you don't mind."

"What do you want it back for?" said Helmholtz.

"To burn it," said Schroeder. "It's trash—pure trash." He smiled wanly. "I'm through with music, Mr. Helmholtz."

"Through?" said Helmholtz, heartsick. "You can't mean it!"

Schroeder shrugged. "I simply haven't got what it takes," he said. "I know that now." He waved his small hand feebly. "All I ask is that you don't embarrass me any more by playing my foolish, crude, and no doubt comical compositions."

He saluted Helmholtz and left.

For the remainder of the period, Helmholtz could not keep his mind on the C Band. All he could think about was Schroeder's shocking and inexplicable decision to give up music entirely.

At the end of the period, Helmholtz set out for the teachers' cafeteria. It was lunchtime. He became gradually aware that he had company. Big Floyd Hires, the genially dumb drummer, was clumping along beside him.

There was nothing casual about Big Floyd's being there. His presence was massively intentional. Big Floyd had something of importance to say, and the novelty of that made him throw off heat like a steam locomotive.

And it made him wheeze.

"Mr. Helmholtz," wheezed Big Floyd.

"Yes?" said Helmholtz.

"I'm—I—I just wanted you to know I'm through loafing," wheezed Big Floyd.

"Excellent," said Helmholtz. He was all for people's trying their hardest, even in cases like Big Floyd's, where the results of trying and not trying were almost certain to be identical.

Big Floyd now flabbergasted Helmholtz by handing him a song he had composed. "I wish you'd look at this, Mr. Helmholtz," he said.

The music was written in great black gobs, and there wasn't much of it. But it must have been about as difficult for Big Floyd as the Fifth Symphony had been for Beethoven.

It had a title. It was called "A Song for Selma."

And there were words to go with the music:

I break the chains that bind me.
I leave the clown I was behind me.
It was wonderful of you to remind me
That if I looked I would find me.
Oh, Selma, Selma, thank you.
I can never say good-bye.

When Helmholtz looked up from the words and music, the poet-composer was gone.

There was a spry debate that noon in the teachers' cafeteria. The subject, as stated by Hal Bourbeau of the chemistry department: "Does the good news about Big Floyd Hires deciding to be a musical genius offset the bad news about Schroeder deciding to withdraw from the field entirely?"

The obvious purpose of the debate was to twit Helmholtz. It was good fun for everybody but Helmholtz, since the problem was regarded as being purely a band matter, and since the band was regarded as being a not very serious enterprise anyway. It was not yet known that Schroeder despaired of amounting to anything in any field of learning.

"As I see it," said Bourbeau, "if a slow student decides to take band music seriously and a genius decides to give it up in favor of chemistry, say, it isn't a case of one person's going up and another person's going down. It's a case of two persons' going up."

"Yes," said Helmholtz mildly, "and the bright boy can give us a new poison gas, and the dumb one can give us a new tune to whistle."

Ernest Groper, the physics teacher, joined the group. He was a rude, realistic, bomb-shaped man, at war with sloppy thinking. As he transferred his lunch from his tray to the table, he gave the impression that he was obeying the laws of motion voluntarily, with gusto—not because he had to obey them but because he thought they were darn fine laws.

"You hear the news about Big Floyd Hires?" Bourbeau asked him.

"The great nucular fizzist?" said Groper.

"The what?" said Bourbeau.

"That's what Big Floyd told me he was going to be this morning," said Groper. "Said he was through loafing, said he was going to be a nucular fizzist. I think he means *nuclear physicist,* but he may mean *veterinarian.*" He picked up the copy of Big Floyd's "A Song for Selma," which Helmholtz had passed around the table a few minutes before. "What's this?"

"Big Floyd wrote it," said Helmholtz.

Groper raised his eyebrows. "He *is* busy these days, isn't he!" he said. "Selma? Selma who? Selma Ritter?" He tucked his napkin under his collar.

"She's the only Selma we could think of," said Helmholtz.

"Must be Selma Ritter," said Groper. "She and Big Floyd sit at the same table in the physics lab." He closed his eyes, rubbed the bridge of his nose. "What a crazy, mixed-up table that is, too," he said tiredly. "Schroeder, Big Floyd, and Selma Ritter."

"They all three sit together?" said Helmholtz musingly, trying to find some pattern.

"I thought Schroeder might help to pull Big Floyd and Selma up," said Groper. He nodded wonderingly. "And he certainly has, hasn't he?" He looked quizzically at Helmholtz. "You don't happen to know what Big Floyd's I.Q. is, do you, George?"

"I wouldn't even know how to find out," said Helmholtz. "I don't believe in I.Q.s."

"There's a confidential file in the principal's office," said Groper. "If you want a real thrill, look up Schroeder, sometime."

"Which one is Selma Ritter?" said Hal Bourbeau, looking through the plate glass partition that separated the teachers' cafeteria from the students' cafeteria.

"She's a little thing," said Groper.

"A quiet little thing," said Eldred Crane, head of the English department. "Shy, and not very popular."

"She's certainly popular now—with Big Floyd," said

Groper. "They've got a big love affair going, from all I can see." He shuddered. "I've got to get those two away from Schroeder. I don't know how they do it, but they certainly manage to depress him."

"I don't see her out there anywhere," said Helmholtz, still scanning the student cafeteria for Selma Ritter's face. He did see Schroeder, who was sitting by himself. The small, brilliant boy was looking very dejected, ruefully resigned. And Helmholtz saw Big Floyd. Big Floyd was sitting alone, too—massive, inarticulate, and inexpressibly hopeful about something. He was apparently thinking prodigiously. He squirmed and scowled, and bent imaginary iron bars.

"Selma isn't out there," said Helmholtz.

"I just remembered," said Eldred Crane, "Selma doesn't eat during the regular lunch hour. She eats during the next period."

"What does she do during the lunch hour?" said Helmholtz.

"She holds down the switchboard in the principal's office," said Crane, "while the staff is out to lunch."

Helmholtz excused himself, and he went to the principal's office to have a talk with Selma Ritter. The office was actually a suite, consisting of a foyer, a meeting room, two offices, and a file room.

When Helmholtz entered the suite, his first impression was that there was no one in it. The switchboard was deserted. The switches buzzed and blinked in dismal futility.

And then Helmholtz heard what was little more than a mouse noise in the file room. He went to the room quietly, peeked in.

Selma Ritter was kneeling by an open file drawer, writing something in her notebook.

Helmholtz was not shocked. He didn't jump to the conclusion that Selma was looking into something that wasn't any of her business—for the simple reason that he didn't believe in secrets. As far as Helmholtz was concerned, there weren't any secrets in Lincoln High School.

Selma took a rather different view of secrecy. What she had her hands in were the confidential files, the files that told, among other things, what everyone's I.Q. was. When Helmholtz caught her red-handed, Selma literally lost her balance, toppled to one side from her precarious kneel.

Helmholtz helped her up. And while he was doing it, he caught a glimpse of the file card Selma had been copying from. The card had unexplained numbers scattered over it, seemingly at random.

The numbers meant nothing to Helmholtz, since he had never used the files. They represented not only an individual's I.Q. but his sociability index, his dexterity, his weight, his leadership potential, his height, his work preferences, and his aptitudes in six different fields of human accomplishment. The Lincoln High School testing program was a thorough one.

It was a famous one, too—a favorite hunting ground for would-be Ph.D.s, since Lincoln's testing records went back more than twenty-five years.

In order to find out what each number meant, Helmholtz would have had to use a decoding card, a card with holes punched in it, which was kept locked up in the principal's safe. By placing the decoding card over the file card, Helmholtz might have found out what all the numbers meant.

But he didn't need the decoding card to find out whose file card Selma had been copying from. The name of the individual was typed big as life at the top of the card.

George M. Helmholtz was startled to read the name.

The name was HELMHOLTZ, GEO. M.

"What is this?" murmured Helmholtz, taking the card from the drawer. "What's this doing with my name on it? What's this got to do with me?"

Selma burst into tears. "Oh, Mr. Helmholtz," she wailed, "I didn't mean any harm. Please don't tell on me. I'll never do it again. Please don't tell."

"What is there to tell?" said Helmholtz, completely at sea.

"I was looking up your I.Q.," said Selma. "I admit it. You caught me. And I suppose I could get thrown out of school for it. But I had a reason, Mr. Helmholtz—a very important reason."

"I have no idea what my I.Q. is, Selma," said Helmholtz, "but you're certainly welcome to it, whatever it is."

Selma's crying abated some. "You won't report me?" she said.

"What's the crime?" said Helmholtz. "If my I.Q. is so interesting, I'll paint it on my office door for all to see."

Selma's eyes widened. "You don't know what your I.Q. is?" she said.

"No," said Helmholtz humbly. "Very submedium, I'd guess," he said.

Selma pointed to a number on the file card. "There," she said, "that's your I.Q., Mr. Helmholtz." She stepped back, as though she expected Helmholtz to collapse in astonishment. "That's it," she whispered.

Helmholtz studied the number. He pulled in his chin,

creating a multitude of echoing chins beneath it. The number was 183. "I know nothing about I.Q.s," he said. "Is that high or low?" He tried to remember when his I.Q. had last been tested. As nearly as he could recall, it hadn't been tested since he himself had been a student in Lincoln High.

"It's very, very, very high, Mr. Helmholtz," said Selma earnestly. "Mr. Helmholtz," she said, "don't you even know you're a genius?"

"What *is* this card anyway?" said Helmholtz.

"It's from when you were a student," said Selma.

Helmholtz frowned at the card. He remembered fondly the sober, little, fat boy he'd been, and it offended him to see that boy reduced to numbers. "I give you my word of honor, Selma," he said, "I was no genius then, and I am not a genius now. Why on earth did you look me up?"

"You're a teacher of Big Floyd's," said Selma. At the mention of Big Floyd, she gained an inch in stature and became radiantly possessive. "I knew you'd gone to school here, so I looked you up," she said, "to see if you were smart enough to realize how really smart Big Floyd is."

Helmholtz cocked his head quizzically. "And just how smart do you think Big Floyd is?" said Helmholtz.

"Look him up, if you want to," said Selma. She was becoming self-righteous now. "I guess nobody ever bothered to look him up before I did."

"You looked him up, too?" said Helmholtz.

"I got so sick of everybody saying how dumb Big Floyd was, and how smart that stupid Alvin Schroeder was," said Selma. "I had to find out for myself."

"What did you find?" said Helmholtz.

"I found out Alvin Schroeder was a big bluffer," said Selma, "acting so smart all the time. He's actually dumb. And I found out Big Floyd wasn't dumb at all. Actually, he's a big loafer. Actually, he's a genius like you."

"Um," said Helmholtz. "And you told them so?"

Selma hesitated. And then, so steeped in crime she could hardly worsen her case, she nodded. "Yes—I told them," she said. "I told them for their own good."

From three until four that afternoon, Helmholtz was in charge of an extracurricular activity, the Railsplitters, the glee club of Lincoln High. On this particular occasion, the sixty voices of the Railsplitters were augmented by a grand piano, a brass choir of three trumpets, two trombones, and a tuba, and the bright, sweet chimes of a glockenspiel.

The musicians who backed the glee club so richly had been recruited by Helmholtz since the lunch hour. Helmholtz had been frantically busy in his tiny office since lunch, making plans and sending off messengers like the commander of a battalion under fire.

When the clock on the wall of the rehearsal room stood at one minute until four, Helmholtz pinched off with his thumb and forefinger the almost insufferably beautiful final chord of the song the augmented glee club had been rehearsing.

When Helmholtz had pinched it off, he and the group looked stunned.

They had found the lost chord.

Never had there been such beauty.

The undamped voice of the glockenspiel was the last to die. The high song of the last chime struck on the glockenspiel faded into infinity, and it seemed to promise that it would be forever audible to anyone willing to listen hard enough.

"That's it—that's certainly it," whispered Helmholtz raptly. "Ladies and gentlemen—I can't thank you enough."

The buzzer on the wall clock sounded. It was four o'clock.

Right on the dot of four, Schroeder, Selma, and Big Floyd came into the rehearsal room, just as Helmholtz had told them to do. Helmholtz stepped down from the podium, led the three into his office, and closed the door.

"I suppose you all know why I've asked you to come," said Helmholtz.

"I don't," said Schroeder.

"It's about I.Q.s, Schroeder," said Helmholtz. And he told Schroeder about catching Selma in the file room.

Schroeder shrugged listlessly.

"If any of you three talks about this to anybody," said Helmholtz, "it will get Selma into terrible trouble, and me, too. I haven't reported the very bad thing Selma's done, and that makes me an accessory."

Selma paled.

"Selma," said Helmholtz, "what made you think that one particular number on the file cards was an I.Q.?"

"I—I read up on I.Q.s in the library," said Selma, "and then I looked myself up in the files, and I found the number on my card that was probably my I.Q."

"Interesting," said Helmholtz, "and a tribute to your modesty. That number you thought was your I.Q., Selma—that was your weight. And when you looked up the rest of us here, all you found out was who was heavy and who was light. In my case, you discovered that I was once a very fat boy. Big Floyd and I are far from being geniuses, and small Schroeder here is far from being a moron."

"Oh," said Selma.

Big Floyd gave a sigh that sounded like a freight whistle. "I told you I was dumb," he said to Selma wretchedly. "I told you I wasn't any genius." He pointed helplessly at Schroeder. "He's the genius. He's the one who's got it. He's the one who's got the brains to carry him right up into the stars or somewhere! I told you that!"

Big Floyd pressed the heels of his hands against his temples, as though to jar his brains into working better. "Boy," he said tragically, "I sure proved how dumb I was, believing for even one minute I had something on the ball."

"There's only one test to pay any attention to," said Helmholtz, "and that's the test of life. That's where you'll make the score that counts. That's true for Schroeder, for Selma, for you, Big Floyd, for me—for everybody."

"You can tell who's going to amount to something," said Big Floyd.

"Can you?" said Helmholtz. "I can't. Life is nothing but surprises to me."

"Think of the surprises that are waiting for a guy like me," said Big Floyd. He nodded at Schroeder. "Then think of the surprises that are waiting for a guy like him."

"Think of the surprises that are waiting for everybody!" said Helmholtz. "My mind reels!" He opened his office door, indicating that the interview was at an end.

Selma, Big Floyd, and Schroeder shuffled from Helmholtz's office into the rehearsal room. Their chins were not held high. The talk from Helmholtz hadn't inspired them much. On the contrary, the talk, like so many pep talks on the high school level, had been fairly depressing.

And then, as Selma, Big Floyd, and Schroeder shuffled past the glee club, the glee club and the musicians in support of it stood up.

At a signal from Helmholtz, there was a brilliant fanfare of brass.

The fanfare brought Selma, Big Floyd, and Schroeder to a halt and to startled attention.

The fanfare went on and on—intricately. And the grand piano and the glockenspiel joined the fanfare—clanged, banged, and pealed triumphantly, like church bells celebrating a great victory.

The seeming church bells and the fanfare died reluctantly.

The sixty voices of the glee club began to murmur sweetly, to murmur low.

And then the sixty voices, crying out wordlessly, began to climb. They reached a plateau, and they seemed to want to stay there.

But the brasses and the grand piano and the glockenspiel taunted them into climbing again, taunted the voices into overcoming all obstacles above them, taunted the voices into aspiring to the stars.

Up and up the voices went, to unbelievable heights. And as the wordless voices climbed, they seemed to promise that, when they reached the uppermost limits of their aspirations, they would at last speak words. They seemed to promise too that, when they spoke those words, those words would be stunning truth.

The voices now could go no higher.

They strained melodramatically. Melodramatically, they could rise no more.

And then, musical miracle of miracles, a soprano sent her voice not a little above the rest, but far, far, far above the rest. And, soaring so far above the rest, she found words.

"*I break the chains that bind meeeeeeeeeeee,*" she sang. Her voice was a thread of pure sunlight.

The piano and the glockenspiel both made sounds like breaking chains.

The glee club groaned in harmonic wonder at the broken chains.

"*I leave the clown I was behind me,*" sang a rumbling bass.

The trumpets laughed ironically, and then the entire brass choir sang a haunting phrase from "Auld Lang Syne."

"*It was wonderful of you to remind me,*" sang a baritone, "*That if I looked I would find me.*"

In very swift order, the soprano sang a phrase from "Someday I'll Find You," the full glee club sang a phrase from "These Foolish Things," and the piano played a phrase from "Among My Souvenirs."

"*Oh, Selma, Selma, Selma, thank you,*" sang all the basses together.

"Selma?" echoed the real Selma in real life.

"You," said Helmholtz to Selma. "This is a song Big Floyd, the well-known genius, wrote for you."

"For me?" said Selma, astonished.

"Sh!" said Helmholtz.

"*I can never—*" sang the soprano.

"*Never, never, never, never, never, never, never, never—*" chanted the glee club.

"*Say—*" rumbled the basses.

"*Good*—" piped the soprano.

And now the entire ensemble, Helmholtz included, joined in a hair-raising final chord, "*Byeeeeeeeeeeeeeeeeeeeeeeee eeeeeeeeeeeeeeeeeeeeeeeeeeeeeeeeeeeeeeeeeee!*"

Helmholtz pinched off the final chord with his thumb and forefinger.

Tears streamed down Big Floyd's cheeks. "Oh my, oh my, oh my," he murmured. "Who arranged it?" he said.

"A genius," said Helmholtz.

"Schroeder?" said Big Floyd.

"No," said Schroeder. "I—"

"How did you like it, Selma?" said Helmholtz.

There was no reply. Selma Ritter had fainted dead away.

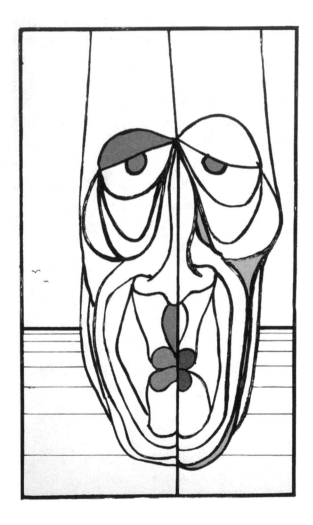

HALL OF MIRRORS

There was a parking lot, and then a guitar school, and then Fred's O.K. Used Car Lot, and then the hypnotist's house, and then a vacant lot with the foundation of a mansion still on it, and then the Beeler Brothers' Funeral Home. Autumn winds, experimenting with the idea of a hard winter, made little twists of soot and paper, made the plastic propellers over the used car lot go *frrrrrrrrrrrrrrrrrrrrrrrrrrrrr.*

The city was Indianapolis, the largest city not on a navigable waterway in the world.

It was to the hypnotist's house that the two city detectives came. They were Detectives Carney and Foltz, Carney young and dapper, Foltz middle-aged and rumpled. Carney went up the hypnotist's steps like a tap dancer. Foltz, though he was going to do all the talking, trudged far behind. Carney's interest was specific. He was going straight for the hypnotist. Foltz's attention was diffused. He marveled at the monstrous architecture of the hypnotist's twenty-room house, let his mournful eyes climb the tower at one corner of the house. There had to be a ballroom at the top of the tower. There were ballrooms at the tops of all the towers that the rich had abandoned.

Foltz reached the hypnotist's door at last, rang the bell. The only hint of quackery was a small sign over the doorbell. K. HOLLOMON WEEMS, it said, HYPNOTIC THERAPY.

Weems himself came to the door. He was in his fifties, small, narrow-shouldered, neat. His nose was long, his lips full and red, and his bald head had a seeming phosphorescence. His eyes were unspectacular—pale blue, clear, ordinary.

"Doctor Weems?" said Foltz, grumpily polite.

" 'Doctor' Weems?" said Weems. "There is no 'Doctor' Weems here. There is a very plain 'Mister' Weems. He stands before you."

"In your line of work," said Foltz, "I'd think a man would almost have to have some kind of doctor's degree."

"As it happens," said Weems, "I hold two doctor's degrees—one from Budapest, another from Edinburgh." He smiled faintly. "I don't use the title Doctor, however. I wouldn't want anyone to mistake me for a physician." He shivered in the winds. "Won't you come in?"

The three went into what had been the parlor of the mansion, what was the hypnotist's office now. There was no nonsense about the furnishings. They were functional, gray-enameled steel—a desk, a few chairs, a filing cabinet, a bookcase. There were no pictures, no framed certificates on the high walls.

Weems sat down behind his desk, invited his visitors to sit. "The chairs aren't very comfortable, I'm afraid," he said.

"Where do you keep your equipment, Mr. Weems?" said Foltz.

"What equipment is that?" said Weems.

Foltz's stubby hands worked in air. "I assume you've got something you hypnotize people with. A light or something they stare at?"

"No," said Weems. "I'm all the apparatus there is."

"You pull the blinds when you hypnotize somebody?" said Foltz.

"No," said Weems. He volunteered no more information, but looked back and forth between the detectives, inviting them to state their business.

"We're from the police, Mr. Weems," said Foltz, and he showed his identification.

"You are not telling me the news," Weems said.

"You were expecting the police?" said Foltz.

"I was born in Romania, sir—where one is taught from birth to expect the police."

"I thought maybe you had some idea what we were here about?" said Foltz.

Weems sat back, twiddled his thumbs. "Oh—generally, generally, generally," he said. "I arouse vague fears among the simpler sorts wherever I go. Sooner or later they coax the police into having a look at me, to see if I might not be performing black magic here."

"You mind telling us what you do do here?" said Foltz.

"What I do, sir," said Weems, "is as simple and straightforward as what a carpenter or any other honest workman does. My particular service has to do with the elimination of undesirable habits or unreasonable fears." He startled young Carney by gesturing at him suddenly. "You, sir, obviously smoke too much. If you were to give me your undivided attention for two minutes, you would never smoke again, would never want to smoke again."

Carney put out his cigarette.

"I must apologize for the chair you're sitting on, sir," said Weems to Carney. "It's brand-new, but something's wrong with the cushion. There's a small lump on the left side. It's a very small lump, but after a while it makes people quite un-comfortable. It's surprising how a little thing like that can ac-tually induce real pain. Curiously enough, people usually feel the pain in the neck and shoulders rather than in the lower spine."

"I'm all right," said Carney.

"Fine," said Weems. He turned to Foltz again. "If a man had a fear of firearms, for instance," he said, "and his work made it necessary for him to be around them, I could elimi-nate that fear with hypnosis. As a matter of fact, if a police-man, say, were only a moderately good pistol shot, I could steady his hand enough by means of hypnosis to make him an expert. I'll steady your hand, if you like. If you'll take out your pistol and hold it as steadily as possible—"

Foltz did not draw his pistol. "Only two reasons I ever take my pistol out," he said. "Either I'm gonna clean it, or I'm gonna shoot somebody with it."

"In a minute you'll change your mind," said Weems, and he glanced at his expensive wristwatch. "Believe me— I could make your hand as steady as a vise." He looked at Carney, saw that Carney was standing, was massaging the back of his neck. "Oh, dear," said Weems, "I did warn you about that chair. I should get rid of it. Take another chair, please, and turn that one to the wall, so no one else will get a stiff neck from it."

Carney took another chair, turned his first chair to the wall. He carried his head to one side. His neck was as stiff as a bent crowbar. No amount of rubbing seemed to help.

"Have I convinced you?" Weems said to Foltz. "Will you tell my friends and neighbors that I'm not practicing witch-craft or medicine without a license here?"

"I'd be glad to do that, sir," said Foltz. "But that isn't the main thing we came to see you about."

"Oh?" said Weems.

"No, sir," said Foltz. He took a photograph from the inside pocket of his coat. "What we really wanted to ask you was, do you know this woman, and do you have any idea where we could find her? We've traced her here, and nobody seems to know where she went after."

Weems took the photograph without hesitation, identified it promptly. "Mrs. Mary Styles Cantwell. I remember her well. Would you like to know the exact dates when she was here for treatment?" He opened a card file on his desk, searched for the card of the missing woman, found it. "Four visits in all," he said. "July fourteenth, fifteenth, nineteenth, and twenty-first."

"What did you treat her for?" said Foltz.

"Would you mind pointing that thing somewhere else?" said Weems.

"What?" said Foltz.

"Your pistol," said Weems. "It's pointing right at me."

Foltz looked down at his right hand, discovered that it really did hold a pistol, a pistol aimed at Weems. He was embarrassed, confused. Still, he did not return the pistol to its holster.

"Put it away, please," said Weems.

Foltz put it away.

"Thank you," said Weems. "Surely I'm not being that uncooperative."

"No, sir," said Foltz.

"It's the heat in the room," said Weems. "It puts everybody's nerves on edge. The heating system is very bad. It's always boiling hot in this room, while the rest of the house is like the North Pole. It's at least ninety degrees in here. Won't you gentlemen please take off your coats?"

Carney and Foltz took off their coats.

"Take off your suit coats, too," said Weems. "It must be a hundred in here."

Carney and Foltz took off their suit coats, but sweltered still.

"You both have splitting headaches now," said Weems, "and I know how hard it must be for you to think straight. But I want you to tell me everything you know about me or suspect about me."

"Four women who've been reported missing have been traced here," said Foltz.

"Only four?" said Weems.

"Only four," said Foltz.

"Their names, please?" said Weems.

"Mrs. Mary Styles Cantwell, Mrs. Esmeralda Coyne, Mrs. Nancy Royce, Mrs. Caroline Hughs Tinker, and Mrs. Janet Zimmer."

Weems wrote the names down, just the last names. "Cantwell, Coyne, Royce . . . Selfridge, did you say?"

"Selfridge?" said Foltz. "Who's Selfridge?"

"Nobody," said Weems. "Selfridge is nobody."

"Nobody," echoed Foltz blankly.

"What do you think I did with these women?" said Weems.

"We think you killed them," said Foltz. "They were all fairly rich widows. They all drew their money out of the bank after they came to see you, and they all disappeared after that. We think their bodies are somewhere in this house."

"Do you know my real name?" said Weems.

"No," said Foltz. "When we get your fingerprints, we figure we'll find out you're wanted a lot of other places."

"I will save you that trouble," said Weems. "I will tell
you my real name. My real name, gentlemen, is Rumpelstiltskin. Have you got that? I will spell it for you.
R-u-m-p-e-l-s-t-i-l-t-s-k-i-n."

"R-u-m-p-e-l-s-t-i-l-t-s-k-i-n," said Foltz.

"I think you should phone that information in to headquarters immediately," said Weems. He held out absolutely
nothing to Foltz. "Here's the telephone," he said.

Foltz took the nothing he'd been handed, treated it like a
telephone. Using the nonexistent instrument, he put a call
through to a Captain Finnerty, reported gravely that Weems's
real name was Rumpelstiltskin.

"What did Captain Finnerty say when you gave him the
news?" said Weems.

"I don't know," said Foltz.

"You don't know?" said Weems incredulously. "He said
I was the man who made people pass through mirrors,
didn't he?"

"Yes," said Foltz. "That's what he said."

"I admit it," said Weems. "You've got me dead to rights.
I am Rumpelstiltskin," he said, "and I have hypnotized people into stepping through mirrors, into stepping out of this
life and into another on the other side. Can you believe
that?"

"Yes," said Foltz.

"It's certainly possible, once you think about it, isn't it?"
said Weems.

"Yes," said Foltz.

"You believe it, too, don't you?" Weems said to Carney.

Carney was a hunchback now, his neck, shoulders, and head ached so. "I believe it," he said.

"So that explains what happened to the ladies you're looking for," said Weems. "They're far from being dead, believe me. They came to me, very unhappy about the way their lives were going, so I sent them through mirrors to see if things weren't better on the other side. In every case, they chose to remain on the other side. I'll show you in a moment the mirrors they went through, but first I'd like to know if there are any more police outside, or on their way here."

"No," said Foltz.

"Just you two?" said Weems.

"Yes," said Foltz.

Weems clapped his hands lightly. "Well—come along, gentlemen, and I'll show you the mirrors."

He went to the office door, held it open for his guests. He watched them closely as they passed out into the hall, was gratified when they both began to shiver violently, as though struck by bitter cold.

"I warned you it was like the North Pole out here," he said. "You'd better bundle up, though I'm afraid you'll still be quite uncomfortable."

Carney and Foltz bundled up, but continued to shiver.

"Three flights of stairs to climb, gentlemen," said Weems. "We're going to the ballroom at the top of the house. That is where the mirrors are. There is an elevator, but it hasn't run for years."

Not only was the elevator inoperative. It didn't even exist anymore. The elevator, the paneling, the ornate light fixtures, and everything remotely valuable had been stripped from the mansion years before Weems took it over. But Weems invited his guests, even as their feet crunched broken plaster on bare floors, to admire the immaculate and lavish decor.

"This is the gold room, and this is the blue room," he said. "The white swan bed in the blue room is said to have belonged to Madame Pompadour, believe it or not. Do you believe that?" he said to Foltz.

"You couldn't prove it by me," said Foltz.

"Who can be sure of anything in this world, eh?" said Weems.

Carney repeated this sentiment word for word. "Who can be sure of anything in this world, eh?" he said.

"Here is the staircase to the ballroom," said Weems. The staircase was broad. There was a pedestal at its base that had once supported a statue. The original banisters were gone, naked spikes showing where the uprights had once been moored. There was only one banister now, a length of pipe held by clinched nails. The bare steps were studded with carpet tacks. A tack here and there held a twist of red yarn.

"I've spent more money restoring this staircase than I've spent on anything else in the house," said Weems. "The banisters I found in Italy. The statue, a fourteenth-century Saint Catherine from Toledo, I bought from the estate of William Randolph Hearst. This carpet we're walking on, gentlemen, was woven to my specifications in Kerman, Iran. It's like walking on a feather mattress, isn't it?"

Carney and Foltz did not reply, there was so much splendor to appreciate. But they lifted their knees high, as though they were indeed walking on a feather mattress.

Weems opened the ballroom door, a handsome door,

actually. But its handsomeness was spoiled by a message whitewashed across its face. KEEP OUT, said the sign. Two coat hangers hung from the doorknob, tinkled tinnily as Weems opened and closed the door.

The ballroom at the tower's top was circular. Around its walls, full-length mirrors alternated with ghastly leaded-glass windows of purple, mustard, and green. The only furnishings were three bundles of newspapers, tied up as though for a paper sale, two pieces of track from a toy train set, and the headboard of a brass bed.

Weems did not rhapsodize about the glories of the ballroom. He invited Carney and Foltz to give their full attention to the mirrors, which were real. And the play of mirrors on mirrors gave each mirror the aspect of a door leading to infinite perspectives of other doors.

"Sort of like a railroad roundhouse, isn't it?" said Weems. "Look at all the possible routes of travel radiating from us, beckoning to us." He turned to Carney suddenly. "Which route attracts you most?"

"I—I don't know," said Carney.

"Then I'll recommend one in a moment," said Weems. "It isn't a decision to be taken lightly, because a person changes radically when he passes through a mirror—he or she, as the case may be. Handedness changes, of course. That's elementary. A right-handed person becomes left-handed, and vice versa. But a person's personality changes, too—and his future—his or her future, as the case may be."

"The women we're looking for—they went through these mirrors?" said Foltz.

"Yes—the women you're looking for, and about a dozen

more you're not looking for besides," said Weems. "They came to me with the shapeless longings of widows with money, but without confidence, hope, irresistible beauty, or dreams. They had been to physicians and quacks of every sort before they came to me. They could describe neither their ailment nor the hoped for cure. It was up to me to define both."

"So what did you tell them?" said Foltz.

"Couldn't you make a diagnosis on the basis of what I've told you?" said Weems. "It was their futures that were sick. And for sick futures"—and he swept his hand at the seeming doors all around them—"I know only one cure."

Weems shouted now, and then listened as though expecting faint replies. "Mrs. Cantwell? Mary?" he called. "Mrs. Forbes?"

"Who is Mrs. Forbes?" said Foltz.

"That is Mary Cantwell's new name on the other side of the glass," said Weems.

"Names change when people go through?" said Foltz.

"No—not necessarily," said Weems, "though a lot of people decide to change their names to go with their new futures, new personalities. In the case of Mary Cantwell—she married a man named Gordon Forbes a week after passing through." He smiled. "I was the best man—and, in all modesty, I don't think anyone ever deserved the honor more."

"You can go in and out of these mirrors any time you want?" said Foltz.

"Certainly," said Weems. "Self-hypnosis, the easiest and commonest form of hypnosis."

"I'd sure like a demonstration," said Foltz.

"That's why I'm trying to call Mary or one of the others back," said Weems. "Hello! Hello! Can anybody hear me?" he shouted at the mirrors.

"I thought maybe *you'd* go through a mirror for us," said Foltz.

"It's a thing I don't care to do, really, except on very special occasions," said Weems, "like Mary's wedding, like the Carter family's first anniversary on the other side—"

"The who family?" said Foltz.

"The Carter family," said Weems. "George, Nancy, and their children, Eunice and Robert." He pointed over his shoulder at a mirror behind him. "I put them all through that mirror there a year and a quarter ago."

"I thought you just specialized in rich widows," said Foltz.

"I thought that's what you specialized in," said Weems. "That's all you asked about—rich widows."

"So you put a family through, too?" said Foltz.

"Several of them," said Weems. "I suppose you want the exact number. I can't give you that number off the top of my head. I'll have to check my files."

"They had bad futures, sick futures," said Foltz, "these families you—uh—put through?"

"In terms of life on this side of the glass?" said Weems. "No—not really. But there were far better futures to be had on the other side. No danger of war, for one thing—a much lower cost of living, for another."

"Um," said Foltz. "And when they went through, they left all their money with you. Right?"

"They took it with them," said Weems, "all of it, with the exception of my fee, which is a flat hundred dollars a head."

"It's too bad they can't hear you yell," said Foltz. "I'd sure like to talk to some of these people, hear about all the nice things that have been happening to them."

"Look in any mirror, and see what a long, complicated corridor my voice has to carry down," said Weems.

"Guess it's up to you to put on the demonstration, then," said Foltz.

"I told you," said Weems, very uneasy now, "I am very reluctant to do it."

"You're afraid the trick won't work?" said Foltz.

"Oh, it'll work all right," said Weems. "It's likely to work too well, is all. If I get on the other side of the glass, I'm going to want to stay on the other side. I always do."

Foltz laughed. "If it's so heavenly on the other side," he said, "what could keep you here?"

Weems closed his eyes, massaged the bridge of his nose. "The same thing that makes you an excellent policeman," he said. He opened his eyes. "A sense of duty." He did not smile.

"And what is it this duty of yours makes you do?" said Foltz. He asked the question mockingly. His air of being dazed, of being in Weems's power, had dropped away.

Weems, seeing the transformation, became in turn a small and wretched man. "It makes me stay here, on this side," he said emptily, "because I am the only one I know of who can help others pass through." He shook his head. "You aren't hypnotized, are you?" he said.

"Hell no," said Foltz. "And neither is he."

Carney relaxed, shuddered, smiled.

"If it makes you feel any better," said Foltz, taking his handcuffs from his hip pocket, "it's a couple of brother hypnotists who are taking you in. That's how we got this assignment. Carney and I've both played with it some. Compared to you, we're mere amateurs, of course. Come on, Weems—Rumpelstiltskin—hold out your wrists like a good boy."

"This was a trap, then?" said Weems.

"Right," said Foltz. "We wanted to get you to talk, and you certainly did. The only problem now is to find the bodies. What did you plan to do with Carney and me—get us to shoot each other?"

"No," said Weems simply.

"I'll tell you this," said Foltz, "we respected hypnotism enough not to take any chances. There's another detective right outside the door."

Weems had not yet held out his thin wrists like a good boy. "I don't believe you," he said.

"Fred!" Foltz called to the detective on the staircase outside. "Come on in, so Rumpelstiltskin can believe in you."

In came the third detective, a pale, moonfaced, huge, young Swede. Carney and Foltz were elated and smug. The man named Fred didn't share their delight. He was worried and watchful, had his gun drawn.

"Please," Weems said to Foltz, "tell him to put his gun away."

"Put your gun away, Fred," said Foltz.

"You guys are really all right?" said Fred.

Carney and Foltz laughed.

"Fooled you, too, eh?" said Foltz.

Fred didn't laugh. "Yeah—you sure did," he said. He looked closely at Carney and Foltz, did it impersonally, as though they were department store dummies. And Carney and Foltz, in their moment of triumph, really did look like dummies—stiff, waxen, with mortuary smiles.

"For the love of God," Weems said to Foltz, "tell him to put his gun away."

"For the love of God," said Foltz, "put the gun away, Fred."

Fred didn't do it. "I—I don't think you guys know what you're doing," he said.

"That's the funniest thing I ever heard," said Weems.

Carney and Foltz burst out laughing. They laughed so hard and long that their bellies ached and their weeping eyes bugged, and they gasped for air.

"That's enough," said Weems, and they stopped laughing instantly, became department store dummies again.

"They *are* hypnotized!" said Fred, backing away.

"Certainly," said Weems. "You've got to understand what sort of a house you're in. Nothing is seen, said, felt, or done here that I don't want seen, said, felt, or done."

"Come on—" said Fred queasily, waving his gun, "wake 'em up."

"Straighten your tie," said Weems.

"I said wake 'em up," said Fred.

"Straighten your tie," said Weems.

Fred straightened his tie.

"Thank you," said Weems. "Now, I'm afraid I have rather frightening news for you—for all of you."

Consternation filled every face.

"A tornado is coming," said Weems. "It will blow you all away unless you handcuff your left hands to that steam radiator."

The three detectives, clumsy with terror, handcuffed themselves to the radiator.

"Throw your keys away, or you'll be struck by lightning!" said Weems.

Keys flew across the room.

"The tornado missed you," said Weems. "You're safe now."

The three detectives wept at their miraculous deliverance.

"Pull yourselves together, gentlemen," said Weems. "I have an announcement to make."

The three were avid for the news.

"I'm going to leave you," said Weems. "In fact, I'm going to leave everything about this existence behind." He went to a mirror, tapped it with his knuckles. "I'm going to step through this mirror in a moment. You will see me and my reflection meet and blend, shrink to the size of a pinhead. The pinhead will grow again, not as me and my reflection, but as my reflection alone. You will then see my reflection walk away from you, down the long, long corridor. See the corridor I'm going to walk down?"

The three nodded.

"You will see me pass through the mirror," said Weems, "when I say the words 'Black magic.' When I say the words 'White magic,' you will see me reappear in every mirror in this room. You will shoot at each of those images, until every mirror is broken. And when I say, 'Good-bye, gentlemen,' you will shoot each other down." Weems strolled to the attic door. Nobody watched him do it. All eyes were on the mirror he'd said he was going to pass through.

"Black magic," said Weems softly.

"There he goes!" cried Foltz.

"Like going through a door!" said Carney.

"God help us!" said Fred.

Weems stepped out of the ballroom and onto the stairs. He left the door open a crack. "White magic," he said.

"There he is!" said Foltz.

"All around us!" said Carney.

"Get him!" said Fred.

There was a pandemonium of shots and yells and shattering glass.

Weems waited for the silence that would tell him that all mirrors had been broken, that it was time at last to say good-bye.

The farewell was poised on his lips when bullets ripped through him and the door against which he leaned.

Weems sank dying to the staircase, about to roll all the way down it. He was not thinking of the lifeless roll to come. He was remembering too late—that on the other side of the ballroom door had been a mirror.

THE NICE
LITTLE PEOPLE

It was a hot, dry, glaring July day that made Lowell Swift feel as though every germ and sin in him were being baked out forever. He was riding home on a bus from his job as a linoleum salesman in a department store. The day marked the end of his seventh year of marriage to Madelaine, who had the car, and who, in fact, owned it. He carried red roses in a long green box under his arm.

The bus was crowded, but no women were standing, so Lowell's conscience was unencumbered. He sat back in his seat and crackled his knuckles absently, and thought pleasant things about his wife.

He was a tall, straight man, with a thin, sandy mustache and a longing to be a British colonel. At a distance, it appeared that his longing had been answered in every respect save for a uniform. He seemed distinguished and purposeful. But his eyes were those of a wistful panhandler, lost, baffled, inordinately agreeable. He was intelligent and healthy, but decent to a point that crippled him as master of his home or an accumulator of wealth.

Madelaine had once characterized him as standing on the edge of the mainstream of life, smiling and saying, "Pardon me," "After you," and "No, thank you."

Madelaine was a real estate saleswoman, and made far

more money than Lowell did. Sometimes she joked with him about it. He could only smile amiably, and say that he had never, at any rate, made any enemies, and that, after all, God had made him, even as he had made Madelaine—presumably with some good end in mind.

Madelaine was a beautiful woman, and Lowell had never loved anyone else. He would have been lost without her. Some days, as he rode home on the bus, he felt dull and ineffectual, tired, and afraid Madelaine would leave him—and not blaming her for wanting to.

This day, however, wasn't one of them. He felt marvelous. It was, in addition to being his wedding anniversary, a day spiced with mystery. The mystery was in no way ominous, as far as Lowell could see, but it was puzzling enough to make him feel as though he were involved in a small adventure. It would give him and Madelaine a few minutes of titillating speculation. While he'd been waiting for the bus, someone had thrown a paper knife to him.

It had come, he thought, from a passing car or from one of the offices in the building across the street. He hadn't seen it until it clattered to the sidewalk by the pointed black toes of his shoes. He'd glanced around quickly without seeing who'd thrown it; had picked it up gingerly, and found that it was warm and remarkably light. It was bluish silver in color, oval in cross section, and very modern in design. It was a single piece of metal, seemingly hollow, sharply pointed at one end and blunt at the other, with only a small, pearl-like stone at its midpoint to mark off the hilt from the blade.

Lowell had identified it instantly as a paper knife because he had often noticed something like it in a cutlery window he passed every day on his way to and from the bus stop downtown. He'd made an effort to locate the knife's owner by holding it over his head, and looking from car to car and from office window to office window, but no one had looked back at him as though to claim it. So he had put it in his pocket.

Lowell looked out of the bus window, and saw that the bus was going down the quiet, elm-shaded boulevard on which he and Madelaine lived. The mansions on either side, though now divided into expensive apartments, were still mansions outside, magnificent. Without Madelaine's income, it would have been impossible for them to live in such a place.

The next stop was his, where the colonnaded white colonial stood. Madelaine would be watching the bus approach, looking down from the third-story apartment that had once been a ballroom. As excited as any high school boy in love, he pulled the signal cord, and looked up for her face in the glossy green ivy that grew around the gable. She wasn't there, and he supposed happily that she was mixing anniversary cocktails.

"Lowell:" said the note in the hall mirror. *"Am taking a prospect for the Finletter property to supper. Cross your fingers. — Madelaine."*

Smiling wistfully, Lowell laid his roses on the table, and crossed his fingers.

The apartment was very still, and disorderly. Madelaine had left in a hurry. He picked up the afternoon paper, which was spread over the floor along with a pastepot and scrapbook, and read tatters that Madelaine had left whole, items that had nothing to do with real estate.

There was a quick *hiss* in his pocket, like the sound of a perfunctory kiss or the opening of a can of vacuum-packed coffee.

Lowell thrust his hand into his pocket and brought forth the paper knife. The little stone at its midpoint had come out of its setting, leaving a round hole.

Lowell laid the knife on the cushion beside him, and searched his pocket for the missing bauble. When he found it, he was disappointed to discover that it wasn't a pearl at all, but a hollow hemisphere of what he supposed to be plastic.

When he returned his attention to the knife, he was swept with a wave of revulsion. A black insect a quarter of an inch long was worming out through the hole. Then came another and another—until there were six, huddled together in a pit in the cushion, a pit made a moment before by Lowell's elbow. The insects' movements were sluggish and clumsy, as though they were shaken and dazed. Now they seemed to fall asleep in their shallow refuge.

Lowell took a magazine from the coffee table, rolled it up, and prepared to smash the nasty little beasts before they could lay their eggs and infest Madelaine's apartment.

It was then he saw that the insects were three men and three women, perfectly proportioned, and clad in glistening black tights.

On the telephone table in the front hall, Madelaine had taped a list of telephone numbers: the numbers of her office, Bud Stafford—her boss, her lawyer, her broker, her doctor, her dentist, her hairdresser, the police, the fire department, and the department store at which Lowell worked.

Lowell was running his finger down the list for the tenth

time, looking for the number of the proper person to tell about the arrival on earth of six little people a quarter of an inch high.

He wished Madelaine would come home.

Tentatively, he dialed the number of the police.

"Seventh precin't. Sergeant Cahoon speakin'."

The voice was coarse, and Lowell was appalled by the image of Cahoon that appeared in his mind: gross and clumsy, slab-footed, with room for fifty little people in each yawning chamber of his service revolver.

Lowell returned the telephone to its cradle without saying a word to Cahoon. Cahoon was not the man.

Everything about the world suddenly seemed preposterously huge and brutal to Lowell. He lugged out the massive telephone book, and opened it to *United States Government.* "Agriculture Department...Justice Department... Treasury Department"—everything had the sound of crashing giants. Lowell closed the book helplessly.

He wondered when Madelaine was coming home.

He glanced nervously at the couch, and saw that the little people, who had been motionless for half an hour, were beginning to stir, to explore the slick, plum-colored terrain and flora of tufts in the cushion. They were soon brought up short by the walls of a glass bell jar Lowell had taken from Madelaine's antique clock on the mantelpiece and lowered over them.

"Brave, brave little devils," said Lowell to himself, wonderingly. He congratulated himself on his calm, his reasonableness with respect to the little people. He hadn't panicked, hadn't killed them or called for help. He doubted that many people would have had the imagination to admit that the little people really were explorers from another world, and that the seeming knife was really a spaceship.

"Guess you picked the right man to come and see," he murmured to them from a distance, "but darned if I know what to do with you. If word got out about you, it'd be murder." He could imagine the panic and the mobs outside the apartment.

As Lowell approached the little people for another look, crossing the carpet silently, there came a ticking from the bell jar, as one of the men circled inside it again and again, tapping with some sort of tool, seeking an opening. The others were engrossed with a bit of tobacco one had pulled out from under a tuft.

Lowell lifted the jar. "Hello, there," he said gently.

The little people shrieked, making sounds like the high notes of a music box, and scrambled toward the cleft where the cushion met the back of the couch.

"No, no, no, no," said Lowell. "Don't be afraid, little people." He held out a fingertip to stop one of the women. To his horror, a spark snapped from his finger, striking her down in a little heap the size of a morning-glory seed.

The others had tumbled out of sight behind the cushion.

"Dear God, what have I done, what have I done?" said Lowell heartbrokenly.

He ran to get a magnifying glass from Madelaine's desk, and then peered through it at the tiny, still body. "Dear, dear, oh, dear," he murmured.

He was more upset than ever when he saw how beautiful the woman was. She bore a slight resemblance to a girl he had known before he met Madelaine.

Her eyelids trembled and opened. "Thank heaven," he said. She looked up at him with terror.

"Well, now," said Lowell briskly, "that's more like it. I'm your friend. I don't want to hurt you. Lord knows I don't." He smiled and rubbed his hands together. "We'll have a welcome to earth banquet. What would you like? What do you little people eat, eh? I'll find something."

He hurried to the kitchen, where dirty dishes and silverware cluttered the countertops. He chuckled to himself as he loaded a tray with bottles and jars and cans that now seemed enormous to him, literal mountains of food.

Whistling a festive air, Lowell brought the tray into the living room and set it on the coffee table. The little woman was no longer on the cushion.

"Now, where have you gone, eh?" said Lowell gaily. "I know, I know where to find you when everything's ready. Oho! a banquet fit for kings and queens, no less."

Using his fingertip, he made a circle of dabs around the center of a saucer, leaving mounds of peanut butter, mayonnaise, oleomargarine, minced ham, cream cheese, catsup, liver pâté, grape jam, and moistened sugar. Inside this circle he put separate drops of milk, beer, water, and orange juice.

He lifted up the cushion. "Come and get it, or I'll throw it on the ground," he said. "Now—where did you get to? I'll find you, I'll find you." In the corner of the couch, where the cushion had been, lay a quarter and a dime, a paper match, and a cigar band, a band from the sort of cigars Madelaine's boss smoked.

"There you are," said Lowell. Several tiny pairs of feet projected from the pile of debris.

Lowell picked up the coins, leaving the six little people huddled and trembling. He laid his hand before them, palm up. "Come on, now, climb aboard. I have a surprise for you."

They didn't move, and Lowell was obliged to shoo them into his palm with a pencil point. He lifted them through the air, dumped them on the saucer's rim like so many caraway seeds.

"I give you," he said, "the largest smorgasbord in history." The dabs were all taller than the dinner guests.

After several minutes, the little people got courage enough to begin exploring again. Soon, the air around the saucer was filled with piping cries of delight, as delicious bonanza after bonanza was discovered.

Lowell watched happily through the magnifying glass as faces were lifted to him with lip-smacking, ogling gratitude.

"Try the beer. Have you tried the beer?" said Lowell. Now, when he spoke, the little people didn't shriek, but listened attentively, trying to understand.

Lowell pointed to the amber drop, and all six dutifully sampled it, trying to look appreciative, but failing to hide their distaste.

"Acquired taste," said Lowell. "You'll learn. You'll—"

The sentence died, unfinished. Outside a car had pulled up, and floating up through the summer evening was Madelaine's voice.

When Lowell returned from the window, after watching Madelaine kiss her boss, the little people were kneeling and facing him, chanting something that came to him sweet and faint.

"Hey," said Lowell, beaming, "what is this, anyway? It was nothing—nothing at all. Really. Look here, I'm just an ordinary guy. I'm common as dirt here on earth. Don't get the idea I'm—" He laughed at the absurdity of the notion.

The chant went on, ardent, supplicating, adoring.

"Look," said Lowell, hearing Madelaine coming up the stairs, "you've got to hide until I get squared away in my mind what to do about you."

He looked around quickly, and saw the knife, the spaceship. He laid it by the saucer, and prodded them with the pencil again. "Come on—back in here for a little while."

They disappeared into the hole, and Lowell pressed the pearly hatch cover back into place just as Madelaine came in.

"Hello," she said cheerfully. She saw the saucer. "Been entertaining?"

"In a small way," said Lowell. "Have you?"

"It looks like you've been having mice in."

"I get lonely, like anybody else," said Lowell.

She reddened. "I'm sorry about the anniversary, Lowell."

"Perfectly all right."

"I didn't remember until on the way home, just a few minutes ago, and then it hit me like a ton of bricks."

"The important thing is," said Lowell pleasantly, "did you close the deal?"

"Yes—yes, I did." She was restless, and had difficulty smiling when she found the roses on the hall table. "How nice."

"I thought so."

"Is that a new knife you have?"

"This? Yes—picked it up on the way home."

"Did we need it?"

"I took a fancy to it. Mind?"

"No—not at all." She looked at it uneasily. "You saw us, didn't you?"

"Who? What?"

"You saw me kissing Bud outside just now."

"Yes. But I don't imagine you're ruined."

"He asked me to marry him, Lowell."

"Oh? And you said—?"

"I said I would."

"I had no idea it was that simple."

"I love him, Lowell. I want to marry him. Do you have to drum on your palm with that knife?"

"Sorry. Didn't realize I was."

"Well?" she said meekly, after a long silence.

"I think almost everything that needs to be said has been said."

"Lowell, I'm dreadfully sorry—"

"Sorry for me? Nonsense! Whole new worlds have opened up for me." He walked over to her slowly, put his arm around her. "But it will take some getting used to, Madelaine. Kiss? Farewell kiss, Madelaine?"

"Lowell, please—" She turned her head aside, and tried to push him away gently.

He hugged her harder.

"Lowell—no. Let's stop it, Lowell. Lowell, you're hurting me. Please!" She struck him on the chest and twisted away. "I can't stand it!" she cried bitterly.

The spaceship in Lowell's hand hummed and grew hot. It trembled and shot from his hand, under its own power, straight at Madelaine's heart.

Lowell didn't have to look up the number of the police. Madelaine had taped it to the telephone table.

"Seventh precin't. Sergeant Cahoon speakin'."

"Sergeant," said Lowell, "I want to report an accident—a death."

"Homicide?" said Cahoon.

"I don't know what you'd call it. It takes some explaining."

When the police arrived, Lowell told his story calmly, from the finding of the spaceship to the end.

"In a way, it was my fault," he said. "The little people thought I was God."

A TREE TRYING TO
TELL ME SOMETHING.
12/21/06.

HELLO, RED

The sun was setting behind the big black drawbridge. The bridge, with its colossal abutments and piers, weighed more than the whole river-mouth village in its shadows. On a revolving stool in a lunchroom at one end of the bridge sat Red Mayo, the new bridge tender. He had just come off duty.

The air of the lunchroom was cut by a cruel screech from a dry bearing in the revolving stool as Red turned away from his coffee and hamburger, and looked up at the bridge expectantly. He was a heavy young man, twenty-eight, with the flat, mean face of a butcher boy.

The frail counterman and the three other customers, all men, watched Red with amiable surmise, as though ready to bloom with broad smiles at the first sign of friendliness from him.

No friendliness was forthcoming. When Red's eyes met theirs briefly, Red sniffed, and returned his attention to his food. He toyed with his tableware, and the big muscles in his forearms fretted under his tattoos, under intertwined symbols of bloodlust and love—daggers and hearts.

The counterman, egged on by nods from the other three customers, spoke to Red with great politeness. "Excuse me, sir," he said, "but are you Red Mayo?"

"That's who I am," said Red, without looking up.

A universal sigh and happy murmur went up. "I knew it was ... I thought it was ... That's who it is," said the chorus of three.

"Don't you remember me, Red?" said the counterman. "Slim Corby?"

"Yeah—I remember you," said Red emptily.

"Remember *me*, Red?" said an elderly customer hopefully. "George Mott?"

"Hi," said Red.

"Sorry about your mother and father passing on, Red," said Mott. "That was years ago, but I never got to see you till now. Good people. *Real* good people." Finding Red's eyes filled with apathy, he hesitated. "You remember me, Red— George Mott?"

"I remember," said Red. He nodded to the other two customers. "And that's Harry Childs and that's Stan West."

"He remembers ... Sure he remembers ... How could Red forget?" said the nervous chorus. They continued to make tentative gestures of welcome.

"Gee," said Slim, the counterman, "I figured we'd never see *you* again. I figured you'd took off for good."

"Figured wrong," said Red. "Happens sometimes."

"How long since you been back, Red?" said Slim. "Eight, nine years?"

"Eight," said Red.

"You still in the merchant marines?" said Mott.

"Bridge tender," said Red.

"Whereabouts?" said Slim.

"This bridge right here," said Red.

"Heeeeeeey—you hear that?" said Slim. He started to

touch Red familiarly, but thought better of it. "Red's the new bridge tender!"

"Home to stay...Got hisself a good job...Ain't that nice?" said the chorus.

"When you start?" said Mott.

"Started," said Red. "Been up there two days now."

All were amazed. "Never heard a word about it...Never thought to look up and see who's there...Two days, and we never noticed him," said the chorus.

"I cross the bridge four times a day," said Slim. "You should have said hello or something. You know—you get to kind of thinking of the bridge tender as just kind of part of the machinery. You must of seen me and Harry and Stan and Mr. Mott and Eddie Scudder and everybody else crossing the bridge, and you never said a word?"

"Wasn't ready to," said Red. "Somebody else I had to talk to first."

"Oh," said Slim. His face went blank. He looked to the other three for enlightenment, and got three shrugs. Rather than pry, Slim tried to fidget his curiosity into thin air with his fingers.

"Don't give me that," said Red irritably.

"Give you what, Red?" said Slim.

"Them innocent looks about who I been talking to," said Red.

"I honest to God don't know, Red," said Slim. "It's so long since you been home, it's kind of hard to figure out *who* you'd want to see *special.*"

"So many people come and gone...So much water under the bridge...All your old friends growed up and settled down," said the chorus.

Red grinned unpleasantly, to let them know they weren't getting away with anything. "A girl," said Red. "I been talking to a girl."

"Ooooooooooh," said Slim. He chuckled lecherously. "You old dog, you old sea dog. All of a sudden got a hankering for some of the old hometown stuff, eh?" His chuckle died as Red glared at him.

"Go on, enjoy yourself," said Red angrily. "Play dumb. You got about five minutes more, till Eddie Scudder gets here."

"Eddie, eh?" said Slim, helpless in the midst of the puzzle.

The chorus had fallen silent, their eyes straight ahead. Red had killed their welcome, and given them only fear and bewilderment in return.

Red pursed his lips prissily. "Can't imagine what Red Mayo'd be wanting to see Eddie Scudder about," he said in a falsetto. He was infuriated by the innocence all around him. "I really forgot what this village was like," he said. "By God—everybody agrees to tell the same big lie; pretty soon, everybody believes it like it was the gospel truth." He hit the counter with his fist. "My own folks, even!" he said. "My own flesh and blood—they never even said a word in their letters."

Slim, deserted by the chorus, was now terribly alone with the surly redhead. "What lie?" he said shakily.

"What lie, what lie?" said Red in a parrot's voice. "Polly wants a crack-*er*, Polly wants a crack-*er*! I guess I've seen just about everything in my travels, but I only seen one thing to come up to you guys."

"What's that, Red?" said Slim, who was now an automaton.

"There was this kind of South American snake, see?" said Red. "Liked to steal kids. It'd swipe a kid, and raise it just like it was a snake. Teach it to crawl and everything. And all the other snakes'd treat it just like it was a snake, too."

In the silence, the chorus felt obliged to murmur. "Never heard of such a thing . . . A snake do that? . . . If that don't take the cake."

"We'll ask Eddie about it when he gets here," said Red. "He always was real good at animals and nature." He hunched over, and stuffed his mouth with hamburger, indicating that the conversation was at an end. "Eddie's late," he said with a full mouth. "I hope he got my message."

He thought about his messenger, and how he'd sent her. With his jaws working, his eyes down, he was soon reliving his day. In his mind, it was noon again.

And it seemed to Red at noon that he was steering the village from his steel and glass booth, six feet above the roadway, on a girder at one end of the bridge. Only the clouds and massive counterweights of the bridge were higher than Red was.

There was a quarter of an inch of play in the lever that controlled the bridge, and it was with this quarter of an inch that Red pretended, God-like, to steer the village. It was natural for him to think of himself and his surroundings as moving, of the water below as standing still. He had been a merchant sailor for nine years—a bridge tender for less than two days.

Hearing the noon howl of the fire horn, Red stopped his steering, and looked through his spyglass at Eddie Scudder's oyster shack below. The shack was rickety and helpless-looking on pilings in the river mouth, connected to the salt marsh shore by two springy planks. The river bottom around it was a twinkling white circle of oyster shells.

Eddie's eight-year-old daughter, Nancy, came out of the shack, and bounced gently on the planks, her face lifted to the sunshine. And then she stopped bouncing, and became demure.

Red had taken the job for the opportunity it gave him to watch her. He knew what the demureness was. It was a prelude to a ceremony, the ceremony of Nancy's combing her bright red hair.

Red's fingers played along the spyglass as though it were a clarinet. "Hello, Red," he whispered.

Nancy combed and combed and combed that cascade of red hair. Her eyes were closed, and each tug of the comb seemed to fill her with bittersweet ecstasy.

The combing left her languid. She walked through the salt meadow gravely, and climbed the steep bank to the road that crossed the bridge. Every day at noon, Nancy crossed the bridge to the lunchroom at the other end, to fetch a hot lunch for herself and her father.

Red smiled down at Nancy as she came.

Seeing the smile, she touched her hair.

"It's still there," said Red.

"What is?" said Nancy.

"Your hair, Red."

"I told you yesterday," she said, "my name isn't Red. It's Nancy."

"How could anybody call you anything *but* Red?" said Red.

"That's *your* name," said Nancy.

"So I got a right to give it to you, if I want to," said Red. "I don't know anybody who's got a better right."

"I shouldn't even be talking to you," she said playfully, teasing him with propriety. There was no mistrust in her mind. Their meetings had a fairy-tale quality, with Red no ordinary stranger, but a genial sorcerer in charge of the wonderful bridge—a sorcerer who seemed to know more about the girl than she knew about herself.

"Didn't I tell you I grew up in this village, just like you're doing?" said Red. "Didn't I tell you I went to high school with your mother and father? Don't you believe that?"

"I believe it," said Nancy. "Only Mother used to say little girls should be introduced to strangers. They shouldn't just start talking to them."

Red kept the needles of sarcasm out of his voice. "Quite an upstanding lady, wasn't she?" he said. "Yup—*she* knew how good little boys and girls should act. Yessirreeee—good as gold, Violet was. Butter wouldn't melt in *her* mouth."

"Everybody says so," said Nancy proudly. "Not just Daddy and me."

"Daddy, eh?" said Red. He mimicked her. "'Daddy, Daddy, Daddy—Eddie Scudder is my great big Daddy.'" He cocked his head watchfully. "You didn't tell him I was up here, did you?"

Nancy blushed at the accusation. "I wouldn't break my word of honor."

Red grinned and wagged his head. "Gee, he'll really get a big boot out of it when I all of a sudden just kind of drop out of the sky, after all these years."

"One of the last things Mother said before she died,"

said Nancy, "was that I should never break my word of honor."

Red clucked piously. "Real serious girl, your mother," he said. "Back when we got out of high school, the other girls wanted to play around a little before they settled down. But not Violet. Nosir. I made my first voyage back then—and when I come back a year later, she was all married and settled down with Eddie, and she'd had you. Course, you didn't have any hair when I saw you that time."

"I've got to go now, and get my daddy's lunch," said Nancy.

" 'Daddy, Daddy, Daddy,' " said Red. " 'Got to do this for Daddy, got to do that for Daddy.' Must be nice to have a pretty, smart daughter like you. 'Daddy, Daddy.' You ask your daddy about red hair, like I told you?"

"He said he guessed it usually ran in families," said Nancy. "Only sometimes it pops up from nowhere, like it did with me." Her hand went up to her hair.

"It's still there," said Red.

"What is?" said Nancy.

"Your *hair*, Red!" He guffawed. "I swear, if anything was to happen to that hair, you'd just dry up and blow away. Comes from nowhere, does it? That's what Eddie said?" Red nodded judiciously. *"He'd* know. I expect Eddie's done a lot of thinking about red hair in his time. Now, you take *my* family: if *I* was ever to have a kid that *wasn't* redheaded, *that'd* start everybody to figuring and wondering. Been a redheaded family since the beginning of time."

"That's very interesting," said Nancy.

"Gets more interesting, the more you think about it," said

Red. "You and me and my old man are about the only red-heads this village ever had, that *I* know of. Now that the old man's gone, that just leaves two of us."

Nancy remained serene. "Huh," she said. "Bye, now."

"Bye, Red."

As she walked away, Red picked up his spyglass, and looked down at Eddie's oyster shack. Through the window, he could see Eddie, blue-gray in the twilight interior, shucking oysters. Eddie was a small man, with a large head majestic in sorrow. It was the head of a young Job.

"Hi," whispered Red. "Guess who's home."

When Nancy came back from the lunchroom with a warm, fat paper bag, Red stopped her again.

"Saaaaaay," he said, "maybe you'll grow up to be a nurse, after taking such good care of old Eddie. I wish there'd been nice nurses like you at the hospital I was at."

Nancy's face softened with pity. "You were in a hospital?"

"Three months, Red, in Liverpool, without a friend or a relative in this world to come see me, or even send me a get-well card." He grew wistful. "Funny, Red—I never realized how lonely I was, till I had to lie down and stay down, till I knew I couldn't ever go to sea again." He licked his lips. "Changed me, Red, like *that.*" He snapped his fingers.

"All of a sudden, I needed a home," he said, "and somebody to care about me, and keep me company—maybe in that little cottage out there on the point. I didn't have nothing, Red, but mate's papers that wasn't worth the paper they were printed on for a man with one leg."

Nancy was shocked. "You've only got one leg?"

"One day I was the crazy, tough kid they all remember down there," said Red, including the village in a sweep of his hand. "The next day I was an old, old man."

Nancy bit her knuckle, sharing his pain. "Haven't you got a wife or a mother or a lady friend to look after you?" she said. By her stance, she offered her services as a daughter, as though it were a simple thing that any good girl would do.

Red hung his head. "Dead," he said. "My mother's dead, and the only girl I ever loved is dead. And the lady friends, Red—they're never what you'd call *real* friendly, not if you can't love *them,* not if you're in love with a ghost."

Nancy's sweet face twisted as Red forced her to look at the grisliness of life. "Why do you live up the river, if you're so lonesome?" she said. "Why don't you live down here, where you'd be with your old friends?"

Red raised an eyebrow. "Old friends? Funny kind of friends to have, who wouldn't even drop me a postcard to tell me Violet's kid had bright red hair. Not even my folks told me."

The wind freshened, and on the wind, from seemingly far away, came Nancy's voice. "Daddy's lunch is getting cold," she said. She started to walk away.

"Red!"

She stopped, and her hand went up to her hair. She kept her back to him.

Red wished to God he could see her face. "Tell Eddie I want to talk to him, would you? Tell him to meet me in the lunchroom after I get off work—about ten after five."

"I will," she said. Her voice was clear, calm.

"Word of honor?"

"Word of honor," she said. She started walking again.

"Red!"

Her hand went up to her hair, but she kept on walking.

Red followed her with his spyglass, but she knew she was being watched. She kept her head turned, so he couldn't see her face. And seconds after she went into the oyster shack, a shade was drawn across the window that faced the bridge.

For the rest of the afternoon, the shack might as well have been empty for all the life Red could see. Only once, toward sunset, did Eddie come out. He didn't so much as glance up at the bridge, and he kept *his* face hidden, too.

The screech from his own stool in the lunchroom brought Red back to the present. He blinked at the sunset, and saw the silhouette of Eddie Scudder crossing the bridge, big-headed and bandy-legged, carrying a small paper bag.

Red turned his back to the door, reached into a jacket pocket, and brought forth a packet of letters, which he set on the counter before him. He put his fingertips on them, like a cardplayer standing pat. "Here's the man of the hour," he said.

No one spoke.

Eddie came in without hesitation, with a formal greeting for everyone, Red last of all. His voice was surprisingly rich and deep. "Hello, Red," he said. "Nancy said you wanted to see me."

"That's right," said Red. "Nobody here can figure out what I'd have to say to you."

"Nancy had a little trouble figuring it out, too," said Eddie, without a trace of resentment.

"She finally got the drift?" said Red.

"She got it, about as well as an eight-year-old could," said

Eddie. He sat down on the stool next to Red's, and set his bag on the counter, next to the letters. He showed mild surprise at the handwriting of the letters, and made no effort to hide his surprise from Red. "Coffee, please, Slim," he said.

"Maybe you'd rather have this private," said Red. He was a little disconcerted by Eddie's equanimity. He'd remembered Eddie as a homely clown.

"Makes no difference," said Eddie. "It's all before God, wherever we do it."

The straightforward inclusion of God in the meeting was also unexpected by Red. In his daydreams in his hospital bed, the resounding lines had all been his—irrefutable lines dealing with man's rights to the love of his own flesh and blood. Red felt the necessity of puffing himself up, of dramatizing his advantages in bulk and stature. "First of all," he said importantly, "I wanna say I don't care what the law has to say about this. This is bigger than that."

"Good," said Eddie. "Then we agree first of all. I'd hoped we would."

"So's we won't be talking about two different things," said Red, "lemme say right out that I'm the father of that kid—not you."

Eddie stirred his coffee with a steady hand. "We'll be talking about exactly the same thing," he said.

Slim and the three others looked out the windows desperately.

Around and around and around went Eddie's spoon in his coffee. "Go on," he said happily.

Red was rattled. Things were going faster than he had expected—and, at the same time, they were seemingly going nowhere. He'd passed the climax of what he'd come home to say, and nothing had changed—and nothing seemed about to change. "Everybody's gone right along with you, pretending she was your kid," he said indignantly.

"They've been good neighbors," said Eddie.

Red's mind was now a mare's nest of lines he hadn't used yet, lines that now didn't seem to fit anywhere. "I'm willing to take a blood test, to find out who's her father," he said. "Are you?"

"Do we all have to bleed, before we can believe each other?" said Eddie. "I told you I agreed with you. You are her father. Everybody knows that. How could they miss it?"

"Did she tell you I'd lost a leg?" said Red hectically.

"Yes," said Eddie. "That impressed her more than anything. That's what *would* impress an eight-year-old the most."

Red looked at his own reflection in the coffee urn and saw that his eyes were watery, his face bright pink. His reflection assured him that he'd spoken well—that he was being trifled with. "Eddie—that kid is mine, and I want her."

"I'm sorry for you, Red," said Eddie, "but you can't have her." For the first time, his hand trembled, making his spoon click against the side of his cup. "I think you'd better go away."

"You think this is a little thing?" said Red. "You think a man can back away from something like this like it was nothing—back away from his own kid, and just forget it?"

"Not being a father myself," said Eddie, "I can only guess at what you're going through."

"Is that a joke?" said Red.

"Not to me," said Eddie evenly.

"This is some smart way of saying you're more her old man that I am?" said Red.

"If I haven't said it, I will say it," said Eddie. His hand

shook so uncontrollably that he was obliged to set his spoon down, to grip the counter's edge.

Red saw now how frightened Eddie was, saw how phony his poise and godliness were. Red felt his own strength growing, felt the flow of booming good health and righteousness he'd daydreamed of. He was suddenly in charge, with plenty to say, and plenty of time in which to say it.

It angered him that Eddie had tried to bluff and confuse him, had nearly succeeded. And on the crest of the anger rode all Red's hate for the cold and empty world. His whole will was now devoted to squashing the little man beside him.

"That's Violet's and my kid," said Red. "She never loved you."

"I hope she did," said Eddie humbly.

"She married you because she figured I wasn't ever coming back!" said Red. He picked up a letter from the top of the packet and waved it under Eddie's nose. "She told me so—just like that—in so many words."

Eddie refused to look at the letter. "That was a long time ago, Red. A lot can happen."

"I'll tell you one thing that didn't happen," said Red, "she never stopped writing, never stopped begging me to come back."

"I guess those things go on for a while," said Eddie softly.

"A *while*?" said Red. He riffled through the letters, and dropped one before Eddie. "Look at the date on that one, would you? Just look at the date on *that.*"

"I don't want to," said Eddie. He stood.

"You're afraid," said Red.

"That's right," said Eddie. He closed his eyes. "Go away, Red. Please go away."

"Sorry, Eddie," said Red, "but nothing's gonna make me go away. Red's home."

"God pity you," said Eddie. He walked to the door.

"You forgot your little paper bag," said Red. His feet danced.

"That's yours," said Eddie. "Nancy sent it. It was her idea, not mine. God knows I would have stopped her if I'd known." He was crying.

He left, and crossed the bridge in the gathering darkness.

Slim and the other three customers had turned to stone.

"My God!" Red cried at them. "My own flesh and blood! It's the deepest thing there is! What could ever make me leave?"

No one answered.

A terrible depression settled over Red, the aftermath of battle. He sucked the back of his hand, as though nursing a wound. "Slim," he said, "what's in that bag?"

Slim opened the bag and looked inside. "Hair, Red," he said. "Red hair."

MAY I
HAVE
THIS
DANCE?

LITTLE DROPS
OF WATER

Now Larry's gone.

We bachelors are lonely people. If I weren't damn lonely from time to time, I wouldn't have been a friend of Larry Whiteman, the baritone. Not friend, but companion, meaning I spent time with him, whether I liked him particularly or not. As bachelors get older, I find, they get less and less selective about where they get their companionship—and, like everything else in their lives, friends become a habit, and probably a part of a routine. For instance, while Larry's monstrous conceit and vanity turned my stomach, I'd been dropping in to see him off and on for years. And when I come to analyze what *off and on* means, I realize that I saw Larry every Tuesday between five and six in the afternoon. If, on the witness stand, someone were to ask me where I was on the evening of Friday, such and such a date, I would only have to figure out where I would be on the coming Friday to tell him where I had probably been on the Friday he was talking about.

Let me add quickly that I like women, but am a bachelor by choice. While bachelors are lonely people, I'm convinced that married men are lonely people with dependents.

When I say I like women, I can name names, and perhaps, along with the plea of habit, account for my association with Larry in terms of them. There was Edith Vranken, the

Schenectady brewer's daughter who wanted to sing; Janice Gurnee, the Indianapolis hardware merchant's daughter who wanted to sing; Beatrix Werner, the Milwaukee consulting engineer's daughter who wanted to sing; and Ellen Sparks, the Buffalo wholesale grocer's daughter who wanted to sing.

I met these attractive young ladies—one by one and in the sequence named—in Larry's studio, or what anyone else would call *apartment*. Larry adds to his revenues as a soloist by giving voice lessons to rich and pretty young women who want to sing. While Larry is soft as a hot fudge sundae, he is big and powerful-looking, like a college-bred lumberjack, if there is such a thing, or a Royal Canadian Mounted Policeman. His voice, of course, gives the impression that he could powder rocks between his thumb and forefinger. His pupils inevitably fell in love with him. If you ask *how* they loved him, I can only reply with another question: where in the cycle do you mean? If you mean at the beginning, Larry was loved as a father pro tem. Later, he was loved as a benevolent taskmaster, and finally, as a lover.

After that came what Larry and his friends had come to call *graduation,* which, in fact, had nothing to do with the pupil's status as a singer, and had everything to do with the cycle of affections. The cue for graduation was the pupil's overt use of the word *marriage.*

Larry was something of a Bluebeard, and, may I say, a lucky dog while his luck held out. Edith, Janice, Beatrix, and Ellen—the most recent group of graduates—loved and were loved in turn. And, in turn, given the ax. They were wonderful looking girls, every one of them. There were also more like them where they had come from, and those others were boarding trains and planes and convertibles to come to

New York because they wanted to sing. Larry had no replacement problem. And, with plenty of replacements, he was spared the temptation of making some sort of permanent arrangement, such as marriage.

Larry's life, like most bachelors' lives, but far more so, had every minute accounted for, with very little time for women as women. The time he had set aside for whatever student happened to be in favor was Monday and Thursday evenings, to be exact. There was a time for giving lessons, a time for lunch with friends, a time for practice, a time for his barber, a time for two cocktails with me—a time for everything, and he never varied his schedule by more than a few minutes. Similarly, he had his studio exactly as he wanted it—a place for everything, with no places begging, and with no thing, in his eyes, dispensable. While he might have been on the fence about marriage as a young young man, marriage soon became impossible. Where he might once have had a little time and space to fit in a wife—a cramped wife—there came to be none, absolutely none.

"Habit—it's my strength!" Larry once said. "Ahhhh, wouldn't they love to catch Larry, eh? And remake him, eh? Well, before they can get me into their traps, they've got to blast me out of my rut, and it can't be done. I love my cozy little rut. Habit—*Aes triplex.*"

"How's that?" I said.

"Aes triplex—triple armor," he said.

"Oh." *Aes Kleenex* would have been closer to the truth, but neither one of us knew that then. Ellen Sparks was around, and ascendant in Larry's heavens—Beatrix Werner having been liquidated a couple of months before—but Ellen was showing no signs of being any different than the rest.

I said I liked women, and gave as examples some of Larry's students, including Ellen. I liked them from a safe distance. After Larry, in his amorous cycle with a favorite, ceased to be a father away from home and eased into a warmer role, I in turn became sort of a father. A lackadaisical, slipshod father, to be sure, but the girls liked to tell me how things were going, and ask my advice. They had a lemon of an adviser in me, because all I could ever think of to say was "Oh well, what the hell, you're only young once."

I said as much to Ellen Sparks, an awfully pretty brunette not likely to be depressed by thoughts or want of money. Her speaking voice was pleasant enough, but when she sang it was as though her vocal cords had risen into her sinuses.

"A Jew's harp with lyrics," said Larry, "with Italian lyrics in a Middle Western accent, yet." But he kept her on, because Ellen was a lot of fun to look at, and she paid her fees promptly, and never seemed to notice that Larry charged her for a lesson whatever he happened to need at the moment.

I once asked her where she'd gotten the idea to be a singer, and she said she liked Lily Pons. To her that was an answer, and a perfectly adequate one. Actually, I think she wanted to get away from the home reservation and have some fun being rich where nobody knew her. She probably drew lots to see whether the excuse would be music, drama, or art. At that, she was more serious-minded than some of the girls in her situation. One girl I know about set herself up in a suite with her father's money, and broadened herself by subscribing to several newsmagazines. One hour out of every day, she religiously underlined everything in them that seemed important. With a thirty-dollar fountain pen.

Well, as New York father to Ellen, I heard her, as I had

heard the others before her, declare that she loved Larry, and that she couldn't be sure, but she thought he might like her pretty well, too. She was proud of herself, because here she was making headway with a fairly famous man, and she'd only been away from home five months. The triumph was doubly delicious in that, I gathered, she'd been looked upon as something of a dumb twit in Buffalo. After that, she confided haltingly about evenings of wine and heady talk of the arts.

"Monday and Thursday evenings?" I asked.

She looked startled. "What are you, a Peeping Tom?"

Six weeks later she spoke guardedly of marriage, of Larry's seeming at the point of mentioning it. Seven weeks later she graduated. I happened to drop by Larry's on my Tuesday call for cocktails, and saw her seated in her yellow convertible across the street. By the way she slouched down in the cushions, defiant and at the same time completely licked, I knew what had happened. I thought it best to leave her alone— being, for one thing, dead sick of the same old story. But she spotted me, and raised my hair with a blast of her horns.

"Well, Ellen, hello. Lesson over?"

"Go on, laugh at me."

"I'm not laughing. Why should I laugh?"

"You are inside," she said bitterly. "Men! You knew about the others, didn't you? You knew what happened to them, and what was going to happen to me, didn't you?"

"I knew a lot of Larry's students grew quite attached to him."

"And detached. Well, here's one little girl who won't detach."

"He's an awfully busy man, Ellen."

"He said his career was a jealous mistress," she said huskily. "What does that make me?"

It did seem to me that Larry's remark was a little meatier than necessary. "Well, Ellen, I think you're well off. You deserve someone closer to your own age."

"That's mean. I deserve him."

"Even if you are foolish enough to want him, you can't have him. His life is so petrified with habits, he couldn't possibly accommodate a wife. It'd be easier to get the Metropolitan Opera Company to work in singing commercials."

"I will return," she said grimly, pressing the starter.

Larry's back was to me when I entered. He was mixing drinks. "Tears?" he said.

"Nary a one," I said.

"Good," said Larry. I couldn't be sure he meant it. "It always makes me feel mean when they cry." He threw up his hands. "But what am I to do? My career is a jealous mistress."

"I know. She told me. Beatrix told me. Janice told me. Edith told me." The roster seemed to please him. "Ellen says she won't detach, by the way."

"Really? How unwise. Well, we shall see what we shall see."

When God had been in his heaven as far as Ellen was concerned, when she had been confident that she was about to bring a certified New York celebrity back to Buffalo in a matter of weeks, I had taken her in fatherly fashion to lunch at my favorite restaurant. She seemed to like it, and I saw her there now and then after the breakup.

She was usually with the type of person both Larry and I had told her she deserved—someone closer to her own age. She also seemed to have chosen persons closer to her own amiable vacuity, which made for lunch hours of sighs, long silences, and the general atmosphere of being fogbound often mistaken for love. Actually, Ellen and her companion were in the miserable condition of not being able to think of anything to say, I'm sure. With Larry, the problem had never come up. It was understood that he was to do the talking, and that when he fell silent, it was a silence for effect, beautiful, to be remembered and unbroken by her. When her escorts focused their attention on the matter of paying the check, Ellen, ever aware of her audience, indicated by restlessness and a look of disdain that this wasn't the caliber stuff she was used to. And, of course, it wasn't.

When we happened to be in the restaurant at the same time, she ignored my nods, and—giving less than a damn, really—I gave the practice of nodding up. I think she felt I was part of a *plot,* somehow *in on* Larry's *scheme* to *humiliate* her.

After a while, she gave up young men closer to her age in favor of buying her own lunch. And finally, by a coincidence that surprised us both, she found herself seated at the table next to mine, clearing her white throat.

It became impossible for me to go on reading my paper. "Well, as I live and breathe," I said.

"And how have you been?" she asked coldly. "Still getting lots of laughs?"

"Oh yes, lots and lots. Sadism's on the upswing, you know. New Jersey's legalized it, and Indiana and Wyoming are on the brink."

She nodded. "Still waters run deep," she said enigmatically.

"Meaning me, Ellen?"

"Me."

"I see," I said perplexedly. "By that, you mean there is

more to you than meets the eye? I agree." And I did agree. It was incredible that there should be so little to Ellen—intellectually, mind you—as what met the eye.

"Larry's eye," she said.

"Oh, come on, Ellen—surely you're over that. He's vain and selfish, and keeps his stomach in with a girdle."

She held up her hands. "No, no—just tell me about the postcards and the horn. What does he say about them?"

"Postcards? Horn?" I shook my head. "He hasn't said a word about either one."

"Natch," she said. "Excellent, perfect. But perf."

"Sorry, I'm conf and have an imp app," I said, rising.

"What's that?"

"I said I'm confused, Ellen. And I'd try to understand, but I haven't time. I've an important appointment. Good luck, dear."

The appointment was with the dentist, and, with that grim visit over and the back of the afternoon broken, I decided to find Larry and ask him about the postcards and the horn. It was Tuesday, and it was four, so Larry would naturally be at his barber's. I went to the shop and took the seat next to him. His face was covered with lather, but it was Larry, all right. For years, no one else had been in that chair at four on Tuesday.

"Trim," I said to the barber; and then, to Larry, "Ellen Sparks says you should know still waters run deep."

"Hmmmm?" said Larry through the lather. "Who's Ellen Sparks?"

"A former student of yours. Remember?" This forgetting routine was an old trick of Larry's, and, for all I know, it was on the level. "She graduated two months ago."

"Tough job keeping track of all the alumnae," he said. "That little Buffalo thing? Wholesale groceries? I remember. And now the shampoo," he said to the barber.

"Of course, Mr. Whiteman. *Naturally* the shampoo next."

"She wants to know about the postcards and the horn."

"Postcards and horn," he said thoughtfully. "No, doesn't ring a bell." He snapped his fingers. "Oh yes, yes, yes, yes. You can tell her that she is absolutely destroying me with them. Every morning I get a card from her in the mail."

"What does she say?"

"Tell her the mail arrives as I am eating my four-minute eggs. I lay it all before me, with her card on top. I finish my eggs, eagerly seize the card. And then? I tear it in halves, then quarters, then sixteenths, and drop the little snowstorm in my wastebasket. Then it is time for coffee. I haven't the remotest idea what she says."

"And the horn?"

"Even more horrible punishment than the cards." He laughed. "Hell hath no fury like a woman scorned. So, every afternoon at two-thirty, as I am about to begin practice, what happens?"

"She lifts you off the floor with a five-minute blast on the horns?"

"She hasn't the nerve. Every afternoon I get one little, almost imperceptible *beep*, the shifting of gears, and the silly child is gone."

"Doesn't bother you, eh?"

"Bother me? She was right in thinking I was sensitive, but she underestimates my adaptability. It bothered me for the first couple of days, but now I no more notice it than I notice the noise of the trains. I actually had to think a minute before realizing what you were talking about when you asked about horns."

"That girl's got blood in her eye," I said.

"She'd do well to send a little of it to her brain," said Larry. "What do you think of my new student, by the way?"

"Christina? If she'd been my daughter, I'd have sent her to welding school. She's the kind the teachers in grade school used to call *listeners*. The teachers would put them in the corner during singing class, and tell them to beat time with their feet and keep their little mouths shut."

"She's eager to learn," said Larry defensively. He was sensitive to intimations that his interest in his students was ever anything but professional. And, more or less in self-defense, he was belligerently loyal to the artistic possibilities of his charges. His poisonous appraisal of Ellen's voice, for instance, wasn't made until she was ready to be chucked in the oubliette.

"In ten years, Christina will be ready for 'Hot Cross Buns.'"

"She may surprise you."

"I don't think she will, but Ellen may," I said. I was disturbed by Ellen's air of being about to loose appalling, irresistible forces. And yet, there was just this damn fool business of the cards and horn.

"Ellen who?" said Larry fuzzily, from under a hot towel.

The barbershop telephone rang. The barber started for it, but it stopped ringing. He shrugged. "Funny thing. Seems like every time Mr. Whiteman's in here lately, the phone does that."

The telephone by my bed rang.

"This is Larry Whiteman!"

"Drop dead, Larry Whiteman!" The clock said two in the morning.

"Tell that girl to quit it, do you hear?"

"Fine, glad to, you bet," I said thickly. "Who what?"

"That wholesale groceress, of course! That Buffalo thing. Do you hear? She's got to quit it instantly. That light, that goddamned light."

I started to drop the telephone into its cradle, hoping against hope to rupture his eardrum, when I came awake and realized that I was fascinated. Perhaps Ellen had at last unleashed her secret weapon. Larry had had a recital that night. Maybe she'd let him have it in front of everybody. "She blinded you with a light?"

"Worse! When the houselights went down, she lit up her fool face with one of those fool flashlights people carry on their key chains till the batteries pooh out. There she was, grinning out of the dark like death warmed over."

"And she kept it up all evening? I'd think they'd have thrown her out."

"She did it until she was sure I'd seen her, then out it went. Then came the coughs. Lord! the coughs!"

"Somebody always coughs."

"Not the way she does it. Just as I took a breath to start each number, she'd let go—*hack hack hack*. Three deliberate hacks."

"Well, if I see her, I'll tell her," I said. I was rather taken by the novelty of Ellen's campaign, but disappointed by its lack of promise of long-range results. "An old trouper like you shouldn't have any trouble ignoring that sort of business," which was true.

"She's trying to rattle me. She's trying to make me crack

up before my Town Hall recital," he said bitterly. The professional high point for Larry each year is his annual Town Hall recital—which is always a critical success, incidentally. Make no mistake about that—Larry, as a singer, is very hot stuff. But now, Ellen had begun her lamp and cough campaign with the big event only two months off.

Two weeks after Larry's frantic call, Ellen and I coincided at lunch again. She was still distinctly unfriendly, treating me as though I were a valuable spy, but not to be trusted, and distasteful to deal with. Once more she gave me the unsettling impression of hidden power, of something big about to happen. Her color was high and her movements furtive. After a few brittle amenities, she asked if Larry had said anything about the light.

"A great deal," I said, "after your first performance, that is. He was quite burned up."

"But now?" she said eagerly.

"Bad news for you, Ellen—good news for Larry. He's quite used to it now, after three recitals, so he has calmed down beautifully. The effect, I'm afraid, is zero. Look, why not give up? You've needled him long enough, haven't you? Revenge is the most you can get, and you've got that." She'd made one basic mistake that I didn't feel was up to me to point out: All of her annoyances were regular, predictable, which made it very easy for Larry to assimilate them into the clockwork of his life and ignore them.

She took the bad news in her stride. I might as well have told her that her campaign was a smashing success—that Larry was at the point of surrender. "Revenge is small apples," she said.

"Well, you've got to promise me one thing, Ellen—"

"Sure," she said. "Why shouldn't I be like Larry and promise anything, any old thing at all?"

"Ellen, promise not to do anything violent at his Town Hall recital."

"Scout's honor," she said, and smiled. "The easiest promise I ever made."

That evening, I played back the puzzling conversation to Larry. He was having his bedtime snack of crackers and hot milk.

"Uh-hummmm," he said, his mouth full. "If she *had* made sense, it would have been the first time in her life." He shrugged disdainfully. "She's licked, this Helen Smart."

"Ellen Sparks," I corrected him.

"Whatever her name is, she'll be catching the train home soon. Awful taste! Honestly. I wouldn't have been surprised if she'd thrown spitballs and stuck pins in my doorbell."

Somewhere along the street, a garbage can lid clattered. "What a racket," I said. "Do they have to be that noisy about it?"

"What racket?"

"That garbage can."

"Oh, that. If you lived here, you'd be used to it. Don't know who it is, but they give the can a lick every night"— he yawned—"just at bedtime."

Keeping big secrets, particularly secrets about things of one's own doing, is a tough proposition for even very bright people. It is so much tougher for small brains that criminals, for instance, are constantly blabbing themselves into jail or worse. Whatever it is they've done, it's too wonderful not to bring out in the open for admiration. That Ellen kept a secret for even five minutes is hard to believe. The fact is, she kept a dandy one for six months, for the time separating her breakup with Larry and the two days before his Town Hall recital.

She finally told me at one of our back-to-back luncheons. She phrased the news in such a way that it wasn't until I saw Larry the next day that I realized what it was she'd given away.

"Now, you promised, Ellen," I told her again, "no rough stuff at the recital day after tomorrow. No heckling, no stink bombs, no serving of a subpoena."

"Don't be crude."

"Don't you, dear. The recital's as much for music lovers as it is for Larry. It's no place for partisan politics."

She seemed, for the first time in months, relaxed, like a person who had just finished a completely satisfying piece of work—a rare type these days. Her color, usually tending toward the reds of excitement, mysterious expectancy, was serene pink and ivory.

She ate in silence, asked me nothing about Larry. There was nothing new I could have told her. Despite her persistent reminders—the horn, the cards, the light and coughs, and God knows what else—he had forgotten all about her. His life went its systematically selfish way, undisturbed.

Then she told me the news. It explained her calm. I had been expecting it for some time, and had even tried to coax her in that direction. I wasn't surprised, nor impressed. It was a completely obvious solution to the mess, arrived at by a brain geared to the obvious.

"The die is cast," she said soberly. "No turning back," she added.

I agreed that the die was cast, indeed, and for the best; and I thought I understood what she meant. The only surprise was that she kissed me on the cheek as she stood to leave the restaurant.

The next afternoon—cocktails-with-Larry-at-five time again—I let myself into his studio. He wasn't anywhere to be seen. Larry had *always* been in the living room when I arrived, puttering around with the drinks, elegant in a loud tartan jacket a woman admirer had sent him. "Larry!"

The curtains into his bedroom parted, and he emerged unsteadily, pathetically. As a bathrobe he wore a scarlet-lined, braid-encrusted cape left over from some forgotten operetta. He sank into a chair like a wounded general, and hid his face in his hands.

"Flu!" I said.

"It's some unknown virus," he said darkly. "The doctor can find nothing. Nothing. Perhaps this is the beginning of a third world war—germ warfare."

"Probably all you need is sleep," I said, helpfully, I thought.

"Sleep! Hah! All night I couldn't sleep. Hot milk, pillows under the small of the back, sheep—"

"Party downstairs?"

He sighed. "The neighborhood was like a morgue. It's something inside me, I tell you."

"Well, as long as you've got your appetite—"

"Did I invite you here to torment me? Breakfast, my favorite meal, tasted like sawdust."

"Well, your voice sounds fine, and that's really the heart of the matter just now, isn't it?"

"Practice this afternoon was an utter flop," he said acidly. "I was unsure, rattled, blew up. I didn't feel right, not ready, half naked—"

"You look like a million dollars, anyway. The barber did a—"

"The barber is a butcher, a hacker, a—"

"He did a fine job."

"Then why don't I *feel* like he did." He stood. "Nothing's gone right today. The whole schedule's shot to hell. And never in my life, not once have I had the slightest bit of anxiety about a recital. Not once!"

"Well," I said hesitantly, "maybe good news would help. I saw Ellen Sparks at lunch yesterday, and she said she—"

Larry snapped his fingers. "That's it, that's it! Of course, that Ellen, she's poisoned me!" He paced the floor. "Not enough to kill me; just enough to break my spirit before tomorrow night. She's been out to get me all along."

"I don't think she poisoned you," I said, smiling. I hoped to divert him by being chatty. I stopped, suddenly aware of the awful significance of what I was about to say. "Larry," I said slowly, "Ellen left for Buffalo last night."

"Good riddance!"

"No more postcards to tear up at breakfast," I said casually. No effect. "No more honking of horns before practice." Still no effect. "No more ringing of the barbershop telephone, no more rattling of the garbage can at bedtime."

He grabbed my arms and shook me. "No!"

"Hell yes." I started to laugh in spite of myself. "She's so balled up in your life, you can't make a move without a cue from her."

"That little termite," said Larry hoarsely. "That burrowing, subversive, insidious, infiltrating little—" He hammered on the mantel. "I'll break the habit!"

"Habits," I corrected him. "If you do, they'll be the first ones you ever broke. Can you do it by tomorrow?"

"Tomorrow?" He moaned. "Oh—tomorrow."

"The houselights go out, and—"

"No flashlight."

"You get set for your first number—"

"Where are the coughs?" he said desperately. "I'll blow up like Texas City!" Trembling, he picked up the telephone. "Operator, get me Buffalo. What's her name again?"

"Sparks—*Ellen* Sparks."

I was invited to the wedding, but I'd have sooner attended a public beheading. I sent a sterling silver pickle fork and my regrets.

To my amazement, Ellen joined me at lunch on the day following the wedding. She was alone, lugging a huge parcel.

"What are you doing here on this day of days?" I said.

"Honeymooning." Cheerfully, she ordered a sandwich.

"Uh-huh. And the groom?"

"Honeymooning in his studio."

"I see." I didn't, but we had reached a point where it would have been indelicate for me to probe further.

"I've put in my two hours today," she volunteered. "And hung up one dress in his closet."

"And tomorrow?"

"Two and a half hours, and add a pair of shoes."

"*Little drops of water, Little grains of sand,*" I recited, "*Make the mighty ocean, And the beauteous land.*" I pointed to the parcel. "Is that part of your trousseau?"

She smiled. "In a way. It's a garbage can lid for beside the bed."

GOOD NEWS

THE PETRIFIED ANTS

I

"This *is* quite a hole you have here," said Josef Broznik enthusiastically, gripping the guard rail and peering into the echoing blackness below. He was panting from the long climb up the mountain slope, and his bald head glistened with perspiration.

"A remarkable hole," said Josef's twenty-five-year-old brother, Peter, his long, big-jointed frame uncomfortable in fog-dampened clothes. He searched his thoughts for a more profound comment, but found nothing. It was a perfectly amazing hole—no question about it. The officious mine supervisor, Borgorov, had said it had been sunk a half mile deep on the site of a radioactive mineral water spring. Borgorov's enthusiasm for the hole didn't seem in the least diminished by the fact that it had produced no uranium worth mining.

Peter studied Borgorov with interest. He seemed a pompous ass of a young man, yet his name merited fear and respect whenever it was mentioned in a gathering of miners. It was said, not without awe, that he was the favorite third cousin of Stalin himself, and that he was merely serving an apprenticeship for much bigger things.

Peter and his brother, Russia's leading myrmecologists, had been summoned from the University of Dnipropetrovsk to see the hole—or, rather, to see the fossils that had come out of it. Myrmecology, they had explained to the hundred-odd guards who had stopped them on their way into the area, was that branch of science devoted to the study of ants. Apparently, the hole had struck a rich vein of petrified ants.

Peter nudged a rock the size of his head and rolled it into the hole. He shrugged and walked away from it, whistling tunelessly. He was remembering again the humiliation of a month ago, when he had been forced to apologize publicly for his paper on *Raptiformica sanguinea,* the warlike, slave-raiding ants found under hedges. Peter had presented it to the world as a masterpiece of scholarship and scientific method, only to be rewarded by a stinging rebuke from Moscow. Men who couldn't tell *Raptiformica sanguinea* from centipedes had branded him an ideological backslider with dangerous tendencies toward Western decadence. Peter clenched and unclenched his fists, angry, frustrated. In effect, he had had to apologize because the ants he had studied would not behave the way the top Communist scientific brass wanted them to.

"Properly led," said Borgorov, "people can accomplish anything they set their minds to. This hole was completed within a month from the time orders came down from Moscow. Someone very high dreamed we would find uranium on this very spot," he added mysteriously.

"You will be decorated," said Peter absently, testing a point on the barbed wire around the opening. His reputation had preceded him into the area, he supposed. At any rate, Borgorov avoided his eyes, and addressed his remarks always to Josef—Josef the rock, the dependable, the ideologically impeccable. It was Josef who had advised against publishing the controversial paper, Josef who had written his apology. Now, Josef was loudly comparing the hole to the Pyramids, the Hanging Gardens of Babylon, and the Colossus of Rhodes.

Borgorov rambled on tiresomely, Josef agreed warmly, and Peter allowed his gaze and thoughts to wander over the strange new countryside. Beneath his feet were the *Erzgebirge*—the Ore Mountains, dividing Russian-occupied Germany from Czechoslovakia. Gray rivers of men streamed to and from pits and caverns gouged in the green mountain slopes—a dirty, red-eyed horde burrowing for uranium . . .

"When would you like to see the fossil ants we found?" said Borgorov, cutting into his thoughts. "They're locked up now, but we can get at them anytime tomorrow. I've got them all arranged in the order of the levels we found them in."

"Well," said Josef, "the best part of the day was used up getting cleared to come up here, so we couldn't get much done until tomorrow morning anyway."

"And yesterday, and the day before, and the day before that, sitting on a hard bench, waiting for clearance," said Peter wearily. Instantly he realized that he had said something wrong again. Borgorov's black eyebrows were raised, and Josef was glaring. He had absentmindedly violated one of Josef's basic maxims—"Never complain in public about anything." Peter sighed. On the battlefield he had proved a thousand times that he was a fiercely patriotic Russian. Yet, he now found his countrymen eager to read into his every word and gesture the symptoms of treason. He looked at Josef unhappily, and saw in his eyes the same old message: Grin and agree with everything.

"The security measures are marvelous," said Peter, grinning. "It's remarkable that they were able to clear us in only

three days, when you realize how thorough a job they do."
He snapped his fingers. "Efficiency."

"How far down did you find the fossils?" said Josef
briskly, changing the subject.

Borgorov's eyebrows were still arched. Plainly, Peter had
only succeeded in making himself even more suspicious.
"We hit them going through the lower part of the limestone,
before we came to the sandstone and granite," he said flatly,
addressing himself to Josef.

"Middle Mesozoic period, probably," said Josef. "We
were hoping you'd found fossil ants deeper than that." He
held up his hands. "Don't get us wrong. We're delighted that
you found these ants, it's only that middle Mesozoic ants
aren't as interesting as something earlier would be."

"Nobody's ever seen a fossil ant from an earlier period,"
said Peter, trying halfheartedly to get back into things. Borgorov ignored him.

"Mesozoic ants are just about indistinguishable from
modern ants," said Josef, surreptitiously signaling for Peter to
keep his mouth shut. "They lived in big colonies, were specialized as soldiers and workers and all that. My myrmecolo-
gist would give his right arm to know how ants lived before
they formed colonies—how they got to be the way they are
now. That *would* be something."

"Another first for Russia," said Peter. Again no response.
He stared moodily at a pair of live ants who pulled tirelessly and
in opposite directions at the legs of an expiring dung beetle.

"Have you *seen* the ants we found?" said Borgorov defensively. He waved a small tin box under Josef's nose. He
popped off the lid with his thumbnail. "Is this old stuff, eh?"

"Good heavens," murmured Josef. He took the box tenderly, held it at arm's length so that Peter could see the ant embedded in the chip of limestone.

The thrill of discovery shattered Peter's depression. "An inch long! Look at that noble head, Josef! I never thought I would see the day when I would say an ant was handsome. Maybe it's the big mandibles that make ants homely." He pointed to where the pincers ordinarily were. "This one has almost none, Josef. It *is* a pre-Mesozoic ant!"

Borgorov assumed a heroic stance, his feet apart, his thick arms folded. He beamed. This wonder had come out of *his* hole.

"Look, look," said Peter excitedly. "What is that splinter next to him?" He took a magnifying glass from his breast pocket and squinted through the lens. He swallowed. "Josef," he said hoarsely, "you look and tell me what you see."

Josef shrugged. "Some interesting little parasite maybe, or a plant, perhaps." He moved the chip up under the magnifying glass. "Maybe a crystal or—" He turned pale. Trembling, he passed the glass and fossil to Borgorov. "Comrade, you tell us what you see."

"I see," said Borgorov, screwing up his face in florid, panting concentration. He cleared his throat and began afresh. "I see what looks like a fat stick."

"Look closer," said Peter and Josef together.

"Well, come to think of it," said Borgorov, "it does look something like a—for goodness sake—like a—" He left the sentence unfinished, and looked up at Josef perplexedly.

"Like a bass fiddle, Comrade?" said Josef.

"Like a bass fiddle," said Borgorov, awed...

II

A drunken, bad-tempered card game was in progress at the far end of the miners' barracks where Peter and Josef were quartered. A thunderstorm boomed and slashed outside. The brother myrmecologists sat facing each other on their bunks, passing their amazing fossil back and forth and speculating as to what Borgorov would bring from the storage shed in the morning.

Peter probed his mattress with his hand—straw, a thin layer of straw stuffed into a dirty white bag and laid on planks. Peter breathed through his mouth to avoid drawing the room's dense stench through his long, sensitive nose. "Could it be a child's toy bass fiddle that got washed into that layer with the ant somehow?" he said. "You know this place was once a toy factory."

"Did you ever hear of a toy bass fiddle, let alone one that size? It'd take the greatest jeweler in the world to turn out a job like that. And Borgorov swears there wasn't any way for it to get down that deep—not in the past million years, anyway."

"Which leaves us one conclusion," said Peter.

"One." Josef sponged his forehead with a huge red handkerchief.

"Something could be worse than *this* pigpen?" said Peter. Josef kicked him savagely as a few heads raised up from the card games across the room. "Pigpen," laughed a small man as he threw his cards down and walked to his cot. He dug beneath his mattress and produced a bottle of cognac. "Drink, Comrade?"

"Peter!" said Josef firmly. "We left some of our things in the village. We'd better get them right away."

Gloomily, Peter followed his brother out into the thunderstorm. The moment they were outside, Josef seized him by the arm and steered him into the slim shelter of the eaves. "Peter, my boy, Peter—when are you going to grow up?" He sighed heavily, implored with upturned palms. "When? That man is from the police." He ran his stubby fingers over the polished surface where hair had once been.

"Well, it *is* a pigpen," said Peter stubbornly.

Josef threw up his hands with exasperation. "Of course it is. But you don't have to tell the police you think so." He laid his hand on Peter's shoulder. "Since your reprimand, anything you say can get you into terrible trouble. It can get us both into terrible trouble." He shuddered. "Terrible."

Lightning blazed across the countryside. In the dazzling instant, Peter saw that the slopes still seethed with the digging horde. "Perhaps I should give up speaking altogether, Josef."

"I ask only that you think out what you say. For your own good, Peter. Please, just stop and think."

"Everything you've called me down for saying has been the truth. The paper I had to apologize for was the truth." Peter waited for a rolling barrage of thunder to subside. "I mustn't speak the truth?"

Josef peered apprehensively around the corner, squinted into the darkness beneath the eaves. "You mustn't speak certain kinds of truth," he whispered, "not if you want to go on living." He dug his hands deep in his pockets, hunched his shoulders. "Give in a little, Peter. Learn to overlook certain things. It's the only way."

Together, without exchanging another word, the brothers

returned to the glare and suffocation of the barracks, their feet making sucking noises in their drenched shoes and socks.

"Too bad all our things are locked up until morning, Peter," said Josef loudly.

Peter hung his coat on a nail to dry, dropped heavily on his hard bunk, and pulled his shoes off. His movements were clumsy, his nerves dulled by a vast aching sensation of pity, of loss. Just as the lightning had revealed for a split second the gray men and gouged mountainsides—so had this talk suddenly revealed in a merciless flash the naked, frightened soul of his brother. Now Peter saw Josef as a frail figure in a whirlpool, clinging desperately to a raft of compromises. Peter looked down at his unsteady hands. "It's the only way," Josef had said, and Josef was right.

Josef pulled a thin blanket over his head to screen out the light. Peter tried to lose himself in contemplation of the fossil ant again. Involuntarily, his powerful fingers clamped down on the white chip. The chip and priceless ant snapped in two. Ruefully, Peter examined the faces of the break, hoping to glue them together again. On one of the faces he saw a tiny gray spot, possibly a mineral deposit. Idly, he focused his magnifying glass on it.

"Josef!"

Sleepily, Josef pushed the blanket away from his face. "Yes, Peter?"

"Josef, look."

Josef stared through the lens for fully a minute without speaking. When he spoke, his tone was high, uneven. "I don't know whether to laugh or cry or wind my watch."

"It looks like what I think it looks like?"

Josef nodded. "A book, Peter—a book."

III

Josef and Peter yawned again and again, and shivered in the cold twilight of the mountain dawn. Neither had slept, but their bloodshot eyes were quick and bright-looking, impatient, excited. Borgorov teetered back and forth on his thick boot soles, berating a soldier who was fumbling with the lock on a long toolshed.

"Did you sleep well in your quarters?" Borgorov asked Josef solicitously.

"Perfectly. It was like sleeping on a cloud," said Josef.

"I slept like a rock," said Peter brightly.

"Oh?" said Borgorov quizzically. "Then you don't think it was a pigpen after all, eh?" He didn't smile when he said it.

The door swung open, and two nondescript German laborers began dragging boxes of broken limestone from the shed. Each box, Peter saw, was marked with a number, and the laborers arranged them in order along a line Borgorov scratched in the dirt with his iron-shod heel.

"There," said Borgorov. "That's the lot." He pointed with a blunt finger. "One, two, and three. Number one is from the deepest layer—just inside the limestone—and the rest were above it in the order of their numbers." He dusted his hands and sighed with satisfaction, as though he himself had moved the boxes. "Now, if you'll excuse me, I'll leave you to work." He snapped his fingers, and the soldier marched the two Germans down the mountainside. Borgorov followed, hopping twice to get in step.

Feverishly, Peter and Josef dug into box number one, the one containing the oldest fossils, piling rock fragments on the ground. Each built a white cairn, sat beside it, tailor-fashion,

and happily began to sort. The dismal talk of the night before, Peter's fall from political grace, the damp cold, the
breakfast of tepid barley mush and cold tea—all were forgotten. For the moment, their consciousnesses were reduced to
the lowest common denominator of scientists everywhere—
overwhelming curiosity, blind and deaf to everything but the
facts that could satisfy it.

Some sort of catastrophe had apparently caught the big,
pincerless ants in their life routine, leaving them to be locked
in rock just as they were until Borgorov's diggers broke
into their tomb millions of years later. Josef and Peter now
stared incredulously at evidence that ants had once lived as
individuals—individuals with a culture to rival that of the
cocky new masters of Earth, men.

"Any luck?" asked Peter.

"I've found several more of our handsome, big ants,"
replied Josef. "They don't seem to be very sociable. They're
always by themselves. The largest group is three. Have you
broken any rocks open?"

"No, I've just been examining the surfaces." Peter rolled
over a rock the size of a good watermelon, and scanned its
underside with his magnifying glass. "Well, wait, here's
something, maybe." He ran his finger over a dome-shaped
projection of a hue slightly different than that of the stone.
He tapped around it gently with a hammer, painstakingly jar-
ring chips loose. The whole dome emerged at last, bigger
than his fist, free and clean—windows, doors, chimney, and
all. "Josef," said Peter. His voice cracked several times before
he could finish the sentence. "Josef—they lived in houses."
He stood, with the rock cradled in his arms, an unconscious
act of reverence.

Josef now peered over Peter's shoulder, breathing down his neck. "A lovely house."

"Better than ours," said Peter.

"Peter!" warned Josef. He looked around apprehensively.

The hideous present burst upon Peter again. His arms went limp with renewed anxiety and disgust. The rock crashed down on the others. The dome-shaped house, its interior solid with limestone deposits, shattered into a dozen wedges.

Again the brothers' irresistible curiosities took command. They sank to their knees to pick over the fragments. The more durable contents of the house had been locked in rock for eons, only now to meet air and sunlight. The perishable furnishings had left their impressions.

"Books—dozens of them," said Peter, turning a fragment this way and that to count the now-familiar rectangular specks.

"And here's a painting. I swear it is!" cried Josef.

"They'd discovered the wheel! Look at this wagon, Josef!" A fit of triumphant laughing burst from Peter. "Josef," he gasped, "do you realize that we have made the most sensational discovery in history? Ants once had a culture as rich and brilliant as ours. Music! Painting! Literature! Think of it!"

"And lived in houses—aboveground, with plenty of room, and lots of air and sunshine," said Josef raptly. "And they had fire and cooked. What could this be but a stove?"

"Millions of years before the first man—before the first gorilla, chimp, or orangutan, or even the first monkey, Josef—the ants had everything, *everything.*" Peter stared ecstatically into the distance, shrinking in his imagination down to the size of a finger joint and living a full, rich life in a stately pleasure dome all his own.

It was high noon when Peter and Josef had completed a cursory examination of the rocks in box number one. In all, they found fifty-three of the houses, each different—some large, some small, varying from domes to cubes, each one a work of individuality and imagination. The houses seemed to have been spaced far apart, and rarely were they occupied by more than a male and a female and young.

Josef grinned foolishly, incredulously. "Peter, are we drunk or crazy?" He sat in silence, smoking a cigarette and periodically shaking his head. "Do you realize it's lunchtime? It seems as though we've been here about ten minutes. Hungry?"

Peter shook his head impatiently, and began digging through the second box—fossils from the next layer up, eager to solve the puzzle of how the magnificent ant civilization had declined to the dismal, instinctive ant way of life of the present.

"Here's a piece of luck, Josef—ten ants so close together I can cover them with my thumb." Peter picked up rock after rock, and, wherever he found one ant, he found at least a half dozen close by. "They're starting to get gregarious."

"Any physical changes?"

Peter frowned through his magnifying glass. "Same species, all right. No, now, wait—there *is* a difference, the pincers are more developed, considerably more developed. They're starting to look like modern workers and soldiers." He handed a rock to Josef.

"Mmmm, no books here," said Josef. "You find any?"

Peter shook his head, and found that he was deeply distressed by the lack of books, searching for them passionately. "They've still got houses, but now they're jammed with people." He cleared his throat. "I mean ants." Suddenly a cry of joy escaped him. "Josef! Here's one without the big pincers, just like the ones in the lower level!" He turned the specimen this way and that in the sunlight. "By himself, Josef. In his house, with his family and books and everything! Some of the ants are differentiating into workers and soldiers—some aren't!"

Josef had been reexamining some of the gatherings of the ants with pincers. "The gregarious ones may not have been interested in books," he announced. "But everywhere that you find them, you find pictures." He frowned perplexedly. "There's a bizarre twist, Peter; the picture lovers evolving away from the book lovers."

"The crowd lovers away from the privacy lovers," said Peter thoughtfully. "Those with big pincers away from those without." To rest his eyes, he let his gaze wander to the tool-shed and a weathered poster from which the eyes of Stalin twinkled. Again he let his gaze roam, this time into the distance—to the teeming mouth of the nearest mine shaft, where a portrait of Stalin beamed paternally on all as they shambled in and out; to a cluster of tar-paper barracks below, where a portrait of Stalin stared shrewdly, protected from the weather by glass, at the abominable sanitary facilities.

"Josef," Peter began uncertainly, "I'll bet tomorrow's to-bacco ration that those works of art the pincered ants like so well are political posters."

"If so, our wonderful ants are bound for an even higher civilization," said Josef enigmatically. He shook rock dust from his clothing. "Shall we see what is in box number three?"

Peter found himself looking at the third box with fear and loathing. "*You* look, Josef," he said at last.

Josef shrugged. "All right." He studied the rocks in silence for several minutes. "Well, as you might expect, the pincers are even more pronounced, and—"

"And the gatherings are bigger and more crowded, and there are no books, and the posters are as numerous as the ants!" Peter blurted suddenly.

"You're quite right," said Josef.

"And the wonderful ants without pincers are gone, aren't they, Josef?" said Peter huskily.

"Calm down," said Josef. "You're losing your head over something that happened a thousand thousand years ago—or more." He tugged thoughtfully at his earlobe. "As a matter of fact, the pincerless ants do seem extinct." He raised his eyebrows. "As far as I know, it's without precedent in paleontology. Perhaps those without pincers were susceptible to some sort of disease that those with pincers were immune to. At any rate, they certainly disappeared in a hurry. Natural selection at its ruggedest—survival of the fittest."

"Survival of the somethingest," said Peter balefully.

"No! Wait, Peter. We're both wrong. Here is one of the old type ants. And another and another! It looks like they were beginning to congregate, too. They're all packed together in one house, like matchsticks in a box."

Peter took the rock fragment from him, unwilling to believe what Josef said. The rock had been split by Borgorov's diggers so as to give a clean cross section through the ant-packed house. He chipped away at the rock enclosing the other side of the house. The rock shell fell away. "Oh," he said softly, "I see." His chippings had revealed the doorway of the little building, and guarding it were seven ants with pincers like scythes. "A camp," he said, "a reeducation camp."

Josef blanched at the word, as any good Russian might, but regained his composure after several hard swallows. "What is that starlike object over there?" he said, steering away from the unpleasant subject.

Peter chiseled the chip in which the object was embedded free from the rest of the rock, and held it out for Josef to contemplate. It was a sort of rosette. In the center was a pincerless ant, and the petals looked like warriors and workers with their weapons buried and locked in the flesh of the lone survivor of the ancient race. "There's your quick evolution, Josef." He watched his brother's face intently, yearning for a sign that his brother was sharing his hectic thoughts, his sudden insight into their own lives.

"A great curiosity," said Josef evenly.

Peter looked about himself quickly. Borgorov was struggling up the path from far below. "It's no curiosity, and you know it, Josef," said Peter. "What happened to those ants is happening to us."

"Hush!" said Josef desperately.

"We're the ones without pincers, Josef. We're done. We aren't made to work and fight in huge hordes, to live by instinct and nothing more, perpetuating a dark, damp anthill without the wits even to wonder why!"

They both fell into red-faced silence as Borgorov navigated the last hundred yards. "Come now," said Borgorov, rounding the corner of the toolshed, "our samples couldn't have been as disappointing as all that."

"It's just that we're tired," said Josef, giving his ingratiating grin. "The fossils are so sensational we're stunned."

Peter gently laid the chip with the murdered ant and its attackers embedded in it on the last pile. "We have the most significant samples from each layer arranged in these piles," he said, pointing to the row of rock mounds. He was curious to see what Borgorov's reaction might be. Over Josef's objections, he explained about two kinds of ants evolving within the species, showed him the houses and books and pictures in the lower levels, the crowded gatherings in the upper ones. Then, without offering the slightest interpretation, he gave Borgorov his magnifying glass, and stepped back.

Borgorov strolled up and down the row several times, picking up samples and clucking his tongue. "It couldn't be more graphic, could it?" he said at last.

Peter and Josef shook their heads.

"Obviously," said Borgorov, "what happened was this." He picked up the chip that showed the bas-relief of the pincerless ant's death struggle with countless warriors. "There were these lawless ants, such as the one in the center, capitalists who attacked and exploited the workers—ruthlessly killing, as we can see here, scores at a time." He set down the melancholy exhibit, and picked up the house into which the pincerless ants were crammed. "And here we have a conspiratorial meeting of the lawless ants, plotting against the workers. Fortunately"—and he pointed to the soldier ants outside the door—"their plot was overheard by vigilant workers.

"So," he continued brightly, holding up samples from the next layer, a meeting of the pincered ants and the home of a solitary ant, "the workers held democratic indignation meetings, and drove their oppressors out of their community. The capitalists, overthrown, but with their lives spared by the merciful common people, were soft and spoiled, unable to survive without the masses to slave for them. They could only dillydally with the arts. Hence, put on their own mettle, they soon became extinct." He folded his arms with an air of finality and satisfaction.

"But the order was just the reverse," objected Peter. "The ant civilization was wrecked when some of the ants started growing pincers and going around in mobs. You can't argue with geology."

"Then an inversion has taken place in the limestone layer—some kind of upheaval turned it upside down. Obviously." Borzorov sounded like sheathed ice. "We have the most conclusive evidence of all—the evidence of logic. The sequence could only have been as I described it. Hence, there *was* an inversion. Isn't that so?" he said, looking pointedly at Josef.

"Exactly, an inversion," said Josef.

"Isn't that so?" Borgorov wheeled to face Peter.

Peter exhaled explosively, slouched in an attitude of utter resignation. "Obviously, Comrade." Then he smiled, apologetically. "Obviously, Comrade," he repeated . . .

Epilogue

"Good Lord, but it's cold!" said Peter, letting go of his end of the saw and turning his back to the Siberian wind.

"To work! To work!" shouted a guard, so muffled against the cold as to look like a bundle of laundry with a submachine gun sticking out of it.

"Oh, it could be worse, much worse," said Josef, holding the other end of the saw. He rubbed his frosted eyebrows against his sleeve.

"I'm sorry you're here, too, Josef," said Peter sadly. "I'm

the one who raised his voice to Borgorov." He blew on his hands. "I guess that's why we're here."

"Oh, that's all right," sighed Josef. "One stops thinking about such things. One stops thinking. It's the only way. If we didn't belong here, we wouldn't be here."

Peter fingered a limestone chip in his pocket. Embedded in it was the last of the pincerless ants, ringed by his murderers. It was the only fossil from Borgorov's hole that remained above the surface of the earth. Borgorov had made the brothers write a report on the ants as he saw them, had had every last fossil shoveled back into the bottomless cavity, and had shipped Josef and Peter to Siberia. It was a thorough piece of work, not likely to be criticized.

Josef had pushed aside a pile of brush, and was now staring with fascination at the bared patch of earth. An ant emerged furtively from a hole, carrying an egg. It ran around in crazy circles, then scurried back into the darkness of the tiny earth womb. "A marvelous adjustment ants have made, isn't it, Peter?" said Josef enviously. "The good life—efficient, uncomplicated. Instinct makes all the decisions." He sneezed. "When I die, I think I'd like to be reincarnated as an ant. A modern ant, not a capitalist ant," he added quickly.

"What makes you so sure you aren't one?" said Peter.

Josef shrugged off the jibe. "Men could learn a lot from ants, Peter, my boy."

"They have, Josef, they have," said Peter wearily. "More than they know."

THE HONOR OF
A NEWSBOY

Charley Howes was the police chief in a Cape Cod village. He was in command of four patrolmen in the summer and one in the winter. It was late winter now. The one patrolman was down with the flu, and Charley didn't feel too good himself. On top of that, there'd been a murder. Somebody had given Estelle Fulmer, the Jezebel waitress over at the Blue Dolphin, a beating that had killed her.

They found her in a cranberry bog on Saturday. The medical examiner said she'd been killed Wednesday night.

Charley Howes guessed he knew who'd done it. He guessed Earl Hedlund had done it. Earl was mean enough, and Earl had reason. Estelle had told Earl to go to hell one night at the Blue Dolphin, told him off the way he'd never been told off before. Nobody had ever told Earl off that way before because everybody knew Earl would kill anybody who did.

Charley's wife was bundling up Charley now so he could go up to Earl's house and question him. "If I'd known there was going to be a murder," said Charley, "I never would have taken the job of police chief."

"Now, you watch out for that big dog," said his wife, wrapping a muffler around his neck.

"He's all bark and no bite," said Charley.

"That's what they said about Earl Hedlund, too," said his wife.

The dog they were talking about was Satan. Satan was a crossbreed between a Great Dane and an Irish wolfhound. He was as big as a small horse. Satan didn't belong to Earl Hedlund, but he spent most of his time in Earl's woods, scaring people off the property. Earl fed him off and on, getting a cheap watchdog that way. And the dog and Earl liked each other fine besides. They both liked to make a lot of noise and act like man-eaters.

When Charley drove the patrol car up the long hill to Earl's house, way off in the woods, he expected to find Earl home. It was Saturday afternoon, but Charley would have expected to find Earl home any day of the week. Earl didn't work for a living. He'd inherited just enough money so he didn't have to work—if he was good and stingy, and kept a sharp eye on the stock market. The busiest Earl ever got was when the newspaper came. He'd turn to the financial page and make graphs of what all the stocks were doing.

When Charley got up to the house, he could hear Satan barking from a long way off. And Earl wasn't around, either. The house was locked up tight, and the newspapers had piled up on the front porch.

The newspapers were under a brick, so they couldn't blow away. Charley counted the papers. There were four. Friday's was the top one. Saturday's hadn't come yet. It began to look as though Earl hadn't killed Estelle after all, much as he would have liked to. It looked as though Earl hadn't been around to do the job.

Charley looked at the dates on the untouched papers, and

he discovered something interesting. The Wednesday paper was missing.

The noise of the dog was coming closer now, coming closer fast. Charley figured the dog had got wind of him. Charley had to keep a grip on himself to keep from being scared. Charley had the same feeling about Satan everybody else in the village had. The dog was crazy. Satan hadn't bitten anybody yet—but if he ever did, he'd bite to kill.

Then Charley saw what Satan was barking at. Satan was cantering alongside of a boy on a bicycle, showing teeth like butcher knives. He was swinging his head from side to side, barking, and slashing air with those awful teeth.

The boy looked straight ahead, pretending the dog wasn't there. He was the bravest human being Charley had ever seen. The hero was Mark Crosby, the ten-year-old newsboy.

"Mark—" said Charley. The dog came after Charley now, did his best to turn Charley's thinning hair white with those butcher-knife teeth. If the boy hadn't set such high standards for bravery, Charley might have made a dive for the safety of the patrol car. "You seen anything of Mr. Hedlund, Mark?" said Charley.

"Nosir," said Mark, giving Charley's uniform the respect it deserved. He put the Saturday paper on top of the pile on the doorstep, put it under the brick. "He's been gone all week, sir."

Satan finally got bored with these two unscarable human beings. He lay down on the porch with a tremendous thump, and snarled lazily from time to time.

"Where'd he go? You know?" said Charley.

"Nosir," said Mark. "He didn't say he was going—didn't stop his paper."

"Did you deliver a paper Wednesday?" said Charley.

Mark was offended that his friend the policeman should ask. "Of course," he said. "It's the rule. If the papers pile up and nobody's said to stop, you keep on delivering for six days." He nodded. "It's the *rule,* Mr. Howes."

The serious way Mark talked about the rule reminded Charley what a marvelous age ten was. And Charley thought it was a pity that everybody couldn't stay ten for the rest of their lives. If everybody were ten, Charley thought, maybe rules and common decency and horse sense would have a Chinaman's chance.

"You—you sure you didn't maybe miss Wednesday, Mark?" said Charley. "Nobody'd blame you—sleet coming down, the papers piling up, the long hill to climb, the big dog to get past."

Mark held up his right hand. "My word of honor," he said, "a paper was delivered here Wednesday."

That was good enough for Charley. That certainly settled it once and for all.

Just about the time that was settled, up the road came Earl Hedlund's old coupe. Earl got out grinning, and Satan whimpered and got up and licked Earl's hand. Earl was the village bully of thirty-five years ago—gone to fat and baldness. His grin was still the bully-boy's grin, daring anybody not to love him. He'd never been able to bluff Charley, and he hated Charley for that.

His grin got wider when Charley, as a precaution, reached into his car and took out the ignition key. "You see a cop do that on television, Charley?" said Earl.

"Matter of fact, I did," said Charley. It was true.

"I'm not running off to nowheres," said Earl. "I read in the Providence papers about poor Estelle, and I figured you'd be wanting to see me, so I came back. Thought I could save you from wasting time—thinking it was me that killed her."

"Thanks," said Charley.

"I been at my brother's place in Providence all week," said Earl. "My brother'll swear to that. Every minute's accounted for." He winked. "O.K., Charley?"

Charley knew Earl's brother. Earl's brother had a mean streak, too—but he was too little to beat up on women, so he specialized in lying. All the same, his word might stand up in court.

Earl sat down on his doorstep, took the top paper off the pile, turned to the financial page. Then he remembered it was Saturday. There weren't any market quotations on Saturday. It was easy to see he hated Saturday for that.

"You have many visitors up here, Earl?" said Charley.

"Visitors?" said Earl scornfully. He was reading what little financial news there was. "What I want with visitors?"

"Repairmen? Strangers out for a walk? Kids?" said Charley. "Hunters maybe?"

Earl puffed himself up for his answer. He really enjoyed the idea that everybody was too scared to come near his place. "Anything needs repairing, I repair myself," he said. "And strangers and kids and hunters and anybody else finds out pretty quick from the dog that we don't want no visitors up this way."

"Then who picked up the paper Wednesday night?" said Charley.

Earl let his paper sag for just a second, then he straightened it out again, pretended to read something a lot more important than anything Charley was saying. "What's this bushwah about a Wednesday paper?" he grumbled.

Charley told him what the bushwah was—told him that it might prove that Earl had been back on Cape Cod the night Estelle was murdered. "If you did come back on Wednesday," said Charley, "I can't see you passing up the chance to look in the paper to see what the market was doing."

Earl put down the paper, and he looked straight at Mark. "There wasn't any Wednesday paper on account of the kid was too lazy to bring one," he said.

"He gave his word of honor he brought one," said Charley.

Earl started reading again. "The kid's not only lazy," he said, "he's a liar besides."

Charley was glad he hadn't brought his gun along. If he had, he might have shot Earl Hedlund. Charley forgot all about the murder. Here, for Charley's money, was a crime that was just as bad as murder—and there wasn't any name for it and there wasn't any law against it.

Poor Mark was ruined. The most priceless thing he'd built up for himself in this vale of tears was his word of honor. Earl had spit on it.

"He gave his word of honor!" Charley yelled at Earl.

Earl said a dirty word, didn't look up from his paper.

"Mr. Howes——" said Mark.

"Yes, Mark?" said Charley.

"I—I got something even better than my word of honor," said Mark.

Charley couldn't imagine what that would be. Earl was

curious, too. Even Satan the dog seemed to want to know what could top a ten-year-old's word of honor.

Mark glowed, he was so sure he could prove, even to Earl's satisfaction, that the Wednesday paper had been delivered. "I was sick Wednesday," he said, "so my father delivered the papers." As far as Mark was concerned, he might as well have said God had done the route.

Charley Howes smiled feebly. Mark had just done him out of his one good clue. Mark's father was maybe brave in a lot of ways, but there were two things he wasn't brave about. All his life he'd been scared of Earl Hedlund and dogs.

Earl Hedlund guffawed.

Charley sighed. "Thanks—thanks for the information, Mark," he said. "You go on and carry the rest of your route now." He was going to let it go at that.

But Earl wouldn't let it go that easily. "Kid," he said to Mark, "I hate to tell you this, but that father of yours is the biggest yellow belly in the village." He put the paper aside and stood up, so Mark could see what a real man looked like.

"Shut up, Earl," said Charley.

"Shut up?" said Earl. "A minute ago, this kid was doing his best to get me in the electric chair."

Mark was flabbergasted. "Electric chair?" he said. "All I said was my father brought the paper."

Earl's piggy eyes glittered. The way those eyes glittered and the way Earl hunched over removed all doubt from Charley's mind that Earl was a murderer. Earl wanted to kill the boy. He couldn't do it with his hands with Charley there, so he was doing the next cruelest thing. He was doing it with words.

"Maybe your old man told you he brought the paper," said Earl, "but I promise you right now he wouldn't come near this dog for a million dollars, and he wouldn't come near me for ten million!" He held up his right hand. "Word of honor on that, kid!" He didn't stop there. He told Mark story after story about how Mark's father had run or hidden or cried or begged for mercy as a boy—how he'd slunk away from danger as a man. And in every story danger was one of two things—a dog or Earl Hedlund. "Scout's honor, word of honor, swear on a stack of Bibles—any kind of honor you want, kid," said Earl, "everything I've said is true."

There was nothing left for Mark to do but the thing he'd sworn never to do again. He cried. He climbed on his bicycle, and he rode away.

The dog didn't chase him this time. Satan understood that Mark wasn't fair game.

"Now you git, too," Earl said to Charley.

Charley was so heartsick about Mark, he leaned against Earl's house and closed his eyes for a minute. He opened his eyes and saw his reflection in a windowpane. He saw a tired old man, and he figured he'd grown old and tired trying to make the world be what ten-year-olds thought it was.

And then he saw the newspaper lying on the chair just inside the window, locked up nice and tight inside the house. Charley could read the date. It was Wednesday's paper, open to the financial page. It was proof enough that Earl had gone to Providence to build an alibi—that he'd sneaked back Wednesday to kill Estelle.

But Charley wasn't thinking about Earl or Estelle. He was thinking about Mark and his father.

Earl knew what Charley had seen through the window. He was on his feet, showing his teeth, ready to fight. And he held the dog by the scruff of his neck, getting the dog ready to fight, too.

But Charley didn't close in for a fight. He climbed into the patrol car instead. "Be here when I get back," he said, and he drove down the hill after Mark.

He caught up with Mark at the mouth of the road. "Mark!" he yelled. "Your father delivered the paper! It's up there! He delivered it through the sleet, past the dog and everything!"

"Good," said Mark. There wasn't any joy in the way he'd said it. He'd been through too much to be happy for a while. "Those things Mr. Hedlund said about Father," said Mark, "even if he gave his word of honor—they wouldn't necessarily be true, would they, Mr. Howes?"

There were two ways Charley could answer. He could lie, say no, the stories weren't true. Or he could tell the truth, and hope that Mark would catch on to the fact that all the stories made his father's delivery of the paper to Earl Hedlund's house one of the most glorious chapters in village history.

"Every one of those stories was true, Mark," said Charley. "Your father couldn't help being afraid, on account of he was born that way, just the way he was born with blue eyes and brown hair. You and me, we can't imagine what it's like to be loaded down with all that fear. It's a mighty brave man who can live with all that. So just think a minute how brave your father was to get that paper up to Earl Hedlund's rather than break a rule."

Mark thought, and then he nodded to show he understood.

He was satisfied. His father was what a ten-year-old's father has to be—a hero.

"Did—did Mr. Hedlund do the murder?" said Mark.

"Gosh amighty!" said Charley. He banged the side of his head with the heel of his hand to make his brains work better. "Forgot all about the murder."

He turned the patrol car around and roared up to Earl's house again. Earl was gone, and so was the dog. They'd taken off through the woods.

Two hours later a search party found Earl. He'd been heading for the railroad tracks, and Satan the dog had killed him. At the coroner's inquest, all anybody could offer was theories about why the dog had done it.

The best theory was probably Charley's. Charley guessed that the dog had smelled Earl's fear and seen him running, so he'd chased him. "And Earl was the first person who'd ever let the dog see how scared he was," Charley said at the inquest, "so Satan killed him."

LOOK AT THE BIRDIE

I was sitting in a bar one night, talking rather loudly about a person I hated—and a man with a beard sat down beside me, and he said amiably, "Why don't you have him killed?"

"I've thought of it," I said. "Don't think I haven't."

"Let me help you to think about it clearly," he said. His voice was deep. His beak was large. He wore a black mohair suit and a black string tie. His little red mouth was obscene. "You're looking at the situation through a red haze of hate," he said. "What you need are the calm, wise services of a murder counselor, who can plan the job for you, and save you an unnecessary trip to the hot squat."

"Where do I find one?" I said.

"You've found one," he said.

"You're crazy," I said.

"That's right," he said. "I've been in and out of mental institutions all my life. That makes my services all the more appealing. If I were ever to testify against you, your lawyer would have no trouble establishing that I was a well-known nut, and a convicted felon besides."

"What was the felony?" I said.

"A little thing—practicing medicine without a license," he said.

"Not murder then?" I said.

"No," he said, "but that doesn't mean I *haven't* murdered. As a matter of fact, I murdered almost everyone who had anything to do with convicting me of practicing medicine without a license." He looked at the ceiling, did some mental arithmetic. "Twenty-two, twenty-three people—maybe more," he said. "Maybe more. I've killed them over a period of years, and I haven't read the papers every single day."

"You black out when you kill, do you," I said, "and wake up the next morning, and read that you've struck again?"

"No, no, no, no, no," he said. "No, no, no, no, no. I killed many of those people while I was cozily tucked away in prison. You see," he said, "I use the cat-over-the-wall technique, a technique I recommend to you."

"This is a new technique?" I said.

"I like to think that it is," he said. He shook his head. "But it's so obvious, I can't believe that I was the first to think of it. After all, murdering's an old, old trade."

"You use a cat?" I said.

"Only as an analogy," he said. "You see," he said, "a very interesting legal question is raised when a man, for one reason or another, throws a cat over a wall. If the cat lands on a person, claws his eyes out, is the cat-thrower responsible?"

"Certainly," I said.

"Good," he said. "Now then—if the cat lands on nobody, but claws someone ten minutes after being thrown, is the cat thrower responsible?"

"No," I said.

"That," he said, "is the high art of the cat-over-the-wall technique for carefree murder."

"Time bombs?" I said.

"No, no, no," he said, pitying my feeble imagination.

"Slow poisons? Germs?" I said.

"No," he said. "And your next and final guess I already know: killers for hire from out of town." He sat back, pleased with himself. "Maybe I really *did* invent this thing."

"I give up," I said.

"Before I tell you," he said, "you've got to let my wife take your picture." He pointed his wife out to me. She was a scrawny, thin-lipped woman with raddled hair and bad teeth. She was sitting in a booth with an untouched beer before her. She was obviously a lunatic herself, watching us with the harrowing cuteness of schizophrenia. I saw that she had a Rollieflex with flashgun attached on the seat beside her.

At a signal from her husband, she came over and prepared to take my picture. "Look at the birdie," she said.

"I don't want my picture taken," I said.

"Say *cheese*," she said, and the flashgun went off.

When my eyes got used to darkness of the bar again, I saw the woman scuttling out the door.

"What the hell is this?" I said, standing up.

"Calm yourself. Sit down," he said. "You've had your picture taken. That's all."

"What's she going to do with it?" I said.

"Develop it," he said.

"And then what?" I said.

"Paste it in our picture album," he said, "in our treasure house of golden memories."

"Is this some kind of blackmail?" I said.

"Did she photograph you doing anything you shouldn't be doing?" he said.

"I want that picture," I said.

"You're not superstitious, are you?" he said.

"Superstitious?" I said.

"Some people believe that, if their picture is taken," he said, "the camera captures a little piece of their soul."

"I want to know what's going on," I said.

"Sit down and I'll tell you," he said.

"Make it good, and make it quick," I said.

"Good and quick it shall be, my friend," he said. "My name is Felix Koradubian. Does the name ring a bell?"

"No," I said.

"I practiced psychiatry in this city for seven years," he said. "Group psychiatry was my technique. I practiced in the round, mirror-lined ballroom of a stucco castle between a used car lot and a colored funeral home."

"I remember now," I said.

"Good," he said. "For your sake, I'd hate to have you think I was a liar."

"You were run in for quackery," I said.

"Quite right," he said.

"You hadn't even finished high school," I said.

"You mustn't forget," he said, "Freud himself was self-educated in the field. And one thing Freud said was that a brilliant intuition was as important as anything taught in medical school." He gave a dry laugh. His little red mouth certainly didn't show any merriment to go with the laugh. "When I was arrested," he said, "a young reporter who *had* finished high school—wonder of wonders, he may have even finished college—he asked me to tell him what a paranoiac was. Can you imagine?" he said. "I had been dealing with the insane and the nearly insane of this city for seven years, and that young squirt, who maybe took freshman psychology at

Jerkwater U, thought he could baffle me with a question like that."

"What *is* a paranoiac?" I said.

"I sincerely hope that that is a respectful question put by an ignorant man in search of truth," he said.

"It is," I said. It wasn't.

"Good," he said. "Your respect for me at this point should be growing by leaps and bounds."

"It is," I said. It wasn't.

"A paranoiac, my friend," he said, "is a person who has gone crazy in the most intelligent, well-informed way, the world being what it is. The paranoiac believes that great secret conspiracies are afoot to destroy him."

"Do you believe that about yourself?" I said.

"Friend," he said, "I *have* been destroyed! My God, I was making sixty thousand dollars a year—six patients an hour, at five dollars a head, two thousand hours a year. I was a rich, proud, and happy man. And that miserable woman who just took your picture, she was beautiful, wise, and serene."

"Too bad," I said.

"Too bad it is, *indeed,* my friend," he said. "And not just for us, either. This is a sick, sick city, with thousands upon thousands of mentally ill people for whom nothing is being done. Poor people, lonely people, afraid of doctors, most of them—those are the people I was helping. Nobody is helping them now." He shrugged. "Well," he said, "having been caught fishing illegally in the waters of human misery, I have returned my entire catch to the muddy stream."

"Didn't you turn your records over to somebody?" I said.

"I burned them," he said. "The only thing I saved was a

list of really dangerous paranoiacs that only I knew about—violently insane people hidden in the woodwork of the city, so to speak—a laundress, a telephone installer, a florist's helper, an elevator operator, and on and on."

Koradubian winked. "A hundred and twenty-three names on my magic list—all people who heard voices, all people who thought certain strangers were out to get them, all people, who, if they got scared enough, would kill."

He sat back and beamed. "I see you're beginning to understand," he said. "When I was arrested, and then got out on bail, I bought a camera—the same camera that took your picture. And my wife and I took candid snapshots of the District Attorney, the President of the County Medical Association, of an editorial writer who demanded my conviction. Later on, my wife photographed the judge and jury, the prosecuting attorney, and all of the unfriendly witnesses.

"I called in my paranoiacs, and I apologized to them. I told them that I had been very wrong in telling them that there was no plot against them. I told them that I had uncovered a monstrous plot, and that I had photographs of the plotters. I told them that they should study the photographs, and should be alert and armed constantly. And I promised to send them more photographs from time to time."

I was sick with horror, had a vision of the city teeming with innocent-looking lunatics who would suddenly kill and run.

"That—that picture of me—" I said wretchedly.

"We'll keep it locked up nice and tight," said Koradubian, "provided you keep this conversation a secret, and provided you give me money."

"How much money?" I said.

"I'll take whatever you've got on you now," he said.

I had twelve dollars. I gave it to him. "Now do I get the picture back?" I said.

"No," he said. "I'm sorry, but this goes on indefinitely, I'm afraid. One has to live, you know." He sighed, tucked away the money in his billfold.

"Shameful days, shameful days," he murmured. "And to think that I was once a respected professional man."

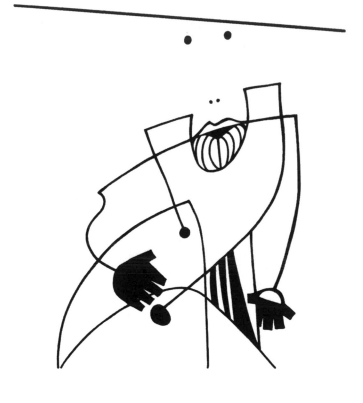

KING AND QUEEN OF
THE UNIVERSE

Mind going back to the Great Depression for a few minutes—
clear back to 1932? It was an awful time, I know, but there
are a lot of good stories in the Great Depression.

Back in 1932 Henry and Anne were seventeen.

At seventeen, Henry and Anne were in love with each
other in a highly ornamental way. They knew how good
their love looked. They knew how good *they* looked. They
could read in the eyes of their elders how right they were for
each other—how right for the society into which they had
been born.

Henry was Henry Davidson Merrill, son of the President
of the Merchants' National Bank; grandson of the late George
Mills Davidson, Mayor from 1916 to 1922; grandson of Dr.
Rossiter Merrill, founder of the Children's Wing of the City
Hospital...

Anne was Anne Lawson Heiler, daughter of the President
of the Citizens' Gas Company; granddaughter of the late federal judge Franklin Pace Heiler; granddaughter of D. Dwight
Lawson, architect, the Christopher Wren of the Middle
Western city...

Their credentials and their fortunes were in order—had
been from the instants of their births. Love like theirs made
no demands beyond good grooming, good sailing, good

tennis, good golf. They remained as untouched by the soul-deep aspects of love as Winnie-the-Pooh, the storybook teddy bear.

It was all so cheerful and easy—so natural and clean.

And, in a Winnie-the-Pooh mood, wherein sordid things could happen only to sordid people, Henry Davidson Merrill and Anne Lawson Heiler crossed a city park late one night—crossed it in evening clothes. They crossed it on their way from an Athletic Club dance to the garage where Henry's car was parked.

The night was black, and the few lights of the park were far apart and sickly pale.

People had been murdered in the park. One man had been butchered for twelve cents, and his murderer was still at large. But he had been a dirty, homeless man—one of those people who were born, seemingly, to be murdered for less than a dollar.

Henry regarded his tuxedo as a safe-conduct pass through the park—a costume so different from that of the natives as to make him immune to their squalid troublemaking.

Henry looked at Anne, and found her correctly bored—a pink bonbon in blue tulle, wearing her mother's pearls and orchids from Henry.

"I wouldn't mind sleeping on a park bench," said Anne loudly. "I think it would be fun. I think it would be fun to be a hobo." She put her hand in Henry's. Her hand was hard, tanned, comradely.

There was no cheap thrill in the meeting of their palms in the dark park. Having grown up together, knowing they would marry and grow old together, neither could surprise or puzzle the other with a touch or a glance or a word—or even with a kiss.

"It wouldn't be much fun to be a hobo in the wintertime," said Henry. He held her hand for a moment, swung it, then let it go without regret.

"I'd go to Florida in the wintertime," said Anne. "I'd sleep on the beaches and steal oranges."

"You can't live on just oranges," said Henry. He was being manly now—letting her know that he understood more about the harshnesses of the world than she did.

"Oranges and fish," said Anne. "I would steal ten cents' worth of hooks from a hardware store, and make a fishline out of string from somebody's wastebasket, and make a sinker out of a stone. Honestly," said Anne, "I think it would be heaven. I think people are crazy to worry about money the way they do."

In the exact middle of the park, what seemed to be a gargoyle on the rim of a fountain detached itself. It revealed itself as a man.

The movement transformed the park into the black River Styx, transformed the lights of the garage beyond into the gates of Paradise—gates a million miles away.

Henry became a foolish, slope-shouldered boy, as ungainly as a homemade stepladder. His white shirt bosom became a beacon for thieves and lunatics.

Henry glanced at Anne. She had become a fuddled butterball. Her hands went to her throat, hiding her mother's necklace. Her orchids seemed to weigh her down like cannonballs.

"Stop—please stop," the man wheezed softly. He coughed boozily, flagged them down with his hands. "Please—whoa, just a second."

Henry felt the sickening excitement of battle billow in his breast, raised his hands to somewhere between fight and surrender.

"Put your hands down," said the man. "I only want to talk to you. The robbers are all in bed by now. Drunks, drifters, and poets are the only ones up this late at night."

He lurched toward Henry and Anne, his own hands raised in a gesture of utter harmlessness. He was small and scrawny, and his cheap clothes wrinkled and crackled like newspaper.

He tipped his head back, exposing his scrawny throat to death at Henry's hands. He smiled slackly. "Big young man like you could kill me with two fingers," he said. Turtlelike, he watched with pop eyes for signs of trust.

Henry lowered his hands slowly, and so did the man.

"What you want?" said Henry. "You want money?"

"Don't you?" said the man. "Doesn't everybody? Bet even your old man could use some more." He chuckled, mimicked Henry. " 'You want money?' "

"My father isn't rich," said Henry.

"These pearls aren't real," said Anne. It came out a series of unbecoming squawks.

"Oh—they're real enough, I imagine," said the man. He bowed slightly to Henry. "And your father has some money, I imagine. Maybe not enough for the next thousand years, but for the next five hundred, anyway." He swayed. His face was mobile, showed in quick succession shame, contempt, whimsy, and finally great sadness. His face showed sadness when he introduced himself. "Stanley Karpinsky is the name," he said. "Don't want your money. Don't want your pearls. Want to talk."

Henry found that he couldn't brush past Karpinsky— couldn't even refuse his hand. Henry Davidson Merrill found that Stanley Karpinsky had become precious to him—had become a small god of the park, a supernatural being who could see into the shadows, who knew what lay behind every shrub and tree.

It seemed to Henry that Karpinsky and Karpinsky alone could lead them safely to the edge of the park so far away.

Anne's terror now turned into hysterical friendliness as Henry shook Karpinsky's hand. "Goodness!" she cried into the night. "We thought you were a robber or we didn't know what!" She laughed.

Karpinsky became reserved, sure of their trust. He studied their clothes. "King and Queen of the Universe—that's what she'd think you were," he said. "By God, if she wouldn't!"

"Beg pardon?" said Henry.

"My mother would," said Karpinsky. "She'd think you were the two most beautiful creatures she ever laid eyes on. Little old Polish woman—scrubbing floors all her life. Never even got up off her hands and knees long enough to learn English. She'd think you were angels." He cocked his head and raised an eyebrow. "Would you come and let her have a look at you?" he said.

In the flaccid idiocy that had followed terror, Henry and Anne accepted Karpinsky's peculiar invitation—not only accepted it, but accepted it with enthusiasm.

"Mother?" babbled Anne. "Love to, love to, love to."

"Sure—where to?" said Henry.

"Just a block from here," said Karpinsky. "We'd go in, let her see you, and then you could leave right away. It wouldn't take over ten minutes."

"O.K.," said Henry.

"O.K.," said Anne. "This is fun."

Karpinsky studied them for a little while longer, taking from his pocket a loose cigarette that had been bent into almost a right angle. Karpinsky didn't bother to straighten it out, but lit it as it was.

"Come on," he said suddenly, flicking the match away. And Henry and Anne found themselves following him, walking very quickly. He was leading them away from the lights of the garage, was leading them toward a side street that was hardly better illuminated than the park.

Henry and Anne stayed right with him. For all the unearthliness of their mission and the park at night, Henry and Anne might have been hurtling through the black vacuum of space to the moon.

The odd expedition reached the edge of the park and crossed the street. The street seemed a murky tunnel through a nightmare, with bright, warm, safe reality at either end.

The city was very quiet. An empty streetcar far away screamed rustily, rang its cracked bell. An automobile horn bleated a reply.

A policeman down the block paused in his rounds to watch Henry, Anne, and Karpinsky. Feeling his protective gaze, Henry and Anne hesitated for an instant, then pressed on. They were committed to seeing the adventure through.

And it wasn't fear that was committing them to it anymore. Exhilaration was driving them now. Henry Davidson Merrill and Anne Lawson Heiler were suddenly, stunningly, dangerously, romantically leading lives of their own.

An old colored man, talking to himself, came from the opposite direction. He stopped and leaned against a building, still talking to himself, to watch them pass.

Henry and Anne met his gaze squarely. They were denizens of the night themselves.

And then Karpinsky opened a door. A steep stairway went up abruptly from the door. On the stair riser that was at eye level for a person standing on the street was a small sign. STANLEY KARPINSKY, M.S., it said, INDUSTRIAL CHEMIST, 3RD FLOOR.

Karpinsky watched Henry and Anne read the sign, and he seemed to draw strength from it. He sobered up, became respectable and grave, became the master of science that the sign proclaimed. He combed his hair with his fingers, straightened his coat.

Until that moment, Henry and Anne had thought of him as old. They could see now that Karpinsky's scrawniness wasn't a withering but a result of his having taken very bad care of himself.

He was only in his late twenties.

"I'll lead the way," said Karpinsky.

The walls of the stairway were sheathed in a bristly fiberboard. They smelled of cabbage. The building was an old house that had been divided into apartments.

It was the first unclean, unsafe building that Henry and Anne had ever been in.

As Karpinsky reached the second floor, an apartment door opened.

"George—that you?" said a woman peevishly. She stepped into the corridor, squinting. She was a big, stupid beast of a woman, holding her bathrobe closed with grubby fists. "Oh," she said, seeing Karpinsky, "the mad scientist—drunk again."

"Hello, Mrs. Purdy," said Karpinsky. He was blocking her view of Henry and Anne.

"You seen my George?" she said.

"No," said Karpinsky.

She smiled crookedly. "Made a million dollars yet?" she said.

"No—not yet, Mrs. Purdy," said Karpinsky.

"Better make it pretty quick," said Mrs. Purdy, "now that your mother's too sick to support you anymore."

"I expect to," said Karpinsky coolly. He stepped aside, letting her look at Henry and Anne on the stairs. "These are two good friends of mine, Mrs. Purdy," he said. "They think a great deal of my work."

Mrs. Purdy was thunderstruck.

"They've been dancing at the Athletic Club," said Karpinsky. "They heard my mother was very ill, and they decided to drop over to see her—to tell her how all the important people at the dance were talking about my experiments."

Mrs. Purdy opened her mouth and closed it again, without having made a sound.

Mrs. Purdy made a mirror of herself for Henry and Anne—showed them images of themselves that they'd never seen before. She showed them how enormously powerful they were, or would be. They had always known that they would be more comfortable and have more expensive pleasures than most—but it had never occurred to them that they would be more powerful, too.

That could be the only explanation of Mrs. Purdy's awe— that she was in awe of their power. "Nice—nice to know you," she said, keeping her eyes right on them. "Good night." She backed into her apartment and closed the door.

The home and the laboratory of Stanley Karpinsky, industrial chemist, were a single, drafty attic room—a room with the proportions of a shotgun. There were two tiny windows, one in each of the gable ends. They rattled in their frames.

The ceiling of the room was wood, the boards of the roof itself, rising to meet at the rooftree. The studs of the wall were bare. Shelves had been nailed between the studs, supporting a meager food supply, a microscope, books, reagent bottles, test tubes, beakers . . .

A great walnut dining table with lions'-claw feet was in the exact center of the room, with a shaded lightbulb over it. This was Karpinsky's laboratory table. A complex system of ring stands, flasks, glass tubing, and burettes was set up on it.

"Whisper," said Karpinsky, as he turned on the light over the table. He put his finger to his lips, and nodded meaningfully at a bed tucked under the eaves. The bed was so deep in shadows that it might have gone unnoticed, if Karpinsky hadn't pointed it out. His mother was sleeping there.

She did not stir. Her breathing was slow. Each time she exhaled, she seemed to be saying, "Thee."

Karpinsky touched the apparatus on the lion-clawed table— touched it with emotions that plainly teetered between love and hate.

"This," whispered Karpinsky, "is what everyone at the Athletic Club was talking about tonight. The captains of finance and industry could talk of nothing else." He raised his eyebrows quizzically. "Your father said I was going to be very rich on account of this, didn't he?" he said to Henry.

Henry managed a smile.

"Say yes," said Karpinsky.

Henry and Anne said nothing for fear of involving their fathers in an unprofitable business enterprise.

"Don't you see what this is?" whispered Karpinsky, his eyes wide. He was playing the magician now. "You mean it isn't self-evident?"

Henry and Anne exchanged glances, shook their heads.

"It's my mother's and father's dream come true," said Karpinsky. "It's what made their son rich and famous. Think of it—they were humble peasants in a strange land, unable to even read or write. But they worked hard in this land of promise, and every tearstained penny they got they put into an education for their son. They sent him not only to high school, but to college! Not only to college, but to graduate school! Now look at him—how successful he is!"

Henry and Anne were too young, too innocent, to recognize Karpinsky's performance for what it was—bloodcurdling satire. They looked at his apparatus gravely, and were prepared to believe that it really would make a fortune.

Karpinsky watched them for a reaction. And, when he got none, he flabbergasted them by bursting into tears. He made as though to grab the apparatus and hurl it to the floor. He stopped just short of doing that, one hand fighting with the other.

"Do I have to spell it out for you?" he whispered. "My father worked himself to death for my future; my mother is dying, killed by the same thing. And now, college degrees and all, I can't even get a job as a dishwasher!"

He closed in on the apparatus with his hands again, again seemed on the verge of destroying it. "This?" he said wistfully. He shook his head. "I don't know. Maybe it's something and maybe it isn't. Take years and thousands of dollars to find out." He looked toward the bed. "My mother hasn't got years to see me be a big success," he said. "She hasn't even got days, probably. She's going to the hospital for an operation tomorrow, and they tell me she hasn't got much of a chance of coming back."

Now the woman awakened. She didn't move, but she spoke her son's name.

"So I've got to be a big success tonight or never," said Karpinsky. "Stand there and admire the apparatus—look at it as though it were the most wonderful thing you ever laid eyes on, while I tell her you are millionaires, and you've come to buy the apparatus for a fortune!"

He went to his mother's side, knelt by the bed, and told her the good news in exulting Polish.

Henry and Anne went to the apparatus self-consciously, their arms limp at their sides.

Now Karpinsky's mother sat up, exclaiming.

Henry smiled glassily at the apparatus. "It's very nice, isn't it?" he said.

"Oh, yes—isn't it?" said Anne.

"Smile!" said Henry.

"What?" said Anne.

"Smile—look happy!" said Henry. It was the first order he had ever given her.

Anne was startled, and then she smiled.

"He's a great success," said Henry. "It's a wonderful thing."

"It's going to make him so rich," said Anne.

"His mother should be very proud of him," said Henry.

"She wants to meet you," said Karpinsky.

Henry and Anne went to the foot of the old woman's bed. She was speechless and radiant.

Karpinsky was wildly happy, too. His deception had paid off stunningly. In less than a minute, his mother had received her full reward, a perfectly gorgeous reward, for a life of awful sacrifices. Her joy shot with the speed of light into her past, illuminating every wretched moment of it with great joy.

"Tell her your names," said Karpinsky. "Any names. Doesn't make any difference."

Henry bowed. "Henry Davidson Merrill," he said.

"Anne Lawson Heiler," said Anne.

It would have been a shame to use any names other than the true ones. What Henry and Anne had just done was, after all, perfectly beautiful—and the first thing they had ever done that was likely to be noticed in Heaven.

Karpinsky made his mother lie down. He went over the good news for her again—crooningly.

She closed her eyes.

Henry and Anne and Karpinsky, their eyes shining, tiptoed away from her, toward the door.

And then the cops broke in.

There were three of them—one with his gun drawn, the other two with their clubs ready. They grabbed Karpinsky.

Right behind them came Henry's and Anne's fathers in tuxedos. They were wild with fear—fear that something awful had happened or was about to happen to their children. They had reported Henry's and Anne's disappearance as a kidnapping.

Karpinsky's mother sat up in bed, saw her son in the hands of the police. This was the last picture to be recorded in her mind in life. Karpinsky's mother groaned and died.

Ten minutes later, it was no longer possible to speak of Henry, Anne, and Karpinsky in a common action, in the same room, or even, poetically, in the same universe.

Karpinsky and the police worked hopelessly to revive Karpinsky's mother. Henry walked dazedly out of the building, with his appalled father begging him to stop and listen. Anne burst into tears that let her think of nothing. She was easily led by her father to his waiting car.

Six hours later, Henry was still walking. He had reached the edge of the city, and the sun was coming up. He had done curious things to his evening clothes. He had thrown away his black tie and his cuff links and his shirt studs. He had rolled up his shirtsleeves, and had ripped the starched white bosom of his shirt, so that it looked something like an ordinary shirt opened at the throat. His once glossy black shoes were the color of city mud.

He looked like a very young bum, which is what he had decided to be. A police cruiser finally found him, took him home. He didn't have a civil word for anybody, and he wouldn't listen. He wasn't a child anymore. He was a badly jangled man.

. . .

Anne cried herself to sleep. And then, just about the time Henry was being brought home, she cried herself awake again.

The light of dawn in her room was as pale as skimmed milk. In that light, Anne saw a vision. Anne's vision was of a book. The name of the author was her own. In the book, Anne Lawson Heiler told the truth about the shallowness and cowardice and hypocrisy of the rich people in the city.

She thought of the first two lines in the book: "There was a depression on. Most of the people in the city were poor and heartbroken, but there was dancing at the Athletic Club." She felt much better. She went back to sleep again.

Just about the time Anne went back to sleep, Stanley Karpinsky opened a window in his attic room. He took the apparatus from the table with the lion's-claw feet, and he dropped the apparatus out the window piece by piece. Then he dropped his books and his microscope and all the rest of his equipment. He took a long time doing it, and some of the things made quite a racket when they hit the street.

Somebody finally called the police about a crazy man dropping things out of a window. When the police came, and they found out who it was that was dropping things, they didn't say anything to Karpinsky about it. They just cleaned up the mess in the street as best they could—cleaned it up sheepishly.

Henry slept until noon that day. And when he got up, he got out of the house before anyone knew he was awake. His mother, a sweet, sheltered person, heard his car start, heard his tires swish in gravel, and he was gone.

Henry drove with elaborate caution, dramatizing every motion he made in controlling the car. He felt that he had a terribly important errand to run—but he wasn't sure what the errand was. His driving, then, took on the importance of the nameless errand.

He arrived at Anne's house while she was eating breakfast. The attitude of the maid who let Henry in was that Anne was a pathetic invalid. This was hardly the case. Anne was eating with gusto, and was writing in a school notebook between bites.

She was writing her novel—angrily.

Anne's mother sat across the table from her, uneasily respecting the unfamiliar rites of creativity. The savagery of her daughter's pencil strokes offended her, frightened her. She knew what the writing was about. Anne had let her read some of it.

Anne's mother was delighted to see Henry. She had always liked Henry—and she was sure Henry would help her to change Anne's very bad mood. "Oh, Henry, dear," she said, "have you heard the good news? Did your mother tell you?"

"I haven't seen my mother," said Henry stolidly.

Anne's mother wilted. "Oh," she said. "I—I talked with her on the phone three times this morning. She's looking forward to having a long talk with you—about what happened."

"Um," said Henry. "What's the good news, Mrs. Heiler?"

"They got him a job," said Anne. "Isn't that swell?" Her wry expression made it clear that she thought the news was something less than swell. She thought Henry was something less than swell, too.

"That poor man—last night—Mr. Karpinsky," said Anne's mother, "he has a job, a wonderful job. Your father and

Anne's father got on the phone this morning, and they got Ed Buchwalter to hire him at Delta Chemical." Her soft brown eyes begged Henry moistly to agree that there was nothing wrong in the world that could not be repaired easily. "Isn't that nice, Henry?" she said.

"I—I guess it's better than nothing," said Henry. He didn't feel a great deal better.

His apathy crushed Anne's mother. "What else could anyone *do*, Henry?" she said beseechingly. "What do you children want us to do next? We feel awful. We're doing everything we can for the poor man. If there were anything we could do for the poor woman, we would. It was all an accident, and anybody in our position would have done the same thing— with all the kidnappings and murders and I don't know what all in the papers." She began to weep. "And Anne's writing a book as though we were some kind of criminals, and you come in here and can't even smile, no matter what anybody tells you."

"The book doesn't say you're any criminal," said Anne.

"It certainly isn't very *complimentary*," said Anne's mother. "You make it sound as though your father and I and Henry's father and mother and the Buchwalters and the Wrightsons and everybody were just tickled pink so many people were out of work." She shook her head. "I'm not. I think the Depression is sickening, just sickening. How do you want us to act?" she asked pipingly.

"The book isn't about you," said Anne. "It's about me. I'm the worst person in it."

"You're a *nice* person!" said Anne's mother. "A *very* nice person." She stopped weeping now, smiled twitteringly, moved her elbows up and down as though they were the wing tips of a happy little bird. "Can't we all cheer up, children? Isn't everything going to be all right?" She turned to Henry. "Smile, Henry?"

Henry knew the kind of smile she wanted, and, twenty-four hours before, he would have given it to her automatically—the kind of smile a child gave a grown-up for kissing a hurt well. He didn't smile.

The most important thing to Henry was to demonstrate to Anne that he wasn't the shallow booby she apparently thought he was. Not smiling helped—but something more manly, more decisive was called for. It suddenly dawned on him what the nameless errand was that he'd set out upon. "Mrs. Heiler," he said, "I think maybe Anne and I should go see Mr. Karpinsky, and tell him how sorry we are."

"No!" said Anne's mother. It was sharp and quick—too sharp, too quick. There was panic in it. "I mean," she said, making erasing motions with her hands, "it's all taken care of. Your fathers have already been down to talk to him. They apologized to him and told him about the job and..." Her voice trailed off. It was apparent even to her what she was really saying.

She was really saying that she could not stand the idea of Henry's and Anne's growing up—the idea of their ever looking closely at tragedy. She was saying that she herself had never grown up, had never looked closely at tragedy. She was saying that the most beautiful thing money could buy was a childhood a lifetime long—

Anne's mother turned away. Her turning away was the closest she could come to telling Henry and Anne to go see Karpinsky and his tragedy, if they felt they had to.

Henry and Anne went.

. . .

Stanley Karpinsky was in his room. He was sitting at the big table with the lion's-claw feet. He was staring into the middle distance, his thumb tips clamped lightly between his teeth. Heaped on the table before him were the few things that had survived the drop from the window at dawn. Karpinsky had salvaged what he could—mostly books in sprung bindings.

Karpinsky now listened to two people coming up the stairs. His door was open, so there was no need to knock. Henry and Anne simply appeared in the doorway.

"Well," said Karpinsky, rising, "the King and Queen of the Universe. I couldn't be more surprised. Come in."

Henry bowed stiffly. "We—we wanted to tell you how sorry we are," he said.

Karpinsky bowed in reply. "Thank you very much," he said.

"Very sorry," said Anne.

"Thank you," said Karpinsky.

There followed an embarrassed silence. Henry and Anne had apparently prepared no speeches other than their first ones, and yet seemed to expect great things of their visit.

Karpinsky was at a loss as to what to say next. Of all the players in the tragedy, Henry and Anne had certainly been the most innocent, the most faceless. "Well!" said Karpinsky. "How about some coffee?"

"All right," said Henry.

Karpinsky went to the gas burner, lit it, put water on. "I have a swell job now," he said. "Suppose you heard." He was no more overjoyed by this belated piece of good luck than Henry and Anne had been.

There was no response from Henry and Anne.

Karpinsky turned to look at them, to guess, if he could, what it was they expected from him. With great difficulty, rising above his own troubles, Karpinsky caught on. They had had a soul-shaking brush with life and death, and now they wanted to know what it had all meant.

Karpinsky, ransacking his brain for some foolish tidbit of thought to give them, surprised himself by finding something of real importance.

"You know," he said, "if we had fooled her last night, I would have considered my life at a satisfactory end, with all debts paid. I would have wound up on skid row, or maybe I would have been a suicide." He shrugged and smiled sadly. "Now," he said, "if I'm ever going to square things with her, I've got to believe in a Heaven, I've got to believe she can look down and see me, and I've got to be a big success for her to see."

This was profoundly satisfying to Henry and Anne—and to Karpinsky, too.

Three days later, Henry told Anne he loved her. Anne told him she loved him, too. They had told each other that before, but this was the first time it had meant a little something. They had finally seen a little something of life.

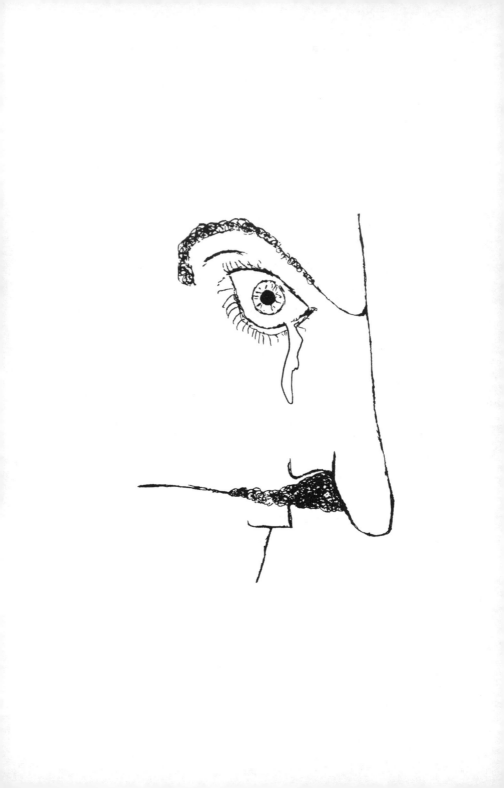

THE GOOD EXPLAINER

The office of Dr. Leonard Abekian was in a bad part of Chicago. It was behind a false front of yellow brick and glass block built out from the first floor of a narrow Victorian mansion whose spine was spiked with lightning rods. Joe Cunningham, treasurer of a bank in a small town outside of Cincinnati, arrived at Dr. Abekian's office by taxicab. He had spent the night in a hotel. Joe had come all the way from Ohio, under the impression that Dr. Abekian had had phenomenal successes in curing sterility. Joe was thirty-five. He had been married ten years without fathering a child.

The waiting room was not impressive. Its walls were goose-fleshed pink Spackle. Its furnishings were cracked leatherette and chromium-plated tubes. Joe had to put down a feeling that the office gave him at once—a feeling that Dr. Abekian was a cheap quack. The air of the place was little more impressive than a barbershop's. Joe put down the feeling, told himself that Dr. Abekian was too absorbed in his work and too little interested in money to put up an impressive front.

There was no nurse or receptionist at the waiting room desk. The only other soul in the room was a boy about fourteen years old. He had his arm in a sling. The nature of this solitary patient disturbed Joe, too. He had expected to find the waiting room filled with people like himself—childless people who had traveled great distances to see the famous Dr. Abekian, to get the final word on what the trouble was.

"Is—is the doctor in?" Joe asked the boy.

"Ring the bell," said the boy.

"Bell?" said Joe.

"On the desk," said the boy.

Joe went to the desk, found a bell button on it, pressed it, heard a buzzer ring somewhere deep in the house. A moment later, a harried-looking young woman in a white uniform came in from the back part of the house, closed a door on the wailing of a child. "I'm sorry," she said, "the baby isn't well. I have to go back and forth between him and the office. Can I help you?"

"Are you Mrs. Abekian?" said Joe.

"Yes," she said.

"I talked to you on the phone last night," said Joe.

"Oh yes," she said. "You made appointments for yourself and your wife?"

"That's right," said Joe.

She referred to an appointment pad. "Mr. and Mrs. Joseph Cunningham?"

"Right," said Joe. "My wife had some shopping. She'll be along. I'll go in first."

"Fine," she said. She nodded at the boy with his arm in a sling. "You go in right after Peter here." She took a blank form from the desk drawer, tried to ignore the squalling of the baby in the back of the house. She wrote Joe's name at the top of the form, and she said, "You'll have to excuse the distractions."

Joe tried a shy smile. "To me," he said, "that's the most beautiful sound in the world."

She gave a tired laugh. "You've come to the right place to hear beautiful sounds like that," she said.

"How many children do you have?" said Joe.

"Four," she said. And then she added, "So far."

"You're very lucky," said Joe.

"I keep telling myself so," she said.

"You see," said Joe, "my wife and I don't have any."

"I'm *so* sorry," she said.

"That's why my wife and I have come to see your husband," said Joe.

"I see," she said.

"We came all the way from Ohio," said Joe.

"Ohio?" she said. She looked startled. "You mean you just moved to Chicago from Ohio?"

"Ohio's still our home," said Joe. "We're up here just to see your husband."

She looked so puzzled now that Joe had to ask, "Is there another Dr. Abekian?"

"No," she said. And then she said, too quickly, too watchfully, too brightly to make Joe think he really had come to the right place, "No, no—there's only one. My husband's the man you want."

"I heard he'd done some wonderful things with sterility cases," said Joe.

"Oh, yes, yes, yes—he has, he has," she said. "May—may I ask who recommended him?"

"My wife heard a lot of talk around about him," said Joe.

"I see," she said.

"We wanted the best," said Joe, "and my wife asked around, and she decided he *was* the best."

She nodded, frowned ever so slightly. "Uh-huh," she said.

Dr. Abekian himself now came out of his office, shepherding a mournful, old, old woman. He was a tall, flashily handsome man—flashy by reason of his even white teeth and dark skin. There was a lot of the sharpness and dazzle of a nightclub master of ceremonies about him. At the same time, Dr. Abekian revealed an underlying embarrassment about his looks, too. He gave Joe the impression that he would have preferred, on occasion anyway, a more conservative exterior.

"There must be something I could take that would make me feel better than I do," the old, old woman said to him.

"You take these new pills," he said to her gently. "They may be just what you've been looking for. If not, we'll try, try, try again." He waved the boy with the broken arm into his office.

"Len—" said his wife.

"Hm?" he said.

"This man," she said, indicating Joe, "this man and his wife came all the way from Ohio to see you."

In spite of herself, she made Joe's trip seem such a peculiar thing that Joe was now dead certain that a big, foolish mistake had been made.

"Ohio?" said Dr. Abekian. His incredulity was frank. He arched his thick, dark eyebrows. "All the way from Ohio?" he said.

"I heard people from all over the country came to see you," said Joe.

"Who told you that?" he said.

"My wife," said Joe.

"She knows me?" said Dr. Abekian.

"No," said Joe. "She just heard about you."

"From whom?" said the doctor.

"Woman talk," said Joe.

"I—I'm very flattered," said Dr. Abekian. "As you can see," he said, spreading his long-fingered hands, "I'm a neighborhood general practitioner. I won't pretend that I'm a specialist, and I won't pretend that anyone has ever traveled any great distance to see me before."

"Then I beg your pardon," said Joe. "I don't know how this happened."

"Ohio?" said Dr. Abekian.

"That's right," said Joe.

"Cincinnati?" said the doctor.

"No," said Joe. He named the town.

"Even if it were Cincinnati," said the doctor, "it wouldn't make much sense. Years ago, I was a medical student in Cincinnati, but I never practiced there."

"My wife was a nursing student in Cincinnati," said Joe.

"Oh, she was?" said the doctor, thinking for a moment that he'd found a clue. The clue faded. "But she doesn't know me."

"No," said Joe.

Dr. Abekian shrugged. "So the mystery remains a mystery," he said. "Since you've come all this distance—if there's anything I can do—"

"They want children," said the doctor's wife. "They haven't had any."

"You've no doubt been to many specialists before coming all this distance," said the doctor.

"No," said Joe.

"At least your own family doctor, anyway—" said Dr. Abekian.

Joe shook his head.

"You haven't taken this matter up with your own doctor?" said Dr. Abekian, unable to make sense of the fact.

"No," said Joe.

"May I ask why not?" said the doctor.

"You'd better ask my wife when she comes," said Joe. "I've been after her to go to a doctor for years. She not only wouldn't go—she made me promise I wouldn't go, either."

"This was a religious matter?" said the doctor. "Is she a Christian Scientist?"

"No, no," said Joe. "I told you—she was a nurse."

"Of course," said the doctor. "I forgot." He shook his head. "But she did agree to see me—under the impression that I was a famous specialist."

"Yes," said Joe.

"Amazing," said Dr. Abekian softly, rubbing the bridge of his nose. "Well—since you haven't even seen a general practitioner, there *is* a chance I can help."

"I'm game—God knows," said Joe.

"All right—fine," said the doctor. "After Peter, then, comes you."

When young Peter was gone, Dr. Abekian called Joe into his office. He had a directory open on his desk. He explained it. "I was trying to find," he said, "somebody with a name remotely like mine—somebody who might be really famous for handling cases like yours."

"What luck?" said Joe.

"There *is* Dr. Aarons—who's done a lot with a psychiatric

approach," said Dr. Abekian. "His name is vaguely like mine."

"Look," said Joe, patiently, earnestly, "the name of the man we were coming to see, the name of the man who was going to do so much for us, the name wasn't Aarons, and it wasn't a name we could very well mix up with another name, because it was such an unusual name. My wife said we should come to Chicago and see Dr. Abekian—A-b-e-k-i-a-n. We came to Chicago, looked up Dr. Abekian—A-b-e-k-i-a-n— in the phone book. There he was—A-b-e-k-i-a-n—and here I am."

Dr. Abekian's sharp, gaudy features expressed tantalization and perplexity. "Tst," he said.

"You say this Aarons uses the psychiatric approach?" said Joe. He was undressing now for a physical examination, revealing himself as a chunky man, with muscles that looked powerful but slow.

"The psychiatric approach is meaningless, of course," said Dr. Abekian, "if there's anything physically wrong." He lit a cigarette. "I keep thinking," he said, "this whole mystery has to have something to do with Cincinnati."

"I'll tell you this," said Joe, "this isn't the only crazy thing that's happened lately. The way things have been going, maybe Barbara and I ought to go over and see Dr. Aarons no matter what the physicals turn up."

"Barbara?" said Dr. Abekian, cocking his head.

"What?" said Joe.

"Barbara? You said your wife's name was Barbara?" said Dr. Abekian.

"Did I say that?" said Joe.

"I thought you did," said the doctor.

Joe shrugged. "There's one more crazy promise down the drain," he said. "I was supposed to keep her name a secret."

"I don't understand," said the doctor.

"Who the hell does?" said Joe, showing sudden fatigue and exasperation. "If you knew all the fights we've had this past couple of years, if you knew how much I had to go through before she'd agree to see a doctor, to find out if there was anything we could do . . ." Joe left the sentence unfinished, went on undressing. He was quite red now.

"If I knew that?" said Dr. Abekian, himself a little restless now.

"If you knew that," said Joe, "you'd understand why I promised her anything she wanted, whether it made sense or not. She said we had to come to Chicago, so we came to Chicago. She said she didn't want people to know what her real name was, so I promised I wouldn't tell. But I did tell, didn't I?"

Dr. Abekian nodded. Smoke from the cigarette in his mouth was making one eye water, but he did nothing to remedy the situation.

"Well—what the hell," said Joe. "If you can't tell a doctor the whole truth, what's the point of going to one? How's he going to help you?"

Dr. Abekian responded not at all.

"For years," said Joe, "Barbara and I were about as happily married as two people could be—I think. It's a pretty town where we live, full of nice people. We've got a nice big house I inherited from my father. I like my job. Money's never been a problem."

Dr. Abekian turned his back, stared at a rectangle of glass block that faced the street.

"And this no kid thing—" said Joe, "much as we both want kids, not having 'em wouldn't be enough to break us up. It's this doctor thing—or was. Do you know she hasn't gone to a doctor for *any* reason? For the whole ten years we've been married! 'Look, sweetheart,' I'd say to her, 'if you're the reason we can't have children, or if I'm the reason—it doesn't make any difference. I won't think any the less of you, if you're to blame, and I hope you won't think any the less of me, if I'm to blame, which I probably am. The big thing is to find out if there's anything we can do.' "

"It really wouldn't make any difference?" said Dr. Abekian, his back still to Joe.

"All I can speak for is myself," said Joe. "Speaking for myself—no. The love I've got for my wife is certainly big enough to rise above something accidental like that."

"Accidental?" said Dr. Abekian. He started to face Joe, but changed his mind.

"What the heck is it but an accident, who can have kids and who can't?" said Joe.

Joe came closer to Dr. Abekian and the glass block window, was surprised to see in every dimple of every glass block a tiny image of his wife, Barbara, getting out of a taxicab. "That's my wife," said Joe.

"I know," said Dr. Abekian.

"You know?" said Joe.

"You can get dressed, Mr. Cunningham," said the doctor.

"Dressed?" said Joe. "You haven't even looked at me."

"I don't have to," said Dr. Abekian. "I don't have to look at you to tell you that, as long as you're married to that woman, you can never have children." He turned on Joe with startling bitterness. "Are you a marvelous actor, Mr.

Cunningham?" he said. "Or are you really as innocent as you seem?"

Joe backed away. "I don't know what's going on, if that's what you mean," he said.

"You came to the right doctor, Mr. Cunningham," said Dr. Abekian. He gave a rueful smile. "When I told you I wasn't a specialist, I was very much mistaken. In your particular case, I'm as specialized as it's possible for a man to be."

Joe heard the sharp heels of his wife as she crossed the waiting room outside. He heard her ask someone else out there whether the doctor was in. A moment later, the buzzer rang in the back of the house.

"The doctor is in," said Dr. Abekian. He raised his arms in mock admiration of all he was. "Ready for anything," he said.

Out in the waiting room, the door to the back of the house opened. The baby was still crying. Dr. Abekian's wife was still harassed.

Dr. Abekian strode to his office door, opened it on Barbara and his wife. "The doctor is in, Mrs. Cunningham," he said to Barbara. "He can see you right away."

Barbara, a little woman, a glistening trinket brunette, walked into the office, looking at everything with great curiosity. "You finished with Joe that fast?" she said.

"The faster the better, wouldn't you say?" said Dr. Abekian tautly. He closed the door. "I understand you haven't been quite honest with your husband," he said.

She nodded.

"We know each other, you see," Dr. Abekian said to Joe.

Joe licked his lips. "I see," he said.

"You now wish to be completely honest with your husband?" Dr. Abekian said to Barbara. "You want me to help you achieve that honesty?" he said.

Barbara shrugged weakly. "Whatever the doctor thinks best," she said.

Dr. Abekian closed his eyes. "The doctor thinks," he said, "that Mr. Cunningham should know that his wife, while a student nurse, was pregnant by me. An abortion was arranged for, the job was botched, and the patient was made sterile ever after."

Joe said nothing. It would be some time before anything coherent came to him.

"You went to a lot of trouble to bring this moment about," said Dr. Abekian to Barbara.

"Yes," she said emptily.

"Is the revenge sweet?" said Dr. Abekian.

"It isn't revenge," she said, and she went over to look at the thousands of identical images in the glass blocks.

"Then why would you go to so much trouble?" said the doctor.

"Because you were always so much better than I was at explaining why everything we did was all for the best," she said, "every step of the way."

ILLUSTRATIONS

www.vonnegut.com

ABOUT THE AUTHOR

KURT VONNEGUT was a master of contemporary American literature. His black humor, satiric voice, and incomparable imagination first captured America's attention in *The Sirens of Titan* in 1959 and established him, in the words of *The New York Times,* as "a true artist" with the publication of *Cat's Cradle* in 1963. He was, as Graham Greene declared, "one of the best living American writers." Mr. Vonnegut passed away in April 2007.

ABOUT THE TYPE

This book was set in Bembo, a typeface based on an old-style Roman face that was used for Cardinal Bembo's tract *De Aetna* in 1495. Bembo was cut by Francisco Griffo in the early sixteenth century. The Lanston Monotype Company of Philadelphia brought the well-proportioned letterforms of Bembo to the United States in the 1930s.